Stepping Out of Line

Reina F McKenzie

First Printing: December 2011

ISBN-10: 978-1463562472
ISBN-13: 1463562470

DEDICATION

~For anyone who has ever stood up for what they believe in and tried to make a change for the better…this is for you~

A Quick Note to the Reader

Hyko and her people speak a fictional language. Yup, that's right; it's not actually real! Don't worry about not understanding it, though. Whenever there is a phrase or word used, it will either be a) Self explanatory, such as the word "noka," which means no

or

b) Translated either right after or right before the word/phrase's use

Also, the vowels are not pronounced as they are in English. Well, mostly. A makes only the "ah" sound; E makes only the "eh" sound; I and Y make only the "ee" sound; O makes only the "oh" sound; U makes only the "uh" sound.

Please Enjoy This Book!!

~Reina

ACKNOWLEDGMENTS

Without the LORD, I know none of this would've been possible...thank You for my gift. Thanks to Christy Yang for pushing me to get this published; without you, this story would've never left the computer. Mi hermanita, Rachel, I thank you for being supportive, listening to my questions and all of our "photo shoots"; you might not think it was a help, but it was! To all my teachers who have ever read my pieces and encouraged me to keep writing, I thank you also. To my family, thank you for your love and support, and for letting me hog the computers; it is very much appreciated! Lastly, but most certainly not least, thanks to AHJKSR, The Original Nine, Ryan Jennings and anyone else that I know or have ever met through all of the activities I participate in; you are all a part of this story, for you inspire me in everything you do every day.

GESOWUU
DREAM

Hyko had healed many wounds, but this was, by far, the strangest she'd ever encountered. A thin, metal rod was buried deep within Gisipeh's flesh. The skin around it was bruising oddly. As Hyko pressed Nipperbree leaves against his arm, the young man flinched, groaning in pain. Hyko shook her head and dipped a rag in water. She then placed the rag over the leaves.

"Doh deshoney, Gisipeh," she told him as a smirk came across her lips. "Yeioy dojeino tatsui...you've really gotten yourself in trouble now. How do you manage to keep coming back to me every weija?"

"Every week? Don't you think that's a bit exaggerated?" Gisipeh teased. He tried to sit up, but Hyko pushed him back down. At that instant, Hanjeha entered, sweat dripping from her brow. She set a basket of roots and herbs at Hyko's feet, and then began to spread them out and organize them into groups. She was dressed in her usual outfit, a sleeveless brown top and long faded green skirt. Her wild, tight curls were bunched together at the top of her head in a bun. She let out an obnoxious, squawking noise and slapped her knee.

"Aah! Gisipeh-sosii," she exclaimed. "You squirm too much. Let Hyko do her work so you may be off and hunting once more."

"It is not as simple as you say," Gisipeh chuckled. His amusement lasted no more than a few short moments, for Hyko spread some herbal cream over his injury. "This haowo, this pain…you're always on the other side of it, eh?"

It was a very true thing. Hyko had never been on the receiving end of the care and nursing because she was never out where she could be hurt as the men were. In the village of Tattao, the women very rarely stepped out of the boundaries. Past the boundaries was the woods and the paths, where mostly children played and men hunted. A few selected women went out each morning to gather herbs, roots, flowers, plants and berries for the healers or for cooking. Other than that, the women stayed within the boundaries at all times, with the exception of the Samnba gatherings each month. There was no time and no way for Hyko to injure herself as the hunters did, even if she wished for it.

"Hoi, Hyko!" Hanjeha barked suddenly. "Your head is always in the clouds. What is on your mind now?"

"Oh, me?" Hyko's daydream hadn't been of anything particularly new. She'd often times reflect on her culture and the ways of her people. "Da samnba. Ta ne tojo, eh? It's tonight, isn't it?" Hanjeha smiled broadly, letting out her infamous cackle as she finished up her sorting. She stood, basket on her hip and patted Hyko on the shoulder.

"Oh, child, of course, of course!" she hooted. "Samnba. That is tonight. And tonight, there is a great reason to be excited, I suppose, for a young lady such as yourself?"

"Of course, Moro Hanjeha," Gisipeh teased. "Hyko is always excited at the time of Samnba. It's the only time she gets to see that boy-"

"Shetteme, the both of you!" Hyko cried. She gave Gisipeh a friendly slap on his uninjured arm. "You know I'm not excited because of that. I just…forgot if tonight was the right day or not."

"Nondeque, Hyko." Hanjeha continued her guffaws and laughter and "of course" comments all the way out of the room. Gisipeh attempted once more to sit up as Hyko shut her mouth due to embarrassment.

"Don't mind us, Hyko," he laughed. "You know we're just messing with you." Hyko knew that. Gisipeh never ceased with his joking while Hanjeha was just a load of trouble. People often mistook the most respected healer of all the villages for a kind, gentle old lady. But within that woman was a fiery spirit that never stopped burning. "Hyko? May I leave now?"

"Natte? Oh, um, yes," Hyko said at last. "Just don't hunt for two days, alright?"

"Fine." With a grunt, Gisipeh lifted himself off the bed using the rest of his body. His hurt arm hung limply at his side as he stood.

"How did you manage to get that injury, anyway?" Hyko asked, eyeing the sliver of metal she'd extracted from his arm. She certainly had never seen anything like it, nor heard hunters speaking of it while telling tales of their day.

"I was near the setuji," Gisipeh explained. This still made no sense to Hyko, though; the setuji were nothing more than shrubs and weedy roots that, at worst, would snag at one's clothing and leave them with a few scrapes upon returning home. Hyko opened her mouth to question her friend further, but he was gone in an instant and Hyko decided to save her inquiries for later.

Hyko left the healer's hut early that day. There had been few patients after Gisipeh had left, and Hanjeha was beginning to get on Hyko's nerves. Besides, the air was refreshing, as was the light breeze on that rather warm day. Usually, her healer duties took up most of the day, and it was nice to receive a break every now and again. It was only on her break days that she had much time to interact with her family and a few of her friends.

Hyko often times felt a bit alienated from the others her age in the village. She was the only one to receive a healer's path on the day of her Whispering. While most of the young women received housewife, teacher or gatherer, Hyko alone had received healer. It had been exciting at first, until she'd discovered that she'd be spending the best of her days with old, wrinkly women with attitudes.

"I'm home!" Hyko yelled as she slipped off her shoes at the entrance of her kytah.

"So early?" Ohn-Tsung didn't look up from her paintings even when she'd heard her older sister come through the door. "Did you get out early for Samnba?"

"Sort of," Hyko lied, taking a seat on the floor by her sister. Ohn-Tsung had been in love with artwork since she was a mere few years old. At age eight, she spent most of her days painting with liquid sand or sketching with chalk. The village leaders were often displeased with Ohn-Tsung, who, unlike other kids her age, "wasted her days" playing with paints and oils. Hyko and her parents got all kinds of grief for Ohn-Tsung's talent. Hyko couldn't care less; her sister loved art and her pictures turned out beautiful every time. "Hey, Umnii, you ever see this before?" She held up the small metal rod. Ohn-Tsung eyed it carefully before giving an answer.

"Noka," she said plainly. "Never seen it."

"Nothing like it? Ever?"

"Noka." Ohn-Tsung was once more engrossed in her painting. "Oh, and amam said that we're out of bread, so we need more wheat. Will you get some later?" Hyko sighed; if her hands weren't constantly covered with oils, Ohn-Tsung would be perfectly capable of fetching the wheat herself.

Her path was a walkway of stars. As Hyko rose slowly, she treaded the pathway cautiously, focused intently on who stood waiting patiently at the other end. There was no mistaking Naura, the lovely spirit of Saiytah. This wasn't the first time the lovely spirit had come to the young healer in a dream.

"Lovely Naura, is there...is there something that is wrong?" Hyko asked, but the spirit said nothing. Naura's red ringlets blew gently in the breeze. She held out her hand and pointed in the direction of the village of Fayune, a village covered completely in ice and snow. Hyko took two steps towards the village, but Naura held her back by placing a hand on her shoulder. Hyko still managed to get a good view of the activity going on in Fayune despite her limited movement. Other than the elderly and their

caretakers, most of the village was on their way to Tattao for Samnba, leaving most of the homes empty and without activity. But as Hyko concentrated on the village, she noticed strange men dressed in thick clothing wandering aimlessly around the village center. Hyko's eyes widened. Never in her life had she ever seen men with skin that color before. She turned to the lovely spirit.

"Lovely Naura, Whatta arei telkje dojei tun?" Hyko asked. "What are they doing there? What's going on? Is Fayune in trouble?" Naura said nothing. She released Hyko from her grasp and disappeared down the walkway of stars.

Hyko awoke with a start, a shiver running down her spine. *When did I fall asleep?* She wondered groggily. *Where did I fall asleep?* Whatever room she'd passed out in, there was a window a few feet away. The sun was setting, and the village was gathering at the village center to prepare for Samnba.

"Hyko!" Hyko jumped to her feet the moment she heard her name called; it was Gisipeh calling to her, waving frantically from outside. "Beinei te citon! Come on! We're gonna be starting soon!" Samnba was the most exciting part of a young person's life. The five villages would gather five times each year in a different village to share stories, trade items and fellowship. This time, Samnba was in their village of Tattao, and everyone was going out of their minds preparing for it. Even Ohn-Tsung had stopped her painting to assist in decorating the homes for the arrival of the four sister villages.

Hyko met up with Gisipeh out front after changing into her celebration dress. Gisipeh looked sharp in his fresh shirt, which was unlike the dingy hunting clothes he'd been dressed in earlier.

"How's the arm?" Hyko asked. It didn't seem quite as limp as earlier. Gisipeh shrugged before taking her hand.

"It's fine," he answered. "Come on, I hear there's something big going on this time. But first, I gotta show you something." The two friends weaved through the crowd, careful not to get stopped by too many people. Gisipeh seemed so bent on getting to wherever it was they were going that he didn't stop to greet anyone, elders included.

"Gisipeh, what's up with you?" Hyko came to a sudden halt as they entered the woods and crossed her arms across her chest. She gave Gisipeh a smirk, but furrowed her eyebrows at the same time. "Why the rush?"

"What rush?" Gisipeh called from ahead. He was using an old switchblade to hack at plants standing in their way. Even then, he was moving so quickly that the weeds and plants were flying up in Hyko's face.

"This rush! Hadassah! Slow down!" she laughed, though she truly was curious as to what was on his mind. Then again, that was just his personality, in a way; Gisipeh always had to be up and running, doing something and occupying his time. That was part of the reason why he was constantly returning to the healer's hut; he was like a little kid, never sitting still and getting into everything.

"I had a dream," he began to explain. "The spirit Bujetu showed me this spot in the woods with...kokoro! Look!"

Hyko's attention immediately went to the ground, but she saw nothing.

"You dummy, there's nothing there!" Hyko exclaimed, paying more attention to Gisipeh than to where she was headed. A second later, the ground seemed to move beneath her and she grunted, landing with her face flat on the ground. Hyko groaned as she felt a sharp pain on her palm. *Just a bruise,* she told herself, though she checked to be sure. It had to be a hunter's wire net or something of the sort. She lifted her hand to examine it, finding no blood but noticing that her celebrations dress was completely ruined.

"These things are everywhere," Gisipeh muttered.

"What-" As Hyko put her hand out to push herself up, she suddenly felt something cool and metallic. Hyko rolled it around in her fingers, bringing it up to her eyes; a small rod, similar to the one that had hurt Gisipeh earlier. "What...where did these things come from?"

"You think I know?" Gisipeh asked. "I'm just as confused as you, dyoku." Hyko frowned, refusing to take her eyes off the small metal object. Her people knew of metal; one of their sister villages, Delfusio, used it a lot and sent blocks to the other villages in exchange for rare herbs that didn't grow near the mountains. However, this small rod...it was unlike anything Hyko had ever seen sent down from the mountains, with the exception of the other one she'd removed from Gisipeh that afternoon. In any case, Tattao village was much too far from Delfusio for fragments of metal to be scattered on forest trails.

"So...you say Buteju came to you in a dream and showed you these?" Hyko mused aloud. "And who's to say it wasn't someone else? What if it was the trouble-making spirit, Kee, playing a trick on you?"

"Hyko, you know that the spirits don't work like that," Gisipeh said. That was true, according to the village elders. Many aspects of life in the villages depended on the dreams the spirits gave the people. If a dream had a lesson to it or made you realize something, it was from Nanoho, the spirit of wisdom. If a dream was terrifying, it was from the trouble-making spirit, Kee. Most good dreams were from lovely Naura, but some of her dreams were hazy and unclear...sort of like Hyko's earlier one. "Hyko? You listening?"

"Natte? Oh, um...yeah, sonno. Sorry." Hyko got to her feet and brushed herself off the best she could. She tore her attention away from the metal for a moment to gaze at the sun. It was getting lower in the sky, and its rays shone brightly through the branches of the trees. "We should get going. It's pretty late."

"Ahown," Gisipeh replied, and picked up one of the metal objects.

"Whatta arei yeioy dojei?" Hyko asked. "What are you doing? You don't know what those are!"

"Yes, but we can figure it out." He began walking back in the direction of Tattao. "We can show them to some of our friends from Delfusio. They might know what they are." As Gisipeh ended his sentence, he heard a low horn echoing through the forest, disturbing the birds and causing them to flee from their nests in the trees. "They're here. Come on!" Gisipeh broke into a sprint, leaving Hyko to follow without warning. She sighed and shook her head, yet smiled inwardly at her friend.

LOUYE
MYSTERY

By the time Hyko and Gisipeh returned to the village, their sister villages Fayune, Kainau and Sasse had arrived. Delfusio, unfortunately, had not. The village elders were speaking proudly, their faces shining despite their old age. Wrinkles marked years of leadership on each of the elder's faces. They greeted each other and anyone else who happened to pass by them.

"We can't get stopped by them or they'll ask what happened," Gisipeh hissed, his mouth right by Hyko's ear. Hyko nodded, noting her attention-drawing, shrubbery-covered outfit.

"We won't tell them?" she asked. Gisipeh's response was a quick shake of his head.

Hyko opened the door to her home and swiftly pulled Gisipeh inside. "I'm gonna change and then we can go."

"Who said that?" The oddly familiar voice was a surprise for the two friends, who took several steps backwards. The house had been empty when Hyko had left not so long ago. The wooden floor boards creaked as a little old woman emerged from one of the backrooms. Her messy curls and bags under her eyes showed she had been napping peacefully. She was dressed in a jade-colored robe and a golden hair ornament adorned the mop atop her head. Her face was nearly wrinkle free, but still looked aged. Gisipeh relaxed and exhaled loudly as he recognized who it was.

"Elder Agenee," he sighed. "Soyqueay alkeno. Nice to see you again. But...may I ask why you're in Hyko's kytah?"

"Aah! How can you ask such a thing when you are a guest yourself?" Elder Agenee scolded, causing Gisipeh to clamp his mouth shut. "If you must know, Hyko's mother was kind enough to allow me to reside here since my husband, Elder Hele, has passed on to be in Saiytah." The Tattao village elder ran her hand through her curls momentarily, getting out a few of the worst kinks. "I apologize for that little scare I gave you back there."

"Essako, no big deal," Hyko replied. "We, uh, were just going to get me a new anneta." She pointed at the one she'd ripped and torn while out in the woods. "This one is ruined."

"Shay, hejikoro bendao tsu, my dear...you will need to change that for sure," Elder Agenee said. "Ah me vehaja, how did you do such a thing to that lovely anneta?" Hyko smacked Gisipeh playfully on the arm.

"Ask this guy." She grinned at Gisipeh who shook his head. Elder Agenee chuckled.

"Ah, you two. The best of friends since your young years." The woman looked off at nothing, her eyelids droopy. She said no more on the matter, or anything else at all. The quiet was unnerving, and Hyko cleared her throat.

"Uh, well...I'll just go up and change," she announced softly, beginning to make her way up the stairs. Gisipeh followed right behind her.

"Gisipeh! Stozien! Stop right there!" Elder Agenee called out, suddenly awake from her trans. "You think you're going to go up with her? Young man, think again! Stay down here. You have no need to look at her while she changes her clothing."

"What?" Gisipeh's caramel-colored skin was dark, but not so dark where his blush wasn't visible. "I-"

"Boy, sit yourself down here!" Elder Agenee said sharply. Gisipeh didn't try to argue.

By sundown, Samnba was in full swing. Children told each other vivid stories and tried to act them out. Adults laughed and drank sweet sap punch. Teens caught up on the past few months or kept track of their younger siblings. Gisipeh and Hyko had joined the festivities shortly before the High Elder (although Gisipeh liked to call him "the really old guy") asked the blessing of the feast. Their old friends, Iatso, Issiio and Awa'hi had glared at them when they entered, but didn't question them until later on.

"What did you two sneak off and do?" Awa'hi teased, a wicked grin on her lips. Iatso and Issiio, the infamous twins from Sasse, snickered uncontrollably. In the village of Sasse, it was assumed by all the young people that Gisipeh and Hyko were madly in love with each other. In the village of Tattao, everyone knew that this was not the case, but they thought that she was in love with Iatso, the soft spoken twin.

"Shetteme, lleigehs!" Hyko cried, pretending to be defensive. "We didn't sneak off anywhere! I had to change after Gisipeh and I-" Awa'hi burst into laughter, a scowl coming across Hyko's face. Awa'hi was a character. Although they were friends, the two girls would sometimes butt heads due to their clashing personalities.

"Actually, we went to the woods earlier," Gisipeh began, hesitantly. Iatso, Issiio and Awa'hi turned to him, listening intently. "But only because I had a dream about these little metal things."

"Koomo dasamundio? What in the world?" Issiio asked. "Little metal things?"

"Yes, little metal things." The four of them took a seat on the grass, setting their drinks down on the ground. "I was hurt by one this morning, when I went to look for the place in the woods I had dreamed about. I didn't get a chance to go back until this evening before Samnba, with Hyko." Awa'hi gave the both of them looks of amusement, assuming that they were hiding the truth. The twins, on the other hand, were no longer thinking of Gisipeh and Hyko's suspected romance.

"You sure they weren't something the hunters put out?" Iatso asked, trying to think logically.

"Iatso, I am a hunter." Gisipeh flicked a small pebble off his thumb and sipped from his drink. "I put out traps myself. This wasn't anything like a trap." By then, Awa'hi was much less concerned with Hyko's current romance and was wondering more about the metal rods. She glanced over by where most of the partying was going on; no one seemed to be looking for them.

"The Elders haven't called us in for the meeting yet," Awa'hi told the group. "You guys wanna go check it out?" The four of them stood quickly, and began making their way back to the village center. It took longer than anticipated to weave through the crowd. Several people stopped them to say hello or talk about the food that had been prepared or the beautiful décor. Just as the teens were stepping out onto the forest path, they were stopped.

"What are you all doing?" Hanjeha had Hyko by the shoulder, her nails digging into the fabric of her dress. "Eh? Answer me; where are you all running off to?"

"We were just-"

"Save your explanations." The healer shoved them all forward towards the gathering of people at the village center. "The meeting is to begin shortly." Before they knew it, the four friends were settled neatly with the rest of the adults and children in the village center. The twins grumbled frustrated while Awa'hi drew her mouth into a thin line. Gisipeh and Hyko wondered to themselves what the meeting was on this time. Mostly, the meetings consisted of boring updates on the villages; who had died, what mothers had given birth, how the crops were doing; Hyko had learned how to tune all that out ages ago. It was the interesting, juicy stuff that she wanted to hear. Occasionally, the spirits brought an elder a peculiar message to be shared. Usually, though, it was the elders babbling.

"One young woman and young man in our villages have been chosen by the spirits to wed," Elder Opi announced with a wide grin on his face. "Usually, brides and grooms are selected by parents once they have come of age. This time, I will do as the spirits told me in a dream." He paused and outstretched his arm to the crowd. "Hyko, my dear. Please stand."

Hyko froze. She couldn't breathe. Her throat felt constricted. The world around her seemed to be spinning. Gisipeh patted her arm to try and bring her back to reality, but it didn't appear to be working.

"Hyko! Keil tsu! Go up there now!" Issiio hissed urgently. Ever so slowly, Hyko stood and made her way to the Elder on shaky legs. She tried to keep her composure, but she feared that she had already lost it.

"Hyko, the spirits came to me in a dream, child, saying that you will soon marry," the elder continued. "The man you will marry is strong and fierce. He will always be able to protect you and keep you fed. Should you be blessed with children, he will be a wonderful father and train his children to have confidence and courage." He paused to point towards the crowd once more. "Yonej! Young man, please come forward." Hyko stared blankly ahead as Yonej came forward.

Young man? Yonej was nearly ten years older than her! His skin was dark like all her people of all the villages, but he was exceedingly so due to the summer sun. His hair was neatly braided and reached down to his shoulder blades. It was even longer than Hyko's own hair. His smile was warm yet intimidating. He reached Hyko within a few strides and Hyko looked up at him to see his expression. He seemed rather chipper, much happier than she was.

"Yonej, you and Hyko will be wed!" The villages erupted with cheers and applause. When Yonej lifted her hand to kiss it, Hyko felt sick. She pulled away from him, and the crowd suddenly grew silent.

"No!" she cried. "Noka, noka! I can't...you can't do that!"

"Hyko-jete, it's custom-"

"Don't call me that!" Hyko spat, stepping backwards. "I won't marry you!" The villages began to murmur, their eyes wide and on Hyko. Yonej winced at her words. Elder Opi stepped in.

"You dare defy the spirits like this?" he bellowed. "You dare speak out against the spirits, myself and Yonej, your future husband?"

"He isn't my future *anything!*" Hyko knew that saying such things would come back to bite her in the butt sooner than later. It was against the laws of the spirits to disrespect a man. She wasn't only disrespecting a man, but a man of power, no less...in front of hundreds of people. Still, she wasn't ready for marriage, and certainly would not marry someone she barely knew. "I'm not marrying *him* or *anyone else* anytime soon." Elder Opi grasped Hyko by the wrist and threw her down. She landed on her knees hard and gritted her teeth.

"Young lady, the spirits have spoken." He let go of her wrist. "This is over and done. You and Yonej will have several months to bond. But by autumn's end, you will be married."

The villagers from Fayune, Sasse and Kainau were dispersed amongst the homes in Tattao to spend the night. No one was assigned to Hyko's kytah, for too many people were living there already. Besides, no one wanted to room with Hyko's "discourteous mouth". Gisipeh said nothing to her after what had happened with Elder Opi and Yonej. The twins and Awa'hi hadn't even looked Hyko in the eye when she'd sat back down by them immediately following the announcement of her engagement.

The walk back to Hyko's kytah was even worse than her treatment at the meeting. Her mother and her father walked several paces ahead of her, refusing to acknowledge her presence. Ohn-Tsung wasn't rude or particularly friendly towards her sister, but was kinder than her parents. She spoke briefly about a game she'd played with some cousins from another village. Hyko hadn't been paying enough attention to her sister's babbling to catch which cousins they were or which village they had been from. The moment the door to Hyko's kytah clicked shut, she was knocked down to the floor when a hand forcefully met her cheek.

"How dare you embarrass our family like that!" Hyko's father bellowed. Hyko hated when her father lost his temper. It usually resulted in her receiving some sort of bodily harm. "How dare you step out of line like that!"

"Adad, I-" Her words earned her another slap in the face.

"Do not speak!" he growled. "You are of age, and you *will* marry Yonej." Hyko's lip quivered as she lay on the ground, her face to the floor."You *will* learn to hold your tongue and respect a man before you leave this house." He said nothing more before he headed to the backroom that he and Hyko's mother shared. Ohn-Tsung passed by to go upstairs wordlessly, as did her mother. Only Elder Agenee stopped and pulled Hyko up.

"Child, things aren't as bad as they seem," she soothed.

"I'm marrying a man that I don't even know!" Hyko cried, tears streaming down her cheeks. "He'll probably want children that I'm not ready to have right now..." Sobs stopped her from continuing on. Elder Agenee patted her shoulder.

"Dear Hyko...I'm sure the spirits have something big planned for you. Be patient and see."

RARROSO
STRANGER

The week following Samnba, Hyko busied herself with work at the healer's hut. She wondered why Delfusio had never joined them; she and Gisipeh still had questions on the metal rods for them.

She met with Yonej twice, and he didn't seem so bad. He was a hunter and a constructor, so his muscles were very chiseled. He knew a lot about the land and wished to travel past Kainau one day.

"And I always wanted a big family," he'd said one afternoon, causing Hyko to lean backwards, eyes wide.

"Devas? Really?" she'd asked. "And, um...how big, exactly, is 'big'?"

"Five or six kids...maybe seven."

Hyko had felt sick.

Aside from wanting a family the size of an army, she liked him alright. She didn't particularly want to marry him, but he was a kind enough man.

Nearly two weeks after Samnba, Gisipeh came to Hyko while she was at work. He wasn't wearing his usual hunter's attire.

"Hey...can I come in?" Hyko glanced up from her herb arrangements. He seemed solemn, oddly so for Gisipeh's personality. She scooted over to offer him a seat next to her. He pulled her into a long and tight embrace upon sitting, his warmth making Hyko tingle all over.

"Um...Gisipeh?" she asked, pulling back. "What's all this about?"

"I haven't gotten a chance to talk with you about...you know," he sighed. Hyko lowered her gaze, her heart sinking.

"There's nothing to say."

"Now that's sheekey and you know it," Gisipeh said, his tone slightly playful. "Come on, I know you. You don't want to marry Yonej."

"But the spirits-"

"Maybe they'll change their minds." Hyko shook her head and chuckled, swatting playfully at Gisipeh's arm. She highly doubted that the spirits would be changing their minds, but Gisipeh's words helped put her mind at ease.

"Thanks," she told him. "I needed that." The two joked around for a while longer, poking fun at Hanjeha if she walked through. They avoided conversation on the metal rods and Delfusio. They both just wanted a break from anything serious. Hours passed, and as the sun started sinking in the sky, Hyko's mood was lifted.

"Let's go to the trader's hut," Gisipeh suggested. "I've got some stuff we can trade for candied sap." Hyko's mouth watered at the thought of a sweet treat. She was definitely up for it. The two exited the healer's hut, continuing to laugh and joke like they used to when they were younger. As they walked the other villagers gave her dirty looks, or looked away altogether; Hyko simply tried to pass it off as nothing. Hyko knew why that was so; nobody could completely shake from their memories what had happened at Samnba.

Both Gisipeh and Hyko noticed immediately that something was not right when they entered the trader's hut. Several men conversed in hushed tones, leaning in towards each other over a barrel of flour. One man with curly strands of hair covering parts of his face turned to glower at Hyko when they stepped in.

"This is a private conversation," he growled. "That young lady will need to leave." Hyko glared right back at him, sticking out her tongue and mocking him.

"I'm not going anywhere," she snapped. "Just keep whispering. Don't worry, I'm not listening." The man stepped away from the others he'd been speaking with to back Hyko up against a wall.

"So, you have not yet learned to watch your tongue."

"I guess not." Hyko grinned smugly as she watched the man grow angrier. Gisipeh stepped in then. He pushed the man away from Hyko and pulled her away from the wall.

"Hey, Gusto, leave her be," Gisipeh warned. "We just want some-"

"It doesn't matter in the least what she *wants*," Gusto snapped. "I told her to leave. She didn't. She must now be punished." Hyko felt her throat grow dry. Not even a month ago would she have spoken back to a man like that. It was the law amongst her people that all women obey men without question, or dire consequences could be carried out; Hyko was in no way anxious to know what those consequences were.

Gisipeh seemed ready to fight. He curled his hands into fists. Hyko noticed his jaw tighten.

"Don't," she told him, touching his arm, but he brushed her off.

"Someone...someone, peleiko...zze..." Hoarse cries stopped the beginnings of the fight that otherwise could've ended with bloodshed. A middle-aged hunter, most likely not from Tattao, limped into the traders hut. His hands were scratched and bleeding, blood pouring from what appeared to be a terrible stab wound in his chest. He fell to his knees, his body trembling. He struggled to breathe, shallow breaths making their way into his lungs as he gasped for air. Gusto shoved Hyko forward until she was standing in the hunter's blood.

"You are a healer, yes?" he asked. Hyko nodded. "You have to do something." Hyko's blood boiled; how dare he put her on the spot like that? Nevertheless, there was no time to argue. The man had already lost a lot of blood and was losing more every second she wasted thinking about it. She bent down and tore open his shirt, revealing his chest, sticky with blood. The stab wound was not like any she'd ever seen. It was far too clean cut to even be caused by a knife. What, then, had caused it? The unfamiliarity of the man's injury caused Hyko to panic.

"Well, what's wrong with him?" Gusto's impatience was in no way helpful, and made Hyko even more nervous. Her hands hovered over the injured young man's chest as she hesitated.

"I...I don't know."

"Koomo? What do you mean you don't know?"

"I mean I don't know!" she wailed, but brought her tone down to finish. "I-I thought it was a stab wound, but-"

"This child doesn't know what she's doing," Gusto grumbled. "Somebody go get Hanjeha." Hyko leaned back, her eyes blankly focused on the floor, her brow furrowed. She had failed. It was as simple as that. The hunter was nearly dead and there was nothing she could do.

"Is he from this village?" one of the other men asked, starting a commotion in the hut.

"No, I think he's from Fayune! Look at the design on his attire."

"No, that's what Delfusio wears during the cool spells...besides, what would a Fayune hunter be doing way out here? He's definitely from Delfusio."

"It's the middle of summer! Why would he be dressed in such thick clothing?"

"It can get cold-"

"What does it matter? He was obviously hurt on the way here. Seriously so."

"Shouldn't we send word back to his village that he's hurt?"

"Shetteme, tsu! Shut up now, *all of you!*" Hyko hissed. Every man in the hut turned to Hyko, their eyes wide. "You sound like a bunch of bickering old women." The men began to snap at her, insults flying from their mouths along with droplets of spit. Hyko tuned all of it out. She kneeled, her knees in a puddle of the man's blood, monitoring his vitals until Hanjeha made it to the hut with herbs and medicines. She called Hyko over to her and Hyko did as she was instructed without hesitation. Hanjeha was a feisty old woman with a sense of humor like a teenager; but when there was serious work to be done, she was not someone to be messed with. Hanjeha worked furiously to examine the wound and stop the bleeding. Hyko mixed any herbs she needed and smeared them on the man's chest. It was ages before Hanjeha leaned back and groaned with frustration.

"This is a wound I have never seen in all my years," she grumbled. "I do not have the slightest idea of what to do for this man. He is in the hands of the spirits now, I'm afraid." In spite of the situation, Hyko gave the impatient Gusto a smug look. The man didn't bother to scowl back. Instead, he looked down and made his way out of the hut silently. Hyko didn't look up again until Gisipeh placed a hand on her shoulder. He helped her to her feet and Hyko sulked on the way out of the hut to the village center without showing her face.

Hyko's entire family was gathered along with half the others in Tattao at the center. Women gossiped to pass the time. Men scolded children for running up to the village elders and asking questions improperly. Ohn-Tsung ran right up to Hyko, knocking her backwards into Gisipeh. Gisipeh steadied her as best he could, but Hyko tore away from him.

"Ohn-Tsung, koomo he yeioy gorrono?" she hissed. "Watch it! What do you want?" Ohn-Tsung grimaced at her sister before she continued.

"Sheesh, calm yourself, sis!" she spat. "I was just gonna ask if you knew what happened to that Fayune hunter." The look on Hyko's face hardened, her glare turning icy cold.

"I know probably what you know," she growled. "Now stop asking dumb questions and find Amam." Ohn-Tsung's lip quivered, but the girl still obeyed her older sister and went off to find her mother. Gisipeh wacked Hyko upside the head the moment Ohn-Tsung was out of view.

"Koomo kaheil?" She cursed.

"I was about to ask you the same thing," Gisipeh said, angrily. "Why would you treat your sister like that? She doesn't know what happened in there!"

"It was none of her business!" Hyko insisted. She poked out her lip to pout, but her heart was aching. Not just for the man she couldn't save, but for her innocent sister who'd done nothing but ask a question. When Gisipeh continued to scowl, she heaved a sigh. "Okay, *fine*, I was wrong. You happy now?" Instead of replying, Gisipeh gave her a look of disgust and disappeared off into the crowd of confused villagers.

"People of Tattao!" Elder Agenee announced, and instantly, every head-young and old-turned their attention to her, listening intently. "There must be strangers among us! We know not how dangerous they are, but since their arrival, strange wounds our hunters have had to endure." The old, gossiping women started their murmurings again as Elder Agenee continued. "It is advised that no one visit our sister villages until we know more about these strangers." The crowd that had gathered was dying to know more, but Elder Agenee waved them all away.

* * * * *

At last, the never-ending ice and snow was beginning to thaw. They'd been trekking through snow a foot high for what had seemed like weeks. The men stopped to rest a few times, but mostly, it was miles and miles of trudging through a frozen wasteland with virtually no breaks.

A couple of times, they'd run into the natives when they'd first arrived at the snow-covered terrain. They'd seen a small child playing gleefully in a pile of snow twice as big as him. Upon seeing the men, he'd yelled something in a language they couldn't understand, and taken off. When they'd followed him, they'd discovered a village. It seemed like the men, women and children were all settling in from a long journey.

"Jaedon." He came back to reality when he heard his name being called. It was Bryce, a scowl finally not plastered on his face like it usually was. Jaedon kicked at some slush and mud puddles in his path. He remembered feeling so relieved when they were finally leaving the frozen lands behind them that he nearly dropped down to his knees and thanked the Lord. However, after three days of mud, he wished in his head that he was back in the snow.

"Whatchu want?" he mumbled. The scowl returned to Bryce's awkwardly oblong face.

"Check yourself, brah," he admonished. "You're lucky they let you off easy by allowing you to come on with us." Jaedon rolled his eyes and let his mind wander. He wondered what was going on back at that village they'd seen.

"Tristan's not gonna mess with em,' right?" When Bryce said nothing in response, Jaedon froze. "Right...? Yo, Bryce!"

"I heard you, man," Bryce snapped, turning his head. His sea green eyes seemed to be piercing Jaedon's skin. "I ain't answering for a reason." Jaedon didn't ask anymore, and trudged on at the end of the line for hours.

SUSEOKSEN
BUSY

"There is no way I'm going out there in this weather!" Ohn-Tsung whined, refusing to put away her pastel chalk. "Amam, it's raining like crazy."

"It matters not!" her mother said. "All you need to do is run to Covi gadon Kytah and ask for some extra flood bags." Ohn-Tsung hated the middle of summer. Tattao never failed to get enough rain to flood half the huts and drench the fields. Amam never failed to become as cranky as Adad. Hyko never failed to fall ill right when work was being done, leaving Ohn-Tsung to fetch this and borrow that from all the neighbors. She groaned inwardly, but put on a pleasant look as well as her sandals. If she'd learned anything from her sister, it was that putting up too much of a fight when dealing with adults was the worst thing you could do by far. Not only did it upset the spirits and your parents, but if word got out, your reputation would be turned to dust.

Ohn-Tsung regretted her decision to stop protesting the minute she got outside. Already, the water was up to her ankles, pulling the sandals off her feet as she sloshed across the way to Covi's home. She would've kept on and followed her mother's instructions if it hadn't been for Hyko.

"Sosii, whatta arei yeioy dojei ton?" she hissed at her older sister, who had a bag thrown over her shoulder and a thick throw thrown over her shoulders. "What're you doing here? I thought you were sick!"

"Stupid, you really haven't figured it out by now?" Hyko snapped. "I only pretend to be sick so that I don't have to run Amam's dumb errands during mid-summer. And to answer your question, I'm going out into the woods."

"In *this* weather?" Ohn-Tsung's eyes grew wide. "You have definitely lost your mind." Hyko stared at her sister for a couple of seconds and then sighed.

"I...I had a dream again," she explained. "It came to me from the Spirit of Nanoho. And even before that, Naura came to me in a dream. Maybe it was Nanoho disguised as Naura...?"

"Uh-huh, I get it, confusing dreams given by you don't know who," Ohn-Tsung interrupted impatiently. "Get on with it."

"Well, the last time, I had a dream that strange people came to Fayune...their skin...it was so...pale. Like the color of a Sakora flower." Ohn-Tsung tried to picture someone with skin that color. The Sakora flower was a pale peach color, and was used by Hyko and her people to make creamy dessert fillings. But a person with skin that light...?

"Impossible," Ohn-Tsung whispered.

"Oh, and that's not even all there is! This time, I dreamed that I ran into one in the woods. He was struggling-"

"Whoa, wait, hold on," Ohn-Tsung said. "You wanna go *towards* the people in the woods? What if they try to kill you?" She paused, her jaw dropping as she made an upsetting connection. "What if they're the strangers that Elder Agenee warned us about?" Hyko shrugged. She had no good answer. Ever since her first dream before Samnba, things that had always been the same had started to change. She had been one of the most respected youth in the village due to her work at the healer's hut; now, she was looked down upon and whispered about behind her back. She shivered as she thought of the dead man from Fayune, and how she'd done next to nothing for him. It made no sense to her; healing the wounds of others had always come so easily. Yet, at a time when her skills had mattered the most, she hadn't been able to do a thing. He could've been a husband and a father, and what did she do?

Sit there and watch him join the spirits in Saiytah, unable to do anything.

"There may be answers in the woods," Hyko said finally. "And if I can find answers and prevent what happened to that man from happening to anybody else...well, I'll be thanking the spirits." She felt a tug at her heart and bit her lip, unwilling to explain anymore to her sister. Without telling Ohn-Tsung goodbye, she sloshed off towards the east village gate, where the puddles of water were shallow. Hyko clutched tightly at her throw, the only source of warmth she had. Despite the rain, she was determined to learn something more on the pale strangers. *Forget the rules and sheekey*, she thought to herself. *Maybe we could learn something from these people...*

The rain started to let up after a few minutes of walking. Before long, Hyko encountered one of the metal rods that Gisipeh and her had discovered weeks ago. They'd never gone back to the spot to check them out again, Hyko realized. She lifted one up to her eyes and felt its cool, smooth texture. She scraped it against the skin of her bare arm; it left a scratch mark, but did not puncture.

"This thing is like an overgrown splinter!" she laughed to herself. It was thin, small and could be removed if anyone ever was punctured with one as Gisipeh had been. She walked on, picking up any of the little rods that she came across. There were dozens of them scattered about.

"What on earth are these for?" she muttered, gathering them all into her left hand. After collecting nearly thirty rods, she noticed yet another strange object she'd yet to encounter in all her years. It was much like the metal rod, yet not as thin or cylindrical. It was a bit heavier than the rods as well.

"Mei yukuyo..."

"You wonder what?" Hyko gasped and looked up, surprised to see Yonej so deep in the woods. He wore a hooded throw, his hands shoved in his pockets. On his face was an amused smirk.

"I, um..." Yonej stepped closer and wrapped his arms around her, surprising her even more than his presence. "What was *that* for?"

"You looked cold," he said simply. "Now, tell me, please. Why are you out so deep in the woods in this weather?" Hyko considered telling him about her dreams and her self-resolutions, then decided against it with a sigh.

"You probably wouldn't believe me if I told you," she said. "Or think it a good idea." Yonej's embrace around her tightened briefly, then he let her go and started to walk away.

"Well then, let's get back to the village," he told her. "I'm sure the women could use some help with the flood bags." Hyko frowned.

"But I-"

"Hyko. Come on. This is ridiculous, you out here in the middle of a flood." His expression hardened. He was no longer being friendly; he was demanding that she head back to the village with him. Hyko clenched her fists tightly, feeling the prick of the rods in her left hand.

"So what?" she challenged. "I'm busy. I'll return to the village in a little while." Yonej stared at her as if not believing what he was hearing. He made it over to her in a couple of quick strides, his nose a mere few inches from hers. She sucked in a breath.

"I did not tell you to come back in a *little while*. I told you to come back *now*." Hyko's gaze did not falter as she clenched her fists tighter and furrowed her brow. From her mouth came one of the most dangerous words she could've said.

"No."

The fierce fire in his eyes scared Hyko enough to make her regret her decision to be so defiant. His breathing was ragged from anger. He grabbed a handful of Hyko's throw and pulled her to him, lifting her feet a couple of inches off the ground. She could feel him trembling as he held her slightly suspended in the air, but made no attempts to break free.

"You and I," he growled, "are going to have a lot of problems if you don't learn to hold your tongue and do as I say." He let go of her abruptly, dropping her to the ground. Hyko grunted and pushed herself up with her bloody hands. The rods had punctured her palms terribly, a few of them still stuck in her flesh. Yonej ignored the blood. With a scowl, he grunted and said, "Now. Let's try this again." He held out his hand. "Let's go back to the village. Right. *Now*."

"Look here, Yonej," Hyko hissed. "I. Am. Busy. I will come back to the village when I am finished. Unditiyo?" Yonej looked as if he wanted to hit her. His hands had curled into fists. Hyko braced herself. But, a punch never came. Not even so much as a slap.

"Hyko, you are a beautiful woman," he said. The sudden gentle tone took her aback, though her surprise only lasted a moment. His voice lowered to a menacing growl once again. "But I promise you, if you do not watch what you say…" He shook his head and walked off, leaving Hyko to struggle with her wounded hands.

"Child, what have you done to yourself?" Hanjeha squawked, walking in on Hyko as she was bandaging her hands. The girl had been correct about the rods; they were like overgrown splinters, except normal splinters weren't nearly as painful or hard to extract from the skin. Three had gotten stuck in her flesh, and she'd only successfully removed two of them when Hanjeha entered. The last one wasn't coming out without a fight.

"I was out in the woods," she explained, whimpering as she finally managed to pull the last rod out.

"You are one crazy girl, you know?" Hanjeha laughed quietly. "Going out in the woods in the rain…by the way, Yonej came by looking for you. Did you see him?" Hyko thought grimly of their encounter back in the woods and grimaced.

"Yeah," she grumbled. "I saw him." The threatening look that had lit his eyes on fire. The way his lips had curled into a disgusted scowl; she'd seen it all. Hanjeha noted the girl's expression, how the name of her husband-to-be had caused her to frown.

"Hyko, is something the matter?"

"*Yes*, Hanjeha, something *is* the matter!" she cried. "Something is very much the matter! Yonej, he-"

"Hush, girl, you know better than to speak like that!" Hanjeha scolded, setting down the herbs that she'd been putting up on shelves. "I know you're not completely ready for this all, but sometimes, the spirit call upon us to-"

"The spirits *have* called upon me for something," Hyko interrupted. "The strangers; I think they want me to find out more about them." Hanjeha stared as Hyko continued to ramble. "I mean, I figured out what these metal rods do, how to take em' out. And obviously, the strangers put them there, because they weren't there before..." She stopped when she noticed Hanjeha's tired eyes closed, her brow furrowed as she shook her head.

"Hyko..." The old woman said nothing more for a long few moments of silence. "I pray you'll be careful, for I fear you could be right. I am not one to speak against the spirits if they call you to do something. Piso, peleiko...be careful, I beg you." Hyko nodded, wincing as she finished wrapping her hands.

Apparently, careful was not one of her greatest personality traits. Inquisitive, though, was one of them. She figured that since the man who'd died had been from Fayune, the strange pale men were traveling down from there. She then considered Delfusio, who had failed to show at Samnba. Perhaps they were being held captive? Had the strangers been the reason why Delfusio never came? Hyko's mind then returned to the metal rods, which were on the soil of her own village. Were the strangers hiding out right under Tattao's noses?

MENOSAI MISSION

Hyko never thought she'd be thanking the spirits for illness, but she found herself doing so the day after her woods encounter with Yonej. Many of the young men who'd been assisting with the fields during the flooding had fell ill with a cough, leaving few messengers. In fact, they were so short on messengers that they didn't bother to protest when Hyko volunteered to do what was considered a man's job.

"*You*. You're going to be a messenger?" Gisipeh nearly doubled over with laughter when Hyko broke the news to him. "You've always said that messengers are sweaty and irritable."

"Yeah, and I still think that...mostly," Hyko admitted, then bit her lip. She couldn't let Gisipeh find out about the real reason behind her becoming a messenger. If he discovered the truth, he'd hold her back. "But, they also get to travel and see all of the land. I think that's exactly what I need right now." Gisipeh smiled warmly at his friend, indicating that he was done teasing her. Lucky for Hyko, her old friend was being incredibly understanding while she fretted over the idea of getting married to Yonej. He'd fallen for her excuse in a heartbeat. A "getaway-from-Tattao" trip was the perfect cover-up for the mission "find-the-strangers" she was really on.

Hyko had little time to train for the job, and most of her preparations involved an irritated Gusto grumbling in a gravelly voice about the trails and such. She knew all about the poisonous plants to steer clear of from her experience as a healer, and Gusto skipped over those explanations.

The day her "training" ended happened to be the same day of her first assignment. Gusto came to her in the early afternoon with a bag of letters and packages.

"These are all for different villages," he explained. "A majority of them are for Delfusio, but I would suggest starting by heading over to Kainau or Sasse, since the trails aren't as rugged. Wouldn't want you injured on your first trip as a messenger, now, do we?" Hyko mocked him behind his back and threw the bag over her shoulder.

Hyko's father was less than pleased when he heard his daughter was leaving for her first job as a messenger. He said nothing more than "stay on the trails" as she headed out the door. Hyko's mother, on the other hand, smothered her.

"Hyko, my baby, you'll be careful, won't you?" she said. "You should ask Yonej or Gisipeh to accompany you on your journey. This is your first time, and I don't want you to be hurt. Yes, that's it. Yonej can-"

"Amam, I'll be fine!" Hyko chuckled. "Trust me. I need to do this on my own. Away from Yonej...and Gisipeh. Especially Gisipeh." Once the words escaped her mouth, she thought about which boy she'd rather discover the truth. Gisipeh would try to stop her and lecture her with his never-ending monologues . But Yonej...

I don't think I want to know what he'd do, she thought to herself with a shiver.

The air was warm as she started out, but grew chillier as she made her way deeper into the woods. The shadows of the trees shielded her from the sun's rays, and after a half hour, she put on her throw to cover her bare shoulders. As she pressed on, she found the weight of her bag annoying, especially when it hit her thigh as she walked. Any time one of the packages made noise, she turned her head and her eyes grew wide, in search of the strangers.

To pass the time, she made up several scenarios involving her meeting a stranger in her mind. For half of the little skits, she pictured herself finding one napping in the midday sun underneath a tree. He'd awake with a start and look at her with kind, brown eyes. They'd begin to chat about how hunting was going in the village that he came from or what things the young children did for fun when not learning how to read, write and carry out their duties. In one scenario, she imagined herself asking the stranger if he'd ever been to the City in the Ruins, a city only heard of in legends that was past the village boundaries of Delfusio. Her mind wandered for more than an hour, until the sensation of hunger distracted her.

Her lunch break had turned into a lunch break and nap, setting her back over an hour. By the time she reached Kainau, it was dusk. What struck her most about the village was how deathly silent it was. She'd been to Kainau once before, when she was about nine years old. She remembered traveling through the tropical forest and reaching the clearing where all of the kytahs were built. She remembered being able to see the beach from the window of her cousin's house, and asking her mother why the homes were built in a forest clearing instead of on the beach. She also remembered witnessing a terrible storm with tides so high that they almost reached the kytahs, and how she never asked her mother about houses on the beach after that. It had been a relatively lively place, with music, food and children laughing as they played games. Now, it was not like that in the least.

It was almost completely silent with no one outside their kytah. Hyko cautiously tip-toed into the village and walked around, taking in her surroundings. It looked as though a storm had come through. Supplies and tools were scattered everywhere, along with wood from homes and various other things in the village. Several of the bigger, heavier metal rods she'd seen in the woods near her home were on the ground. Shouts distracted Hyko from the big rods and turned her attention to the village center. Her eyes grew wide and her bag slid off her shoulder, hitting the ground with more noise than she'd hoped.

Walking briskly towards her was a man much like the ones she'd seen in her dreams. His hair was light and straight, cut in a shaggy style that came down over his eyes, though not hiding them completely. They were big, blue and burning with anger. His skin was pale all except for his face, which was red as he neared her.

She'd found the strangers.

PRECHON QUESTIONS

Jaedon was dog tired. He wanted nothing more than to go home...no. Go home? What was there for him? A dozen or so friends who had gotten him into trouble in the first place? A father who couldn't stand to look at him? A mother who busied herself with the needs of only his sisters? No...there was nothing at home for him. *Nothing good, anyway,* he thought sadly to himself. Even if he could travel back to the mainland, the terms of his sentence would be violated and it'd be back to square one for him. *It'd be better than being here with Bryce*, Jaedon thought, and truly believed it to be so.

"Yo, Jadey!" Bryce barged in, a look of sheer amusement on his face. "Ash and I just found another one walk in...she's a cutie. We could have some real fun with her, you get what I'm sayin'?" He laughed and slapped Jaedon on the back before leaving. Jaedon groaned. That was all the men talked about when they saw one of the native women. Ashleigh, London and Bryce were the worst. It was as if they couldn't contain themselves. Jaedon had walked in on a half-naked London lying with a whimpering, trembling native woman at least four times within the past week. Each woman had been different. It didn't help that London and Ash had been placed in charge of the beach town with Bryce being one of their best buddies. They could screw around with pretty much any girl they wanted and Tristan wouldn't say one word.

Jaedon stood and looked out the window. Sure enough, Ash was harassing a native yet again. Jaedon was sick of it. He hated seeing the women being hurt like that, but what could he do? The other men thought he was a wuss because of Bryce teasing him about being the "honorable guy" and trying to be so "squeaky clean with his morals and beliefs." Not only that, but Ash would have his behind dumped in the ocean if Jaedon tried to stop him from fooling around with women.

He stood, throwing on a hoodie over his shirtless body and headed down the stairs. On the lower level of the home (Jaedon wasn't sure what to call it, for it seemed like a hut, but had two stories), several of the natives huddled together, their eyes wide with fear when Jaedon passed by. Three of them were boys under the age of ten, it looked like; one was a girl no older than twelve, and the last was a tall, dark man who seemed at least twenty years older than the rest of them. The father, Jaedon assumed, stepped forward and spoke in a language that Jaedon couldn't understand.

"Jennyu sok mei gadon ajyoka, gentoe!" he pleaded angrily, stepping closer to Jaedon as he spoke. "Mei gadon ajyoka nokae beinei-osko!"

"I'm, um, very sorry, but I can't understand you," Jaedon said. "But...look, I'm just sorry." He left before he could really let the guilt settle in. He walked behind the hut-houses, trying not to let any natives look him directly in the eye with their despondent expressions. That would only worsen his mood. The men from his own group were gathered in the middle of the beach town, cursing and laughing. How could they? Did they feel *nothing?* Nothing at *all?*

He began to feel a little better once he reached the forest. It was cool and damp, but quiet enough to think and forget about the terrible things going on around him.

"Ooh, Lord, I'm sorry...I wish I could do more for these people," Jaedon groaned, running a hand through his hair. He leaned his back against a nearby tree and closed his eyes. He was feeling better, glad to be away from Bryce's menacing green eyes, but he still wished to be *away*. Not at home, but not with the men, either.

As he stood with his eyes closed, he heard the bushes rustle. His eyes shot open. Someone was hiding from him, and it wasn't one of the men. He headed swiftly in the direction of the sound, not bothering to let his eyes lead him, for there was hardly any daylight.

"Hello?" he called out and the rustling paused. "Who is that?" The rustling started again. Jaedon moved. "Please, I just want to know who-" He came to a clearing and glanced to his right. Trying to use the vegetation as a cover was a girl. Her brown eyes shone brightly with terror as she stood there, not daring to breathe as she stared at him. Her skin was the color of chocolate, and she was wearing a simple reddish brown sort of dress that went to her knees. Jaedon's throat went dry as he realized that he felt shy and was staring.

* * * * *

The white boy just kept looking at her. He didn't speak, he just looked. *Just my luck,* Hyko thought. *I leave Kainau to get away from men and I run into another one.* She didn't move, but knew that she should. What if he tried to touch her like those other men? She doubted it; he seemed younger than the others and less threatening. Still, she was wary.

The two of them stood there wordlessly for several awkward minutes. Hyko looked him up and down, taking in his appearance. His hair was dark brown and cut short, though not like the young men of her people. His hair was straight, some parts sticking up. His attire was the strangest she had ever seen. He had on a throw with a hood and long sleeves. His baggy pants only went to his knees, and they were made of a material that looked anything but comfortable. What intrigued her the most about him were his eyes. They were a bright, brilliant blue that seemed to pierce right through her.

"Umm..." The boy cleared his throat and reached his hand up to rub his hair, making some of it stick up even more. Hyko stepped forward. He hadn't done anything yet. If he'd wanted to hurt her, he would've done it by then. "I...well, this is awkward." Hyko continued to look at him. He was so different.

"Ziolen rarroso..." she murmured.

"You speak that language too?" he groaned. "Oh, shoot. Um, okay. I am Jaedon." He pointed to himself and said his name slowly. "Jaaeedon. I am Jaaeedon." His ludicrous voice made Hyko giggle. She sat down and pulled her knees up to her chest. Jaedon sat as well, crossing his legs.

"Yeije Jaedon, mei unditiyosa," she laughed. She pointed to herself. "Mei heje Hyko." Then, just as he'd done, she repeated her name slowly, drawing out the "ee" sound. "Hee-ko. Mei heje Hee-ko." The boy blinked twice and looked at her thoughtfully before his blue eyes lit up once more and he beamed.

"Hyko! Your name...that's what it is, right?" She nodded at his epiphany, and he laughed at his accomplishment. "Sweet! And you know who I am?" She pointed to him.

"Jaedon." She smiled sheepishly and clutched at her throw. She could understand every word that he was saying, and he couldn't understand her at all. But, what he didn't know wouldn't hurt him. He held out his hand. Hyko did nothing but look at it, wondering what he was showing her his palm for.

"Um, it's a hand shake," he explained. He took her right hand and put it in his to shake. Hyko stared wide-eyed at him. *This boy is something else,* she thought, amused. "Nice to meet you."

"Soyqueay alkeno," Hyko replied, translating.

"What?" Jaedon pulled his hand back. Hyko took it again and shook it as he had.

"Mei heje Hyko," she said, slowly. That much she assumed he sort of understood. "Soyqueay alkeno." Jaedon pulled his hand away again and gave her a curious look.

"You...can you understand me?"

"Ahown."

"I don't know what that means and you know it."

"Tyum yoyum!" Hyko smiled sweetly before standing and heading back towards Kainau. She hoped the stranger would follow her. It was entertaining. To her pleasure, he did stand and follow behind her after a few short moments. She could hear his baggy, uncomfortable-looking short pants making nose as he jogged to catch up with her.

"Wait! Please, Hyko, wait!" he called out after her. "Um, soyqueay alkeno to you too!" Hyko stopped suddenly, and Jaedon nearly crashed into her. She pointed to a tree.

"Tattao," she said. "Tattao." She watched as he processed what she was trying to get at. "Tsu, yeioy! Yeioy yasse ta! Tattao."

"Umm...okay, this is weird," Jaedon muttered. He looked from her and her impatient face to the tree. "Um..tattao?" Her face lit up and Jaedon finally understood what she was trying to do. Next, she pointed towards the ground and ran her fingers along a few blades of grass.

"Hyuk," she told him and waited for him to repeat the word. The two of them went on like that until it was too dark to clearly make out the trail ahead of them, the moon their only light. Hyko kept on pointing at rocks, flowers and bushes. Anytime a bird chirped, she'd say the word for that as well . Jaedon tried his best at pronouncing the words, though they sounded funny and not as natural on his own tongue. When she spoke, it all went so smoothly. When he spoke, he sounded like the kids failing in his Mandarin class.

A breeze swept through the forest that caused Jaedon to shiver and wish he'd thrown on some longer pants. Hyko glanced over at him and saw that the language lesson was over.

"Arei yeioy hoquah?" she asked, taking off her throw and handing it to him. He refused, insisting that she needed it more than him. *If I needed it, I wouldn't be giving it to you, now, would I?* she thought to herself, but said nothing aloud. The silence was a comfortable one. When they were almost back at Kainau, she looked up at the sky and the full moon. She pointed up at it, Jaedon's eyes following her finger.

"It's a beautiful moon, isn't it?" he murmured. "How do you say moon?"

"Hyko," she replied and Jaedon looked over at her curiously.

When they reached Jaedon's kytah, he went around to the back. In the village center were three white men with sticks in their mouths, the ends of the sticks burning a dull orange. From her experience earlier, Hyko wanted nothing more than to stay far away from the other strangers. They were nothing like Jaedon, and wouldn't be wanting a language lesson from her if they saw her.

The village was as still and silent as it had been before, and Jaedon continued to stress to Hyko that she shouldn't speak. For once, Hyko was in no mood to protest. He leaned his back against the kytah and Hyko looked at him intently.

"Well, I guess, um...bye," he said quietly.

"Blonto," Hyko translated. Jaedon smiled, his blue eyes relaxing, making Hyko's insides melt.

"Blonto, Hyko." Hyko had to force her feet to take a step back towards the forest with all the strength she could muster. She didn't want to leave him. She didn't want to leave his warm smile and his captivating blue eyes that contrasted beautifully with his dark hair, but she had to. She held up her hand and waved.

"Bye, Jaedon." She waited until she reached the forest once more to giggle to herself with pure delight.

* * * * *

Jaedon found himself serious debating if he should follow Hyko back into the forest instead of going to Ash's impromptu meeting. So far, Hyko was winning; after all, a girl shouldn't be traveling alone at night in the forest, especially with all of Tristan's men spreading out and camping everywhere. If she got jumped...

Jaedon pushed that thought aside.

Then again, if he didn't show up to the meeting, Bryce would begin to question him. Eventually, he'd get the truth and go after Hyko. *Lord only knows what he'll do to her if he catches her again,* Jaedon thought grimly as he headed over to one of the biggest hut-houses (It occurred to Jaedon then that he should've asked

Hyko what those were called). Twenty three men had traveled from the snowy wastelands to the beach town under Ash and London's command. All of them were gathered in the large hut-house, talking amongst themselves. Jaedon didn't bother to take a seat and join in. Instead, he leaned against the wall and hoped no one would notice his presence.

"Jaedon!" Unfortunately, Bryce spotted him the moment he stepped through the door. "Nice of you to show your face to the living."

"Lay off me, Bryce," he grumbled.

"Oh, and what's this you've brought with you? Some attitude!" Bryce exclaimed. "That I do *not* appreciate."

"Please. I'm not in the mood." Before Bryce could say anything more, London cleared his throat to get everyone's attention. London was not one who looked like a leader. He was a scrawny man with thinning, red hair and freckles covering his face and neck. His voice had a scratchy, slurred quality to it, making it sound like he'd recently done some sort of illegal drug.

"Men, I received news from Tristan today," he announced. "The wastelands have been successfully conquered! The last of the natives gave in and surrendered their weapons yesterday evening!" Cheers and applause erupted from the audience. "Now, twenty or so men arrived in the mountains today, making it a grand total of sixty up there. We have just about gained control there as well." More cheers. "We have identified two other towns similar to the three we have discovered already. One of them we have been scouting out, the one that is surrounded by woods."

"You know what that means, right?" Ash joined in. "More native women!" Several of the men voiced their excitement about that while Jaedon frowned.

"Ah, yes, of course that," London laughed. "Have you all been enjoying the lovely ladies here?" More hoots and hollers. Jaedon sank down to the floor and moaned. They were speaking of these people like they were some sort of a delicious food to be enjoyed! Bryce eyed him and kneeled down as well.

"What's up with you?" He stared at Jaedon in silence before saying, "Ooh, I know what this is about. You're jealous because you haven't been *getting' any*, have you? Oh wait, I just remembered! *You're still a virgin by choice*." He chuckled as if someone had told some hilarious joke. Jaedon didn't find it amusing in the least and pushed Bryce down on his butt with more force than he'd wanted. The unexpected shove ticked the man off and he dove at Jaedon, his hands wrapping around his throat. The commotion drew London's attention to the back of the room, a scowl coming across his face.

"Bryce Johnston. Care to explain to me why you're trying to kill Jaedon back there?" Bryce froze, his hands still wrapped tightly around Jaedon's neck as he looked up at his leader. His grip had loosened, and Jaedon took the opportunity to shove Bryce off him and crawl away.

"Nothin', chief," Bryce explained. "Just teaching this worm to watch himself." London narrowed his eyes and glared at him, then turned his attention to Jaedon, who was standing with his back against the door.

"You're in enough of a bind as it is," he hissed. "Don't mess around, or you'll end up regretting it. I'll make sure of that." Jaedon nodded and glanced at the ground.

"Can I leave now?" he mumbled.

"Go. Bryce can fill you in on the rest of this meeting later." Jaedon didn't wait another second and left out as silently as he'd entered.

He collapsed on the bed immediately after pulling off his shirt and hoodie. He didn't bother with pulling the sheets over his bare chest or changing into pajama pants. His neck was sore and his throat was dry as he settled down and gazed out the window at the moon.

Hyko.

The word came to him suddenly and he started to think about his run-in with her. He wondered what she was doing, where she was sleeping. The thought made him blush. In his mind, he ran through all the words she'd taught him. Tattao, tree; hyuk, grass; daunai, bird; ahro ,rock; sai, sky; hyko, moon.

ZEMIDEY
DANGER

Red marks and small, purple bruises covered the palms of Hyko's hands when she removed the bandages she'd put on at least a week before. She dipped her hands into the cool stream that ran through the heart of the forest. She hadn't gotten very far after leaving Kainau the second time. It had been too dark to go anywhere, but she didn't want to stay in the middle of the forest at night. She'd finally settled on climbing a tree and resting soundly in its branches until the sunrise woke her up.

As she washed up in the stream, she realized that she now had an overwhelming amount of options. What with the rest of her village thinking she was off delivering messages, she could use that to her advantage. After all, it had been her original plan to use her job as a messenger as a cover-up so that she could leave the village with a valid excuse. However, Hyko really hadn't planned on running into any of the strangers, only learning more about them. Now that she knew where they were, she wondered if she should warn her people or not, and what the outcome of either decision would be. She could return to Tattao and tell them about the strangers; she could return to Tattao and say nothing about the strangers. She could go on and deliver the letters; she could dump the bag in the stream. She could go back with Jaedon...

But how?

Those other white men seemed less than willing to treat Hyko like an actual person. When they'd been harassing her, she was lucky to get away like she did. There was no way she even wanted to imagine what they would've done to her if she hadn't broken free of their grip, much less if she went back and ran into one again. Besides, what would her people think? What would Gisipeh think?

And Yonej...she'd almost completely forgotten about him. *Which isn't a good thing, seeing as I'll be marrying him,* she groaned inwardly. She'd liked him a little at first, but after they'd argued in the woods, she was positive that she'd never want to marry him. She wasn't even sure if they could become true friends.

That was it, then; going back to Tattao was what she was not going to do. That left her with the choices of going on to deliver the letters, and going back to Kainau with Jaedon...

With a sigh, Hyko grabbed her bag and stood, intent on heading in the direction of Kainau. She still needed to get the letters and packages there if she was to return to Tattao without causing too much suspicion.

Hyko took off her throw and tossed it up in the branches of a nearby tree. It was much warmer than it had been the previous day, and Hyko could kind of understand why Jaedon's pants had only gone to his knees. She walked on for several more minutes before growing tired of the heat and digging through her bag for one of her summertime outfits. As she was doing so, a small moan caught her attention.

"Hiya?" she said warily. Again, she heard a moan. She tried locating the source of the noise, yet saw nothing but plants, trees and rocks. "Hiya? Jaedon? Sok tessa yeioy?"

"Wh...what...Jaedon...?" A weak voice groaned from not too far away. "Who...who is...that...?" All at once, Hyko recognized who it was.

"Awa'hi!" she gasped, and frantically began looking around. When she finally found her old friend, she was appalled. Awa'hi was only half dressed, the clothing she was wearing torn and tattered. Her hair that had once been dark and long was cut short, almost like a boy's. On her cheeks were tear stains. Her eyes bloodshot and her lips cracked.

"Hy...Hyko-jete...what are you...doing here...who...who is Jaedon?" she croaked, attempting to sit up.

"No, noka, Awa'hi," Hyko said. "Don't sit up, just lay there and rest. What happened to you?"

"Is he one of the ziolen rarroso?" she asked, her eyes darting from left to right. "They're not here, are they...? Oh, Hyko, please...don't get...don't get caught by them..."

"Awa'hi, did the strangers do this to you?"

"I was...just coming to see my...my cousin...and when I got here...they were everywhere...and they..." She coughed and moaned, clamping her eyes shut and grimacing. She was in great pain, but Hyko couldn't tell if it was physical or emotional. Whichever one it was, the white strangers had caused it.

"Awa'hi, where does it hurt?" Hyko asked. Her friend just barely opened her eyes and shook her head. She reached up her hands and covered her eyes. When Hyko looked down at her, she noticed blood stains on the tattered hem of her dress as well as on her legs. She sucked in a breath as she realized what had happened.

"*Oh*." She furrowed her brow. "Ah mei vehaja...how could they do this to you?"

"You...you'd better pray to the spirits that...that they never catch you...you better pray...pray long...long and hard..." Awa'hi's eyelids fluttered shut and her countenance relaxed.

* * * * *

"Hey, look! Hyko's back!" Ohn-Tsung and her friends were out during their break from classes. Classes were usually held indoors, but it was warm, and the teacher allowed them a fifteen minute break to run around outside. Gusto had told her family that Hyko wouldn't be returning for at least a week or two, making her presence at the east exit a surprise for Ohn-Tsung. Ohn-Tsung left her friends and their game of ball to rush over to her sister. When she got closer, she stopped dead in her tracks and stared. In Hyko's arms was Awa'hi, one of their friends from Sasse. She looked terrible, with her clothing torn up...and her hair! Ohn-Tsung had always longed for her hair to be as long as Awa'hi's, so that she could put it in one braid that went down to the middle of her back. But to Ohn-Tsung's horror, she saw that Awa'hi's hair had been cut off, reduced to a short little afro atop her hair.

"Umnii, go get Hanjeha," Hyko commanded, sounding worn out. Her legs were shaking. "*Right now*."

Awa'hi did not wake up until well after night had fallen. Hyko had been exhausted from carrying her friend for miles, and collapsed on the floor of the healer's hut, waking up to the smell of the soup that Hanjeha served the patients. Elder Agenee was muttering prayers in the corner and Gisipeh was leaning lazily against a shelf. When he saw Hyko was awake, he pulled her into a tight embrace. He did not let go until they all heard Awa'hi stirring and Hyko was asked to help Hanjeha.

"Hyko found me in the forest," she explained, sipping from the soup Hanjeha had prepared and some herbal tea.

"In the forest?" Hanjeha asked, her voice soft and comforting. "Up by Kainau?"

"Yes, that's right. I was left there after...after..." She paused, a tear falling from her cheek into her soup. "There were these men, and they...did horrible things to me...and it hurt...it hurt so bad and I just wanted them to stop...I begged them to stop, but they just...they just laughed at me..." She clamped her eyes shut. Her lip began to quiver and she clutched at her soup bowl with shaking fingers. Hyko placed a hand on her shoulder, but Awa'hi flinched. "And...and when they were done, they just...they just left me there, and I was bleeding and hurting...and when I cried out for help, no one came..." She moaned loudly, biting her bottom lip. "Why? Spirits, *why? What did I ever do?*"

"Calm yourself, dear," Elder Agenee soothed, but Awa'hi thrashed out, throwing her bowl of soup. The thick broth splattered against the walls and onto Gisipeh's hunting attire.

"I hope they're condemned!" Awa'hi shrieked. *"I hope they are all condemned!"* She began to wail miserably, curling up into a ball. Her sobs shook her entire body. Hanjeha covered her with a blanket and pressed a cool towel across her forehead.

"You all leave," she whispered. "I will keep watch over her. She will...she will need some time to recover."

Hyko could not get her mind off her friend, even when Gisipeh offered to take her down to the stream to fish the next morning. Hyko wondered if Awa'hi would ever get over her traumatic experience with the white men; her spirit had been badly damaged, and she had been utterly humiliated.

"I don't think you should still go out and be a messenger," Gisipeh said. Hyko scowled at the water. After what she'd seen the white men do to Awa'hi, she felt even less secure about them than she had before. But, she still felt compelled to do something more, find out something more. The fact that she'd be able to see Jaedon again was another a huge temptation.

"I have to," she told her friend, tossing the line out into the water. "I never got to deliver the letters Gusto told me to in the first place, and now I have to warn the other villages about these white men. Not to mention let Sasse know that Awa'hi won't be coming home until she settles down." Gisipeh threw a rock into the water. "Hey! We're trying to fish, Ileigeh."

"I know what we're doing," he growled. He stepped forward and grabbed Hyko by the shoulders, spinning her around to face him. "Hyko, have you lost your mind?" Hyko glared defiantly at him.

"Maybe I have," she said. "But I have to do this. I know that this is what the spirits-"

"The spirits have commanded women to listen to the men without question!" Gisipeh snapped. "They've commanded us to love one another and help each other. They've commanded us to respect our elders, *not* go on *suicide missions!*"

"Think what you want, Gisi!" Hyko spat. "But this is what I *know*."

"Yeah, well, this is what *I* know. I know that you will *not* go back out into the woods anymore until these white men, these...these rarroso...they're gone or until we know they're safe."

"Gisi-"

"I'm not asking you, Hyko," he interrupted, firmly. His glare softened, though his tone had grown harsh. He did not loosen his grip on Hyko's shoulders. He could feel his friend shaking, from anger. She hated the men in her village when they thought they owned her. They did and would not own her, not even Gisipeh. He was usually very respectful of her and her opinions. Now, he was being another one of the demanding men. She broke free of his grasp in one violent movement that knocked him backwards.

"Wow," she cried. "Wow! So it's gonna be like that, then? I never thought that you-of all people!-would go against me like this!" She stormed off, brushing his hands off her whenever he tried to touch her shoulder. He said some things to her, words that sounded like apologies. Hyko heard nothing. Her rage made her oblivious to his explanations. She wasn't in the mood. All she wanted was to get far away from Gisipeh. *Men in general,* she thought crossly.

She took the longer route home from the stream, noticing more of the metal rods. What *were* they? The next time she was with Jaedon, she'd ask him to teach her some words too. The next time she was with Jaedon...

That means that I'm planning to risk my life and go back to see him, she thought to herself with a smirk. Something about the boy just seemed so...so innocent and curious, like a little child who was going out of the village for the very first time.

"Hyko." Yonej's voice startled her, made her jump and turn to see him standing behind her. He reached for her and pulled her into an awkward, unnatural hug. "You had us all worried sick! Catahou janneh? What were you thinking? Going out like that with these rarroso-"

"I was doing my job as a messenger," she told him matter-of-factly. Her future husband wrapped his arm around her waist and pulled her along harshly, heading in the direction of his kytah.

"You know good and well that messengers are young men," he growled, not letting on that he was irritated with his facial expression. "Why would you even volunteer to do such a thing?"

"Mei heg ne zze," she said. "I want to help."

"You would be helping everyone if you would just stay in your place and do what a women ought to be doing," he snapped, dragging her inside the kytah. He closed the door and drew in a breath, then let it out slowly. "Aside from that. Where were you just now?"

"Wei Gisipeh; I was with Gisipeh." Hyko thought nothing of it; she was always with Gisipeh. They were best friends, had been for years. Her becoming engaged would not change that. However, when Yonej heard this, he scowled. "Natte?"

"You and him...you aren't lovers, are you?" he asked, and Hyko felt her face heat up.

"*What?* Ai no!" she cried. She couldn't believe that Yonej would think such a thing. She could understand why he would think that they liked each other more than just best friends, but lovers? That was a whole different situation. Lovers weren't looked upon with much respect. Couples that were lovers would live together and commit certain acts that were viewed as unacceptable unless the two were bound by marriage. They usually would sneak away and live outside the land, where they wouldn't be ridiculed. Often times, their affairs wouldn't last for more than a year or two, and the couple would split, returning to normal life. But, she and Gisipeh, lovers...it seemed unimaginable to Hyko.

"You see him more than me," Yonej said. "And most of the time, when you've been together as of recently, you go off into the woods or somewhere secluded."

"Have you been...watching us?"

"I was only wanting to know if the suspicions started by that insolent girl, Awa'hi, were true. She's always assumed that you two were-"

"Shetteme! Shut up!" Hyko yelled. "I'm tired of this! Don't-" Yonej suddenly grabbed a hold of her, his grip painfully tight around her arms.

"Don't *ever* tell me to shut up again," he bellowed. "Do you hear me? *Not ever.*" Without thinking of the consequences, Hyko spat into his face and kicked him. Yonej fell to the ground with a groan, cursing and moaning. That was it for Hyko; she was heading home, grabbing her messenger bag and going back out before the sun was too low in the sky.

Heading back to Tattao while carrying Awa'hi had taken Hyko the better part of the previous day to do. Walking briskly back towards Kainau with only her bag of letters and packages took her less than four hours. She had reached the edge of the Kainau forest just after dusk. The air was warm and smelled of the ocean. The sound of gentle waves broke the odd silence that was still over Kainau.

Hyko couldn't see any white men out on the paths. Despite that, she chose to stay out of sight by walking behind the kytahs until she reached the kytah Jaedon had gone into the day before. When she was positive that none of the white men were around to see her, she darted from behind the kytah to the front. She slipped through the front door and into the main room of the kytah. It was very different from the kytahs in Tattao; the main room was more spacious with larger windows. The walls were made of palm wood, deep red paintings decorating them.

Quietly, she crept up the stairs and turned the corner, heading into the first room she saw. She caught her breath when she entered, for a shirtless Jaedon was laying asleep on a bed. His bare chest was lightly tanned, most likely due to the Kainau sun. Stepping forward, she placed her hands on his chest to shake him awake.

"Jaedon...Jaedon...*Jaedon!*" The third time she called his name, he began to stir and moan.

"Mmm...oh...yess...?" He was only kind of awake.

"Ta mei, Hyko!" she hissed. He turned his head up towards her. His eyelids fluttered open and he gazed drowsily up at her.

"Oh...it's just you..." All of a sudden, his eyes opened completely and he shot up, staring at Hyko. "It's *you!* Oh my...what that-how did you get in here?"

"Da portei," she said, pointing towards the door. Jaedon glanced in that direction, rushing over to close it. He tripped over several piles of clothing as he rushed around the room. *Huh,* Hyko thought. *Beautiful or not, he's still just like most guys...messy.* Her use of the word beautiful caught her off guard. She couldn't believe that she'd just thought of him as more than "the white boy she'd seen a day earlier." She felt her face heat up, then tried to justify her own thinking. He was attractive. It didn't mean anything just to think that a guy was good-looking, white or otherwise.

"You need to be more careful!" he hissed, grabbing her by the shoulders and bringing her back from her own contemplations. She swallowed and nodded her head. She could see he was calming himself down, his breathing slowly returning to normal. He relaxed his muscles and his grip around her arms loosened. Now, he just looked confused. "So...why are you here?" Hyko opened her mouth to speak but closed it a moment later. Why *was* she there? Instead of saying anything, she shrugged her shoulders. He leaned back and smiled. "Are you here to teach me more words in your language?"

"Ahown," she replied, nodding her head. *Why not?* She thought. *That's a good excuse, is it not?*

"Okay, that one I've heard before...is it, like, the word for 'yes'?" he asked, earning a broad grin from Hyko. "Good. I'm getting the hang of this, eh?"

"Donjo ye yam zenje atamo," Hyko chided jokingly. Jaedon stared at her blankly, earning a laugh from her. "Unditiyo?"

"Okay...maybe I'm not all that good at it yet," he laughed. He walked away from her for a moment and watched as she bent down to dig in a pile of clothing. She pulled out a red, short sleeve t-shirt and held it out.

"Tehm ae'losk," she told him.

"Oh...right." He threw it on, his abs still visible through the light, stretchy fabric. "Sorry. I should've, you know, put some clothes on." He smirked at her for a minute before placing a gentle hand on her shoulder. "We should get out of-" Jaedon paused. Hyko stood still, trying to figure out what he was hearing. Footsteps. Coming up the stairs. Walking towards the room they were in. Jaedon shoved her down by the bed, covering her with some clothes and unpacked bags. "Stay right there and please, *don't move*."

The door creaked open a moment later, an tall white man stepping in the room. Hyko didn't like the looks of him, even with dirty socks and unwashed pants limiting her view. His clothes were sloppy and the belt around his waist was unbuckled. He was a rather large man, but he wasn't fat. His green eyes seemed to say "I think everything is a joke."

"Jadey, how ya doin'?" he asked, a half smirk on his face. "Didn't see you earlier today at the-"

"I'm not interested in that, Bryce." Jaedon cut his sentence off short, speaking harshly. "I think you should let those people go and leave them alone."

"What, and have no more free, 'no-strings-attached' fun? You're out of your mind!" He walked forward and put an arm around Jaedon's shoulder. "Listen, Jae. Lay off the goodie two-shoes, squeaky clean guy act. London's not takin' lightly to it. Besides, you're in no position to oppose anything he says. And quite frankly, it's pissin' me off. So. With all that said, please; next time there is something going on around here, you better show up *without* the attitude." He slapped Jaedon on the back twice, then headed for the door. "Oh, and another thing. Get this room cleaned up. I could die trippin' over some shoes in here." Jaedon waited a long while before he told Hyko to come out. She was wary, even when he told her it was okay.

"Don't worry," he reassured her. "Bryce is back at his...his hut-thing, er, whatever, by now."

"Kytah," she corrected him.

"Right, that." He sighed and ran a hand through his hair. "So...we still on for a vocabulary lesson?" Hyko nodded her head.

"Only if you help me with something," she said in English. Her voice sounded heavily accented in Jaedon's ears.

"Whoa. You speak English?"

"Xoupeq," she told him. "Umm...that word I do not know in English. I think it's fluently, or something of the sort." He smiled.

"It's cool. At least I know you know what I'm saying."

"Essa donjo azokon mei kamo-kuai jetitsa Engoosan," she told him. *I'm not lettin' him off easy,* she thought. *I'm still gonna speak my language.* He groaned.

"Oh, so we're back to that again? Just my luck, eh?"

"Shay, yeioy hajekoh cuerete."

Hyko lead Jaedon into the forest, pointing out several herbs and roots as they walked on. She introduced him to old sayings in her language, making him repeat the words until his pronunciation improved. He picked up quickly and was eager to learn more.

"Why are you here?" Hyko asked. The two had been walking on for a while and were growing tired quickly; Jaedon had begun to yawn after every one of his sentences. Hyko had been on her feet for far too long the past few days, and was about ready to collapse. She took a seat on a nearby boulder and patiently awaited Jaedon's answer.

"I was recruited for sort of an expedition. It was either that or...well, never mind."

Hyko blinked. "That or what? You didn't have to come here?"

"The other men would've come no matter what. As for me? The trip was optional for me, and the alternative was pretty...undesirable." Judging from the tone of his voice and his body language, Hyko decided against asking him more about his alternative to coming to her land.

"We call you da ziolen rarroso," Hyko said. "It means white strangers."

"Huh...endearing term," Jaedon commented.

"Well, it's...it's what you are, no?" She was grateful for the fact that her skin was too dark for a blush to be seen. Her face felt so hot that she wondered if maybe he could see it changing shades anyway. Jaedon held up his hand and examined its creamy color. He looked over at Hyko and her darker complexion. Then he shrugged and chuckled to himself.

"Yeah, I guess," he laughed. "There's no one with light skin around here?" Hyko thought about it. There were some in Delfusio with skin a bit lighter. *Not* that *light, though*, Hyko thought. That was the only thing different about them, too; their hair was still in little knotted curls, not straight like the white men. She shook her head.

"Noka...not like you," she muttered, the information striking her as well as Jaedon. There really *was* no one that light on the land she lived on. She looked up at him then, really noticing all of the differences. There were so many of them.

"You...you are so...yeije ahkt denas...so different." She kept gazing at him until she felt it would soon become awkward. She looked away and said quickly, "I don't think I've eaten in a very long while."

"No big deal." He shrugged his shoulders casually. "I've got some food back at the beach town."

"Huh?" Hyko had never heard of a place called beach town... "Oh, Kainau. The, um, beach town, I guess. It's Kainau."

"Oh...right."

Running...she had to keep running. Her feet hit the ground hard with every step, pounding the pavement, aching as they dared to run on. She had to keep running. She had to. She kept telling herself to ignore the pain, that if she kept on, she'd be alright soon. But it wasn't working. She could not calm herself, no matter what little white lies she tried to feed her mind. The road was treacherous, mountains lying dead ahead as well as on every side of her. A few times, she stumbled, tripping over a rock or two. She had several cuts on her knees from her falls.

"You cannot escape." The voice was foreign to her; she could not recognize it no matter how hard she replayed the statement over and over in her head. "You cannot run. Your time is up." She squeezed her eyes shut and ran on. When she opened them once more, she came to a sudden halt. Right in front of her was a ledge. Looking down it, she couldn't see to the bottom of the ravine. If she'd continued on for even a few more steps, she'd have tumbled to her death in the chasm.

A light tap on her shoulder made her spin around. Behind her stood the lovely spirit Naura, her long, flowing dress covered in blood. With her stood the trouble-making spirit Kee. Naura opened her mouth to speak, but only moans and bloodcurdling shrieks of terror escaped her lips.

"Unditiyosa-kuai!"she cried, trying desperately to make sense of Naura's groans. "I don't understand! Naura, what is good about any of this?" Naura said nothing that made any sense. Bewildered, Hyko collapsed to the ground and covered her face with her hands, shielding her eyes from the sight of Naura and her bloody attire. The lovely spirit's screams engulfed her entire being, making her head throb with an excruciating pain.

DESHONEY
FOOLISH

Hyko awoke right at sunrise the next morning. The room was dimly lit and completely quiet, except for the sound of the ocean in the distance and the birds in the forest. She panicked for a few moments when she realized that she had no idea of where she was. The room was far to spacious to be her own, and she wasn't camping in the woods as she'd done a couple of nights earlier. She managed to calm herself a little when she glanced up and saw Jaedon sleeping on the bed.

As she sat up, bit and pieces of the night before came back to her. She remembered teaching Jaedon the word for water and eating something that Jaedon had called a biscuit...she couldn't remember past that, no matter how hard she tried. Her mind was still being haunted by that ugly dream. *You cannot escape*...the words continued to echo in her head, along with the unbearable screams. *It's just the trouble-making spirit Kee playing with my head*, she reasoned in her thoughts.

"You up already?" Jaedon's voice interrupted her thoughts, but frightened her in doing so. She gasped and fell backwards onto the little sleeping pad Jaedon had set up for her. Jaedon ran a hand through his hair. "Sorry...didn't mean to scare you." He yawned.

"It's alright," she murmured. She wanted nothing more than to bury her head in her pillow and drift off into a peaceful sleep. Even so, the sun was up and she no longer felt drowsy. Jaedon shrugged once he heard she was okay and laid back down. Hyko smirked and leaned over him. "What're you doing?"

"Going back to sleep," he told her without opening his eyes. "I'm, how do you say it? Tikkre." She shook his shoulders and he pushed her away playfully. By then, he had a slight smirk on his face.

"Jaedon, sasse sok nanajuka," she said. "You know what that means, right?"

"No."

"It *means* that it's time to get up!" She tugged at his arm impatiently. "What if that man comes back and sees me in here?" Jaedon chortled; Bryce would've been on cloud nine if he thought that Jaedon had been fooling around with one of the native girls.

"I don't think I'd get in trouble," he explained. When he sat up, Hyko saw that he was shirtless again and found herself struggling to keep her eyes on his face. He leaned his head against the wall and sat in bed, his gaze going from the ceiling to her. "They'd just think..."

"I think I know what they'd think," she muttered, suddenly feeling embarrassed. "That's what my people would think as well." She stretched and thought back to what Yonej had said about her and Gisipeh. For a moment, she imagined herself and Jaedon together, as Yonej had thought Gisi and her were. "Um, are you hungry? I would like to eat." Jaedon stood and took in a breath.

"Yeah, sure," he yawned. He slipped into some new socks as well as a pair of shoes, but no shirt yet. He dipped his hands in a bucket of water near a chest at the foot of his bed. He splashed the water on his face and in his hair, ruffling it so that it stood up in every direction.

"What do you eat for your morning meal?" she asked, wandering around the room. "Those biscuit things?"

"Sometimes," Jaedon said with a shrug. "I can find you something else to eat, if you'd like."

"Hmm...do you have usacosia?" Hyko asked. It didn't occur to her that he might not know what those were until he gave her a blank stare. "I guess not...Amam makes them a lot for our morning meal."

"You mean breakfast?"

"Sure, that." She got to her feet and slipped into her shoes. "Generally, there's no dataunai around here, but daunai taste almost the same..." Jaedon recognized the word for bird in an instant. Was she planning on eating birds?

"If I may ask, what are you talking about?" He began digging around in piles of clothing as he spoke. "All I understood was daunai. Are you...gonna eat a bird?"

"What? No, of course not!" Hyko almost laughed at the thought. Birds were only eaten during a famine, and there hadn't been one of those in several years. "I'm going to...you know what? I'll just show you." She grabbed a hold of his wrist and pulled him out the door, not bothering to let him throw on the shirt he had balled up in his hand first.

* * * * *

It was so early that none of the other men were awake. A couple native women made their way silently out of the homes of the men. No doubt they had been "played with" the night before, judging by the disheveled appearance of most of them. What would Hyko say if she found out what his men were doing to her people? Jaedon found himself dwelling on this thought as she continued to pull him into the forest.

For over an hour, Hyko went through the long, drawn out process of making breakfast, or dei mao'oka as she called it. She claimed that it took less time when you already had hudjueh (which Jaedon later learned was the word for eggs), but the procedure was still longer than he was used to. Half the time, the two wandered around the woods looking for bird's nests. Once one was found, they had to see if a bird was in it. When a bird was in it, they had to knock down the nest and kill the bird with one stone. Otherwise, the bird would try to injure them in order to protect its eggs. Once the bird was out of the way, they had easy access to the eggs, so long as they weren't completely smashed. As Jaedon watched them sizzling on a warm rock in the morning sun, Hyko gathered seasoning herbs and roots. As she crushed them up to sprinkle on their usacosia, she told colorful stories that eased Jaedon's mind. It had been a while since he'd been told a story, and it wasn't as if he could go and ask Bryce to break out a story book.

"There is a legend that tells of how the spirits used to tell between a good soul and an evil one," she began. She'd crushed the last of a light brown root and moved on to a deep green one. "Kee and Naura would take a few tahmas-er, twigs-and create an illusion, making the pile of twigs look like a wounded baby daunai. They'd set the baby bird on a path traveled often by the villages and watch from Saiytah to see what travelers would do. Those who stopped to see about the bird were blessed with whatever the spirits saw fit; a new baby, more crops...perhaps even a letter from an old relative in a different village. Anyone who ignored the bird was punished.

"After a while, Kee grew tired of this. She claimed that just because someone didn't stop to care for a baby bird didn't mean that they weren't a good person. Naura disagreed. She said that one who is considerate cares about the feelings and desires of all living things, not just what they think is worth caring about." So far, the story was leaving a sour taste in Jaedon's mouth. He chose not to say anything, though, and Hyko continued.

"One day, a small boy ran through the woods and trampled the bird illusion. He stopped to look at it, but then kept running. Naura was quite upset that the boy had not done anything at all, and punished the boy immediately by making him unable to walk. The boy lay in the woods until another traveler found him and carried him to Sasse. The boy pleaded and pleaded with the traveler to take him to Tattao instead, to gather herbs for his ill father. The boy explained that he'd been in a hurry to get medicines for his father, stopping for nothing as he ran to the village in the woods. He told the traveler also that he must've injured himself when he tripped over the poor baby bird he'd seen on the road. The boy said that on any other day, he would've stopped to help the bird. On that day, however, he'd been preoccupied by his father and hurried past.

"Naura never got over the guilt that had possessed her when she'd stopped the little boy's legs from working. Kee never forgave her either, and the trouble-making spirit's heart grew darker than ever before. From then on, the spirits never tested the hearts of villagers with the baby bird ever again."

"That's a pretty depressing story," Jaedon said. Hyko had begun to sprinkle the herbs onto the fried eggs by then. She used a sharp twig she'd dipped in the stream to divide the eggs into two even portions.

"It has a lesson to it," she explained. "While it is true that one's nature is determined by their actions, some actions can be misunderstood."

"Or that sometimes mistakes can be made?" Jaedon suggested. The eggs that Hyko had made looked and smelled delicious, yet he couldn't bring himself to try them. His stomach felt as if it had been twisted into several knots.

"Yeah, that's a good point," Hyko told him, taking a bite of the usacosia.

"Whatever happened to the boy? Did that Nora girl fix him back?"

"No. The boy never walked again."

"Nora's a bit of a jerk." Jaedon scooped some egg into his mouth with a scowl. "Mmm. These are good...but how could she do that? She should've waited until she knew why the boy trampled the bird, you know? Then, when she found out she made a mistake, she should've fixed him back."

"She couldn't. She didn't have the power to. But she felt very, very sorry."

"I don't think feeling sorry would cut it."

"Some mistakes can't be undone, Jaedon." She stared right at him, and Jaedon shivered. They were such a deep, rich brown. It made Jaedon feel as if she was looking right through him, right into his soul, trying to figure out if he was a good soul or an evil one. They sat in silence for the rest of the meal. Hyko's story wouldn't leave Jaedon's head. Did she know? Had she found out already and was trying to give him a hint by telling him a dismal myth?

"Why did you come back?" Jaedon asked, finally breaking the silence. "I mean, not that I'm not glad you did, but..." Hyko gave him a small grin. It was gone in a moment, though.

"I...I don't wish to go home," she admitted. "Not really. There's only trouble there for me. And, I had a job to do that I didn't finish...actually, now I've got two jobs to do."

"I'm not distracting you, am I?" he asked. "Because if I am, I'll go on and let you work." If he was distracting her, he would need to go. If he needed to go, he couldn't speak with her. Nevertheless, that was the absolute last thing he wanted to do. The girl intrigued him more than anything. All he wanted to do was hang around her and learn more about her world and what was in it, hear more of her stories. In addition to all of that, he wanted to protect her. The men were working their way through more and more of the land every day, taking more and more lives. Mostly, they were interested in the women. They just couldn't get enough "fun," and if one of them saw Hyko walking through the woods alone...

"You are no distraction to me," Hyko reassured him with a smile. "I like your company. I like teaching you." She stood and stretched. "Did you like the usacosia?"

"Yeah, it was deeelish!" He stood as well. "So, this job of yours. What do you need to do?"

"Deliver letters and packages and...umm..." She bit her lip and hesitated to say the last thing. Jaedon looked at her. He opened his mouth to ask her what the third thing was when a noise catches his attention. A voice. Calling for Hyko. Coming closer to where they were.

* * * * *

It didn't take long for Hyko to recognize Gisipeh's voice. She couldn't believe that he'd had followed her all the way out there. *Why?* And why did he have to meet up with her then and there, with Jaedon and her so deep in conversation? Involuntarily, she went into panic mode and backed up slowly. She doubted her stealth would be beneficial; hunting had honed Gisipeh's physical skills, hearing included.

"Stay hidden behind a tree," she hissed, her mouth at Jaedon's ear. She felt him shiver as she placed her hand on his shoulder. "Peleiko, Jaedon. If Gisipeh catches me with you, he might jump to conclusions and hurt you."

"You know-" Before he could get the entire sentence out, Hyko pushed him down and stepped away from his hiding spot. Gisipeh appeared a few short moments later. His shoulders relaxed when he saw her.

"Hyko," he breathed. "Ah mei vehaja, I was going crazy worrying about you. Everyone is. You just left without telling us!" Hyko didn't dare show emotion. Her mouth was a thin, tight line and her eyes gave away nothing.

"I'm well aware of that," she said, impassively. Gisipeh tried to crack a smile.

"Hyko, come on," he pleaded. "I'm sorry. I treated you rudely. Please...come home."

"Get over yourself, Gisi," she hissed. Her friend flinched as if she'd just threatened to hit him. "You aren't the only reason I left Tattao."

"Then...then it's Yonej?"

"I have a job to do," she snapped, completely ignoring his question. "Leave me be."

"You can't be out here all alone with these white men!" The words "white men" left Gisipeh's mouth the same way a cuss word would; filled with venom. "Remember Awa'hi, hmm? Didn't you see what happened to her? Because of a white man?"

"I was the first one to see what happened to her! *Of course I know!*" Hyko cried. She knew where this was going. He'd go on about how it was dangerous and she needed to return home. She needed to swallow her pride and let someone protect her. She needed to do as a man told her. She'd heard it all a million and one times before. Only now did she see that she didn't agree with any of it. She would do what she knew the spirits were telling her to do and warn the other villages before the white men hurt anyone else.

"This has been a nice chat, but I need to go now," Hyko said flatly. She turned to walk away. She heard no noise, which meant Gisipeh wasn't coming after her. He was finally giving up. He was letting her go ahead.

"Hyko, no." A hand grabbed a hold of her wrist tightly. Gisipeh pulled her back to him harshly. The look in his eyes was a fierce one, and for only the second time in her life, Hyko saw his demanding side. "You need to come back to Tattao. I'm serious." Hyko spat in his face.

"I'm serious, too!" she cried. All of a sudden, she heard more bushes rustling. She froze and glanced away from Gisipeh, who was trying to wipe her spit from his eyes. She'd half expected to see the green-eyed white man who'd stormed into Jaedon's room the night before. Instead, Hyko saw Jaedon himself. He marched up to the two arguing friends, looking anything but pleased. Gisipeh's eyes grew wide, and he gawked at the boy as if he was seeing a ghost. Hyko pulled away from Gisipeh, who was too busy staring at Jaedon to try and stop her.

"Hey, man, she said she didn't want to go," Jaedon said, glaring at Gisipeh. Gisipeh took one step back, still in awe.

"Jaedon!" Hyko hissed. Part of her was worried that Jaedon would hurt Gisipeh if he didn't stop insisting she return to Tattao. Another part of her was terrified that Gisipeh would hurt Jaedon, thinking that Jaedon wanted to hurt her. All of her was wanting to do nothing but scream to the heavens and get away from both of them for a few moments and have some peace of mind.

"Hyko...why is this ziolen rarroso here?" Gisipeh growled. He was trembling slightly. Was it from anger, or because he was scared? Jaedon remained where he was, as did Hyko. Gisipeh slowly began backing up. "Hyko...*Hyko!*" Hyko turned to face him then. She knew he was expecting an answer, but what was there to say? For all Gisipeh knew, she was with the "enemy."

"I'm not going-"

"You will come with me right now," Gisipeh insisted. "Don't-"

"*You* go now, Gisipeh! Keil tsu!" Hyko shoved him with such great force that she fell to her knees. She squeezed her eyes shut. One of the boys placed a hand on her shoulder; she didn't have the energy or the desire to look up and see who it was. A few long moments later, she heard one of the boys walk off into the woods, leaving only the boy with his hand on her shoulder.

"Hyko, I'm sorry I caused all that trouble between you and...him." It was Jaedon who had stayed; Gisipeh was gone.

"I think...I think I need to talk with him one last time," Hyko said quietly, standing. She didn't particularly want to speak with him. Nonetheless, there were a few things they needed to work out. "Go back to Kainau. I'll come and find you in a little bit. Don't go anywhere else...please." He nodded slowly, guilt in his eyes. Hyko gave him a weak smile. "Jaedon, you've done nothing wrong. If anything, *I'm* the one causing trouble. Trust me." She didn't wait for his reply. All she could focus on was catching up to Gisipeh before he was too far into the forest. She sprinted furiously, swatting tree branches and shrubbery away from her eyes. It wasn't long before she slammed into him. As she scrambled to get to her feet, Gisipeh started to speak.

"Hyko...why were you with him?" he demanded. "That...that ziolen rarroso, he hasn't hurt you, has he?"

"Not at all," she said. "But, Gisi-"

"Hyko, shut up!" he snapped, his ferocity taking her aback. "You and he...you didn't...you haven't..." Hyko's eyes widened.

"Noka! What kind of a girl do you think I am?" she cried angrily. First, it was Yonej thinking that she and Gisipeh were lovers. Now, Gisi thought that she and Jaedon were...? "I just met Jaedon a few days ago. We haven't done anything...like that. I swear to the spirits." He sighed and ran a hand through his hair, steadily gazing at the ground.

"Hyko, he and his people are bringing changes to our land. Bad changes. Did you know that two other soldiers in Fayune have been seriously injured?"

"Jaedon has done nothing but kind things to me since I have met him," she argued. "Why won't you see my side in all of this? Why can't you trust me and my decisions?"

"Because your choices have been nothing but stupid and rash." He kicked up dirt as he spoke. He still refused look her in the eyes. "You haven't thought anything through. You've been speaking when you shouldn't and stepping out of line."

"Alright, so I've been making some mistakes," she admitted, exasperated. "But I need you to believe me when I say that Jaedon isn't an enemy of ours. I know that Tattao and the other villages won't listen, but I'd thought at least you would."

"Are you out of your mind? These men-"

"Until the rest of the villages will listen, I need you to keep Jaedon a secret. "

"Hyko-"

"Please. Peleiko, Gisi. Don't tell anyone about him and me speaking. *Please*." At last, his gaze moved from the ground to her face. More than anything, he looked tired, Hyko noticed. He looked as if he hadn't been sleeping for days on end. Normally, Hyko would've cracked a joke about the bags under his eyes. Things, however, were far from normal. Hyko was beginning to wonder if they would ever go back to how they'd been before.

* * * * *

Jaedon was put to work as soon as he got back to Kainau. Ash was in a worse mood than usual, increasing everyone's workload by ridiculous amounts. Jaedon was usually the one who was never assigned much of anything. For whatever reason, it was decided that on that day, he would shadow the construction crew as they got to work on improving the quality of the "hut things."

Jaedon trudged on behind the men, focusing more on Hyko than the blueprints they were going over. At least an hour had to have passed since she'd told him to go back to Kainau and wait for her. Had that young man forced her to go back to her village?

I hope not, Jaedon thought. But what if he had? He thought about going out into the woods after her, if that were the case.

"Yo, Jadey!" A tall, burly man slapped Jaedon's shoulder. "Quit daydreaming, man. We gotta get a move on. Ash is trippin' if he thinks we'll have all this up by the end of tomorrow." Jaedon got to his feet reluctantly, following the man to the rest of the group. The sun was high and beads of sweat were dripping down his forehead. He swiped them away and sighed. He was bored out of his mind. The sweltering heat wasn't helping in the least.

"Umm, may I go pee?" he asked. The burly man gave him a look, and Jaedon clamped his mouth shut. He leaned forward and took a look at the designs on the blueprints. He had to admit, the homes they were planning on building were quite impressive. At the same time, he knew that by building on the land, they would be taking over something that did not belong to them.

"Man, these hut things are shabby," a man with blonde hair grunted. The only thing Jaedon remembered about him was that he'd farted a lot on the way over. "How can these sons of-"

"Kytah," Jaedon muttered under his breath. The blonde haired farting man let one loose before turning to gape at Jaedon.

"What did you just say, boy?"

"They're called 'kytahs,' not 'hut things,'" Jaedon clarified. "Hey, what's it take for a guy to be able to pee around here?" A couple of the men continued to stare at Jaedon. He didn't care; all he wanted was to pee.

"Since when are you fluent in the language of these barbarians?" The burly man guffawed, slapping Jaedon on the shoulder again. Jaedon stumbled forward, kicking the blonde man in the knees as he pulled himself up. "Huh? *Jadey!* I'm talking to you, boy!"

"You been hanging with em,' haven't you?" Blonde man snapped. "Is that how you know that word, huh? You been sitting around, sharing beers? Is that it?" Jaedon spit the sand out from his mouth and scowled. The men were watching him, expectantly. *They're waiting for answers I'll never give*, he thought to himself. As he sat in the sand, he felt no anxiety about them getting the truth out of him. Sooner or later, the burly man would grow tired of waiting. Jaedon might get smacked around a little for not responding. But after that, the subject would be dropped and Hyko would remain a secret. All he needed to do was wait it out for a bit longer.

"What's all this about?" Ashleigh came sauntering down to the construction workers, his skin appearing slightly yellow. He leaned against a large boulder in the sand to steady himself. As he lowered himself to his knees, burly man opened his mouth to speak. Ash cut him off too soon, though. "Exactly. Talking; that's exactly what you're doing. It ends. Now. Get to work." Grumbles and complaints filled the air as burly man let the subject drop, just as Jaedon had predicted, and returned to explaining the blueprints. Jaedon was the last to rejoin the group. He stood with a groan, only to be pulled back down by Ash. His fingers were shaky and feeble.

"Ash, man, you don't look so great," Jaedon pointed out. The comment earned him a dirty look from his leader. "Let me rephrase that; you need some water, sir?"

"Shut up, Jadey." As he stood, Ash winced as if in pain. "Hey, you been laid yet?"

"Umm...no. You sure you don't need some water?" Ashleigh narrowed his eyes at Jaedon's question.

"Don't change the subject on me. You'd better get some while it's free and women are readily available." He patted Jaedon's back and began to head towards the village. He mumbled to himself as he waddled away on his weak legs. Ashleigh was never the strongest-looking man around; he did look stronger than London, but he was no body builder. Even with that being so, he'd begun to look much scrawnier since the men's arrival in Kainau.

With Ash gone, Jaedon had no one around to give him orders. The construction crew had made their way down to the other side of the beach. Ash was off being a jerk, as was London. Jaedon was a free man.

"Jaedon." The feminine voice came from nowhere, surprising him enough to make him cuss. He fell ungracefully into the sand, his jaw dropping when he saw Hyko. She had a solemn expression on her face and sweat on her brow. She'd also changed her skirt. She now wore a short, light blue one that blew as a breeze swept through.

"Hyko!" he growled. "What-how'd you get here? What if they see you?" He grabbed a hold of her wrist and broke into a light jog, careful to avoid the direction the construction workers had gone. He entered the village through the south village gate. He knew that only the natives would be near the south; it was the one place they could go during the day without being harassed. Over a dozen native girls and young women were talking amongst themselves when Hyko and Jaedon passed. Few of them looked even a little bit happy. One of the younger girls looked up when she noticed the two rushing by. Her hair was tied into two little puffy pigtails. She wore a dull red dress, almost as dull as her brown, tired eyes.

"Hyko-jete!" the little girl cried, causing the other natives to look up. The little girl started over to Hyko, and Jaedon slowed up a little. The girl's eyes lit up and the beginnings of a smile could be seen on her face. Then, the little girl noticed Jaedon. She froze, all signs of joy vanishing from her face. "Ziolen rarroso! Hyko, Whatta arei yeioy dojei wei yeiho?"

"Mei-"

"Hyko, come on!" Jaedon insisted, placing an arm around her waist and pulling her along.

"Dojei-kuai worletu! Yeioy-yjo heje gwan," she said to the natives just before she couldn't see them any longer. "Don't worry; he is nice! You can trust him!"

KEILKE
TRAVEL

Jaedon didn't stop pulling her until they were deep into the forest. The sun was sinking low in the sky by then. The trails ahead of them would soon be covered in darkness, but they walked on anyway. Finally, Hyko grew tired of the silence and decided to break it.

"This...friendship is...is difficult," she sighed. She'd been contemplating their few-day friendship for a majority of the day. So far, it had been nothing but trouble. Gisipeh was terrified of what the white men could do; the fact that Hyko had befriended one of them scared him even more. He would do any and everything to make sure that they stayed separated. Not to mention fact that all of the villages hated the men for what they'd done to Awa'hi and the other hunters. What with all the preconceived ideas on the fair-skinned men, Hyko knew that it would be hard for the others to accept Jaedon as a friend and not a foe.

"I've noticed," he grumbled. He pulled his shirt up over his head and tossed it aside. "Man, it is still *hot*." Hyko nodded. She didn't have the energy to do much else. The two sat around in the forest, going over more vocabulary and phrases. It wasn't a long lesson for Jaedon, for after a little while, Hyko stood up.

"If I don't get these things delivered, someone else is gonna come after me," she sighed. She adjusted the strap of her messenger bag. "With my luck, someone who will not show so much mercy. But...I really don't feel like going anywhere..."

"Is it because that guy was giving you a hard time?"

"...yeah..." Some of what Gisipeh had said had had some truth to it. The white men *were* dangerous; they had seriously hurt Awa'hi. She'd heard the way the green-eyed white man had spoken. Other than Jaedon, the other men scared her. Jaedon gazed at her, his blue eyes shining.

"Are you afraid?" he asked. All she could do was nod slowly. "Of the men, right? My men?"

"There isn't much I'm afraid of," she explained, quietly. "But, the rest of the ziolen rarroso...they're terrifying."

"I'll come with you," he said quickly. Hyko stared at him, not blinking.

"You'll what?"

"Come with you...uh, in your language, that's...como wei yeioy?" He struggled to finish the sentence, but earned a grin from her when he did. "One of the only places we haven't really been is the desert; we kind of thought there wouldn't be too much out there. Everywhere else, though, is full of my men. I could help you out if we run into any of them on the way."

"Good," Hyko said. "I actually need to go to the desert; good to know that there shouldn't be many rarroso there." She paused. "Are...are you sure? I mean, you don't..." He placed a hand on her shoulder and grinned. Hyko felt her face grow hot.

"I'm sure," he said..

Hyko and Jaedon started heading for Sasse that same evening. Hyko insisted on moving quickly to avoid any animals or scouts in the area. While the trail between Kainau presented few dangers beyond biting, non-venomous spiders, the road to Sasse was a harsher one. Wild animals that were out mostly in the daytime made their nests in the land between the lush forest and the scorching sand. Scorpions nested in some of the caves that travelers would use for refuge. Hyko kept persisting that if they moved quickly, they'd be past the dangers faster.

"Why would we leave the comfort of the tropical Kainau forest to go closer to the freaky stuff?" Jaedon groaned. They were beginning to enter the Middle Grounds, land between all the villages that did not belong to one or the other. It was vast and took a long while to travel through; many villages took several days to travel it when visiting other villages during Samnba.

"To get a move on," she explained. "I told you this already, lleigeh! Some of the deadly bugs and stuff are not out so much at night, also. If we walk mostly at night, maybe I will not have to take poison from a wound of yours."

"You really think I'll get bit by something poisonous?" There was amusement in his voice.

"Several times," she teased. Jaedon smirked at her. "You know nothing about this land. You will get hurt. I know it." She gave him an amused look. "And you'll have no one but me to save you." As Jaedon opened his mouth to make a smart remark, someone gave a shout. He grabbed Hyko's hand suddenly and lowered himself, bringing her with him. She managed to twist out of his grip, though, and back up. She glanced up at the trees.

"What are-" Before he could finish his sentence, Hyko pressed a finger to his lips. She felt them tremble slightly at her touch. She looked him directly in the eyes for what felt like an eternity. Then, she shifted her gaze up towards the trees. As she'd expected, so did Jaedon's. She removed her finger from his soft lips and started up the largest tree closest to them. Jaedon watched incredulously before doing the same.

Hyko had been climbing trees her entire life. She'd learned several times over that they made great hiding places when there were chores that she didn't want to finish. In this case, they made the perfect spot to hide from an angry father and an even angrier fiancée. The both of them came into the clearing Hyko and Jaedon had been resting in a few moments earlier. Yonej threw down his blade in frustration.

"That daughter of yours needs to take a good look at herself and straighten up," he growled. In his eyes was no sign of worry or gentleness at all. Only vehemence. He wasn't worried that she was missing or concerned for her safety; he was beside himself with fury because she hadn't done as she was told and had left the village. Hyko's father emerged from the forest not long after Yonej's comment. The same anger was in his eyes as was in her fiancée's.

"Yes, my daughter is very free spirited," he snapped. "And her attitude does need some adjustment. But by you saying that right to my face, you insult my parenting. You disrespect me and my entire family." Yonej backed off a bit after that. He picked up his knife and began to scan the area. Hyko moved not an inch. She was perched on her knees on a thick branch, carefully concealed from sight by the leaves. Jaedon was a few feet lower than her, awkwardly hanging onto a branch upside down. He kept shifting and changing his weight to better his grip. Each time, he earned a small kick from Hyko.

"What does she want?" Yonej asked quietly. His tone had drastically changed. It was soft and inquisitive now. All of his previous rage had vanished.

"What do you mean?" her father asked.

"I mean, out of life. What does Hyko want?" Hyko listened intently for her father's answer. Did he even know what she wanted?

Did he know she wanted to figure out why women were looked down upon? Did he know she wanted to marry when she felt ready and was in love? Did he know that she wanted to know what had changed inside of Gisipeh and made him so controlling? Did he know that she was almost desperate to learn more about Jaedon before she wed Yonej? Did he know she wanted nothing to do with Yonej at all?

"I...I am her father," her adad sighed. "And...and yet, I do not know what my own daughter wants." His eyes shut tightly as he knelt down. Hyko's jaw dropped. No, of course he knew nothing of what she wanted most in life. Why would he? He only knew what the rest of her people knew; that she was a headstrong girl who couldn't hold her tongue if her life depended on it.

"Perhaps she wants something she feels I cannot give to her?" Yonej muttered.

Yes, that's exactly it, Hyko thought, fiercely. *You cannot give me my freedom. You'd rob me of it the day we got married.*

"You can give her everything she needs, I am sure," Adad said. "She is so stubborn, though. She just-"

Jaedon's weight shifted on the branch, and he nearly disclosed his hiding spot. He grunted while trying to move himself to a safe position. Adad began to watch the trees. Hyko held her breath. She shrank back further on her branch. Yonej was alert and watching now as well. The fierceness was back in his eyes. Jaedon's arms were shaking and his eyes were wide.

"There's something in the tree," Yonej hissed. Adad was searching the trees as well, but in his eyes was less intensity.

"Yonej, it is nothing more than a bird."

"A bird does not make a grunting noise," Yonej grumbled under his breath. He stepped closer. Jaedon's grip slipped again and he moved to stay in the tree. Leaves floated to the ground. Yonej's brow furrowed.

"Leave it be, Yonej. Let's go." Adad started to walk off, but Hyko's fiancée did not follow.

"I swear, if it's a white man-"

"Daunai, Yonej!" Hyko's father bellowed. "It is nothing more than bird!" The noise he made startled several creatures hidden in the trees. Dozens of birds took off into the air. Their noise was loud and an annoyance, but the perfect distraction from Jaedon, who was still trembling and trying to keep himself out of sight. His grip on the branch was weak. Yonej grumbled in frustration, his attention remaining on the tree. However, when Hyko's father shouted for him once more, he tore his gaze away and stalked off after Adad.

As soon as they were out of view, Hyko heaved a sigh. She glanced down at a struggling Jaedon, whose grip had finally slipped. He tumbled to the forest floor and groaned once he'd landed.

"Who...who *were* those people?" he moaned, rolling over onto his back. Hyko slid down the same way she'd gone up and leaned down by him. "They sounded pissed. And, they were either talking a whole lot about the moon or…" He looked up at her curiously.

"That was my father," she explained. "And my f…and a man who thinks he can control me." She silently thanked the spirits that nearly the entire conversation had been in her language and not English.

"Wow. You weren't kidding about the whole 'no mercy' thing because they sounded anything but merciful," Jaedon joked. When she didn't laugh, he grew serious. "What's wrong?" Hyko shook her head and began heading to the north. Luckily, her father and Yonej had gone to the south and were long gone by then.

"It is a long story that maybe I'll tell you later," she sighed. Jaedon let the subject drop and followed her through the woods.

* * * * *

Jaedon was sore and couldn't see. They were well out of the tropical forest now. Jaedon had no idea where they were; it didn't help that the trail was nearly pitch black. The path wasn't as narrow and surrounded by trees as the woods had been. There were more creepy noises, though. Nevertheless, Jaedon trudged on behind Hyko without complaining. All of a sudden, they stepped into a large clearing. In the center was a tree that reached up higher than the others. In some directions, there was more forest. In others, there was mountainous terrain. In one direction, there was a cave.

"This is the Middle Grounds," Hyko explained. "It doesn't belong to any one village. It's just…here. In the middle." She dropped her bag and yawned. "I suppose we can stop here."

"Is there anything dangerous around here at night?" Jaedon asked. He tried not to seem too nervous, but a part of him was a little worried about being away from Kainau and the forest.

"Wild dogs," she replied. "But not a lot. We'll be fine. Follow me."

"Umm...where do we sleep?" Other than the massive tree, a few smaller ones and some shabby, blown-over huts, there was nothing but ground.

"En da tattao," she answered. In an instant, she'd climbed up into one of the trees and set up a small cushion with a blanket. She was dozing off by the time Jaedon had even gotten halfway to where she was.

"Hyko!" he gasped. She blinked and looked at him with her big, brown eyes. He tried to sound angry. "You are out of your mind! How can you sleep in a *tree?*" She flashed him a grin.

"Get used to it," she teased. "Or else, you'll have to find some way to sleep on the ground without getting attacked by wild dogs." Jaedon gave her a look but said nothing more. A light breeze started to blow through the forest, the air finally cooling down. It wasn't long before Hyko was asleep, her light breathing the only sound aside from the wind.

Jaedon tried to settle into the branch and get comfortable, yet sleep refused to come. He gave up with a sigh, and let his gaze fall on Hyko. She'd seemed so exhausted and distraught earlier; now, she was sleeping peacefully. For almost an hour, he watched her sleep. His mind wandered several times. He thought of home for a moment. Mostly, he thought of what Tristan was planning, and how London and Ash were carrying it out. Or rather, how they were only half doing their job. Most of the time, Ash was sick, and London was using the native women for his own personal pleasures. He desperately hoped that none of them would find out about Hyko. If they ever did...Jaedon shuddered at the thought and let his mind wander until he drifted off to sleep.

Mom wouldn't dare look at him the entire time. And, of course, Dad had insisted on watching the entire news report, start to finish. And, of course, the main story was about a young man who'd been convicted of assisting in the murder of Leah Shrells. She hadn't even been fourteen yet when she was killed.

A good twenty minutes following the news reel, Mom broke down in tears. Dad stood in the doorway, his eyes closed, head down.

"Are we going to stand here all night?" the boy hissed. "I told you, I didn't-"

"Joelle and Johannah have school tomorrow," Mom whimpered. "I'm going to make sandwiches for their lunches." She stood slowly, her hands trembling as she left the room. Dad remained where he was. The boy grew frustrated.

"So you're not going to listen, either?" he asked. Dad still said nothing. For several long minutes, the father and son stayed in the room. The only sounds were Mom's sniffling as she cried softly in the kitchen and prepared the sandwiches. That, and the shuffling of the boy's feet.

"There is nothing to listen to," Dad finally grumbled. "The court allowed you two days. If I were you, I'd spend every second of those days praying to God for forgiveness."

"But I-"

"You will not speak to me, or your mother, or your sisters!" he bellowed. "You are no longer to speak a word to anyone in this family." With tired, weary eyes turned towards the ground, Dad trudged down to the basement. It was his self-proclaimed little corner for sulking. It was over. There was no use arguing anymore. The boy knew that the two days he'd been allowed had been gracious. He'd use those days wisely. Arguing with his father about his innocence wasn't on the list of "wise things to do."

As the boy walked up the steps, he saw Joelle. The ten year old's blue eyes were wide and her cheeks were red from crying. Their mother had sent both her and six year old Johannah upstairs before they'd turned on the news. But Joelle was no baby; the boy knew that she'd eavesdropped and heard everything.

"Joelle...I'm...sorry," the boy moaned. She blinked and turned away from him. The ashamed look in her eyes had never ceased to haunt him.

The following day, travel was not nearly as easy. By mid day, Jaedon had removed his shirt and Hyko had changed into thinner clothes twice. There was no doubt that they were heading into the desert. They'd taken a narrow, dirt road that Hyko claimed was the safest way to Sasse. Jaedon had wanted to go through the cave and travel in the shade, but Hyko said it was more dangerous. As the day went on, Jaedon found that it was smarter to follow her directions rather than go his own way. Twice he'd stepped into the same snake hole, and twice Hyko had had to talk him through the tedious ordeal of distracting the snakes to get out. The only reason he'd stepped in the hole in the first place was because he'd refused to use the technique to watch the ground as he walked Hyko had showed him. By the time the sun was setting, Jaedon had gained several new bruises and a large appetite.

"I could go for some steak," he said. He was sitting with his back to a boulder, staring at an ugly purple bruise that was on his upper arm. "Haven't had any of *that* in months."

"Su-teak?" Hyko asked. It was one of the first times she'd struggled to pronounce an English word. "We do not have any of that here."

"No steak?" Jaedon gasped, leaning forward. "How can you live life with *no steak*, woman?" She merely shrugged in response. "You know what? One day, I'm gonna take you back to my homeland and let you eat some steak." Hyko's eyes grew wide.

"Your home?" she asked. "Just to try some su-teak?"

"Well, it's only fair after all that you've shown me," he said with a smile on his face. "I guess I could show you some other stuff, too. And, we could go camping without sleeping in trees."

"Would I get to meet your family?" she asked, her eyes bright. Jaedon's amused look disappeared. He gazed down at his feet.

"That wouldn't be fair," he muttered. "You never let me meet your family. Besides, you wouldn't want to meet my family." His dream from the previous night was still on his mind. The way his father had yelled at him, the way Joelle had looked afraid of him...

The thought of that terrible day made him shiver. Hyko seemed to sense the hurt his family had caused him and let the subject drop.

"We did not travel very wisely today," she grumbled. "We could have run into anything or anyone. And you look..." she suppressed a snicker as she saw his bruises and bumps. They stood out against his light skin.

"Yeah, that's what I get for not listening to you," he said, rolling his eyes. "I'll admit, it's Hyko's way or no way." He paused to lay hack his head on a nearby rock. He flashed her a lazy smile. "So, how close are we to the desert?"

"Hmm...about another day's travel," she explained. "Unless we keep going tonight. Your choice."

* * * * *

Although she'd been before, the heat of Sasse's outskirts was something Hyko doubted she'd ever get used to. Even when she and Jaedon had walked on at night, it was much hotter than Tattao ever got. Jaedon had stuffed his shirt in Hyko's messenger bag and hadn't yet put it back on. Hyko didn't think she could complain about it, though; the boy's chest was tanned and chiseled, and she was surprised that he hadn't caught her staring at him yet.

The sun was rising when Hyko spotted it, at last.

"Over there!" she cried, and darted. Rushing out without watching the ground wasn't the smartest thing to do. But more than anything, she wanted to sleep, and they'd finally reached a place where they could rest peacefully. Jaedon seemed less impressed.

"What is this?" he asked. In a way, Hyko couldn't blame him; all he was probably seeing was a large tree stump, an old shack and some overgrown desert grass. However, Hyko knew that this was much more than a raggedy old hut.

"It's an old hovel that workers used when they were paving the streets of Sasse," she explained. "But now, it's just an old landmark that lets visitors know they've arrived in Sasse." She pushed the door open with great effort. It had practically rusted on its hinges. Inside, it was very apparent that no one had set foot in the hut for decades. The floors were dusty and spider webs hung in every corner. There were two windows and several old blankets; neither of the them looked washed. Hyko dusted off a small space on the floor before setting up her cushion. She fell to the floor and curled up into a ball. It was much cooler in the shack than it was outside. She tried pulling a thin blanket over herself, but it didn't do her much justice.

"Here," Jaedon said, and lowered himself to the ground. He settled down with his body pressed to Hyko's. Hyko sucked in a shaky breath. He was shirtless. Laying next to her. On a bed. Jaedon looked at her, his bright blue eyes very visible even in the dark shack. "That better?"

"Umm..."

"If it makes you uncomfortable, I'll go sleep over there." He pushed himself up onto his elbows. Hyko contemplated it for a short minute, then grabbed his arm and pulled him back down. She wrapped her arms around his arm and snuggled against him, her eyes fluttering shut.

"No," she murmured. "This is much better."

GORR
HATRED

Elder Opi greeted Hyko in a foul mood. She'd slept longer than planned, and awakened at the time that most of the village would be heading to sleep. She'd entered through the North Gate of Sasse, where three Elders had been conversing. Their voices were low and their brows had been furrowed. Elder Opi seemed to be the least pleased when he saw Hyko approach.

"What brings you to Sasse, young Hyko?" Elder Opi pulled away from his conversation with the other Elders to bring Hyko to his kytah. The walls of the kytahs in Sasse were dark in color and looked moist. It was a special type of wood that cooled the homes and protected the families from the harsh heat of the desert. Hyko took a seat on one of the sitting rugs. Elder Opi remained standing.

"Have you been losing any hunters?" she asked, ignoring Elder Opi's question completely. The old man glowers down at her.

"How dare you-"

"Peleiko, Elder Opi! Ta ne akalenpar! It's important!" She shifted in her seat, suddenly feeling restless. The Elder's intense stare was making the situation worse. "There have been changes in our land."

"The spirits are constantly changing the world around us, Hyko," Elder Opi said. He narrowed his eyes. "Surely even *you* would know such a thing as this." Hyko's blood began to boil. *So now men are insulting my intelligence as well,* she thought, crossly. She frowned, but made an effort not to comment directly on the remark the elder had made. She sat up straight and folded her hands in her lap. Hyko figured that maybe seeming like a "proper woman" in appearance might make up for her speaking out of turn.

"Yes, that I know," she replied. She surprised herself with her calm response. "However, I am not speaking of changes such as the seasons, or a child growing to be a man. I speak of bad changes. Great amounts of death. Women and children being harmed."

"We have not-"

"Have you been losing hunters?" Hyko repeated, her voice insistent. Elder Opi's expression grew cold. His dark eyes looked menacing as he leaned his face closer to hers. He smelled of chicken and fish.

"You have disrespected me for the last time," he growled. "Get out of my kytah, you insolent girl." Hyko shot him a defiant look as she got to her feet.

"Besho," she grumbled under her breath as she left. Very rarely did she use such harsh language. She didn't care, though. Elder Opi had been causing her more trouble than she needed. He'd forced her into an unwanted engagement. He'd refused to answer her question about the hunters, which would've done nothing but help him and the entire village.

As she exited the old man's home, Hyko heaved a sigh. She'd failed half of her mission. If Elder Opi wouldn't listen to her explanation of the strangers, it was doubtful that anyone else would. Even less likely was it that they would hear what she had to say about Awa'hi and how she was hurt. Discouraged, she trudged lazily down the streets of Sasse. There were almost no candles burning in any of the windows. A few mothers stood outside their homes speaking as they washed the evening dishes. Some defiant children played in their yards as their mothers yelled for them to come inside. Hyko recognized most of them; there were relatives or old friends of hers in every village. One little boy she knew from Ohn-Tsung's group of friends. She knew that she could tell none of them. What would a mother be able to do with the information? Any man would deny her words and tell her that they were perfectly safe. The same would go for a child. The mothers and children headed inside. Hyko exhaled loudly; she was on the verge of giving up.

The walk back to the shack was a painfully quiet one. She'd dragged Jaedon from the comfort of Kainau to Sasse in vain. He would be angry with her. He would probably want to go home immediately.

Before she'd even gotten comfortable, she started begging for forgiveness.

"Jaedon, I'm so sorry for dragging you into all of this and then failing...if you want to leave, that's fine by me, I'll under..." Hyko paused. The cabin was empty. The blankets the two had shared the night before were scattered about sloppily. Other than that, there were hardly any signs that anyone had been there. It was almost as barren as when they'd first arrived.

Hyko stepped back outside, her head spinning. Where had he gone? Why would he have left when he didn't know where he was? The "where" part didn't matter too much; what *really* mattered was that she had to find him before anyone else or any*thing* else did. There wasn't anywhere he could hide from her people; there were hardly any trees in the desert. Her mind racing, she took off as quickly and cautiously as she could in the direction of the Sasse Abyss. The Sasse Abyss was where the nocturnal wild animals were hunted at night, when the air was cooler. It was the closest area to the shack, excluding the trail that lead out of Sasse and back towards the Middle Grounds.

The Abyss was open and silent. Not even the howling of the wind was audible. No hunters were around, which meant they'd either turned in early for the night, or they weren't out yet. She gazed around nervously. All she could see was sand and the stream off in the distance. *The stream!* That was it! Jaedon had to have gotten thirsty and headed towards the stream. Her spirits lifted, Hyko dashed forward, across the Abyss. As she neared the stream, something caught her eye. It appeared to be a rock from far off, but as she got closer, she saw that the color was off. It wasn't long before the "rock" was shaped less like a rock and more like a person. A person with light skin and short pants...

"Jaedon!" Hyko dropped to her knees at his side. He was laying in an awkward heap in a patch of desert grass. He moaned when she touched his shoulder, and tried to roll over. "Noka, noka...don't move." Jaedon continued to groan softly and clutch at his leg. Hyko gently pried his hand from his leg and saw blood on his palm. His leg was the source of the crimson stain, though. Near Jaedon's ankle was a deep gash, smeared red from his hand touching the wound. The skin surrounding his injury was dark, like his bruises from the other day, as well as swollen.

"I didn't watch...where I was going..." he moaned softly. "And there was...a snake hole..." Hyko's eyes widened. Snake bite remedies were hard to come by so far out in the desert. She needed to get him back to the shack. She grabbed him by the shoulders and tried pulling him up. The entire time, Jaedon flinched and grumbled curse words.

"I need to get you back to the shack so I can extract the poison," Hyko grunted. "If you don't get the poison from your leg soon-"

"Do it here," Jaedon gasped. His face was very pale, his eyes almost bloodshot red. "Do it now."

"What if someone-"

"*Please*...just do it." Hyko sucked in a breath. She didn't even have enough time to weigh the pros and cons of the situation. She let her eyes fall on Jaedon, injured and shaking. Without waiting a minute more, she bent over and began digging in the sand for roots and herbs.

Hyko was constantly learning more and more about Jaedon. That night, she learned that he was heavy. *Very* heavy. It had taken nearly an hour to help him back to the shack after fixing up his snake bite and gash. By the grace of the spirits, they'd run into no one along the way. Once back at the cabin, Jaedon exhaled loudly and dramatically.

"Thank you," he breathed. "That was...painful." Hyko smiled.

"I live to help others," she told him. Her smile faded immediately when she quietly added, "Not that I can live to do much else."

"Huh?"

"Nothing," she said, quickly. From the look on Jaedon's face, Hyko could tell that he was going to ask more. She cleared her throat before he could say anything. "Centuries ago, the spirits held a competition. They gave three men and three women six tasks to complete in six days. The tasks weren't difficult; washing clothes, gathering roots, organizing the tribes-now we're called villages, but it used to be tribes. In the end, the eldest had an easier time with the intellectual tasks, such as anything involving organization or teaching. The women were best at gathering, washing, tending to the children and so on. The men would spend days hunting and building simply because it was fun for them. Well, that, and to show off to their fiancées.

"When the spirits saw what pleased the men, the women, the young and the old, they made a law. The law passed stated that the women were to be home keepers, teachers and healers. When they grew old, they could move into a position of power, an elder. The men were to be the hunters, the builders and the leaders. As time went on, some of the women in the new generations tried to challenge the rules. They tried becoming hunters or builders. Some even tried leading the tribes. All were either punished ruthlessly or banished to the mountains. From then on, it has remained the same. Women are home keepers while the men lead..." Her legend ended on a sour note. When she finished, she pressed her back against an old barrel, dust and dirt collecting on her top. Jaedon was watching her as she slumped over, hiding her face with her hands; she could feel his eyes on her.

Neither of them spoke for the remainder of the evening. Hyko drifted off to sleep long before Jaedon, and when she awoke the next morning, she could hear children playing. She placed a hand on her messenger bag, which was still full of letters and packages. *Might as well do what I should've come here for*, she thought, and rose to her feet.

The streets of Sasse were far busier than Tattao during the day. One would think that a town in the desert would operate mostly at nighttime, when the air was cool. For Sasse, that wasn't the case in the least. Hyko spent quite some time waving to relatives or speaking with a few friends. Some of them asked if she'd seen Awa'hi, and Hyko's heart would ache. She'd say she had seen her, but gave no specifics.

"Well, well! If it isn't meek little Hyko, so far away from home!" One of the infamous twins, Iatso, called out to her. His hair had grown since the last time she'd seen him. That particular day, he looked as if he'd gone down to the Abyss over night without any dinner. Had something changed in the time they'd been apart?

"Iatso!" Hyko cried, rushing to him. She'd never done it before, but she wrapped her arms around him tightly. "Ah mei vehaja, am I glad to see you! Soyqueay alkeno!" He gave her a crooked grin, then a curious look.

"Umm...me, too?" He pulled her to the side, towards a nearby kytah. "Are you...is everything alright? The last time I saw you, you weren't quite..."

"Things are even worse," she answered, taking her friend aback. "They are terrible. Bastane! That's exactly what I'm here to tell you, but Elder Opi won't listen to anything I have to say."

"You know you can always tell me anything."

"Ziolen rarroso," Hyko said right away.

"Okay...now you're not making any sense."

"Ziolen rarroso are on our land," Hyko continued. "Their skin...it is so much lighter than our people's. And their eyes...they can be green and blue as well as brown. A lot of them are here, staying in our kytahs. Building strange things. All of them are men. I do not trust them, for I believe they have been hurting our hunters and women." As she got out the end of her explanation, she paused to see how Iatso was taking it all in. His eyes were wide. He had a lopsided grin on his face, and he was running a hand through his hair.

"Hyko..." he sighed. "Look, I know that you are going through a hard time right now. But, that doesn't mean you should try to get back at Elder Opi by making up these stories-" Hyko scowled. The look of sheer disgust on her face would've been enough to stop Iatso short, but she interrupted him as well.

"Koomo dasamundio?" she snapped. "This is *not* a story!"

"White strangers, Hyko? *That* was what you came up with?" Without thinking, Hyko reached her hand out. She felt her palm connect with his cheek before she even realize what she was doing. The slap sent Iatso reeling, his hands covering his face. *Of all the people I thought I could trust, I cannot trust any of them!* She thought furiously. As she cursed those who had betrayed her in her head, Iatso recovered from the slap. He stood up straight, a dark scowl replacing the smile that had been present just moments ago. Iatso towered over Hyko, glaring down at her as she began to regret slapping him.

"Iatso-kunno...I...I can...sonno-"

"An apology isn't going to do you any good, Hyko." He grabbed her wrist harshly and pushed her down to her knees. "Elder Opi *will* hear about this, and he will *not* be pleased." Hyko opened her mouth to speak only to receive a slap on the mouth. She ran her tongue over her lip after Iatso hit her. She could taste the salty blood as it welled up on her upper lip. Ever so gently, she let the tips of her fingers brush against her mouth to swipe the blood away.

"Besho," Hyko growled. "I'm only trying to help you, and this is how you-"

A scream pierced the air suddenly. Everyone standing outside their kytahs turned to the North Gate. At the gate stood a little boy no older than seven or eight years. His hair was frizzy and his brow was dripping sweat. Barefooted, he raced to the village center, where several hunters and an elder stood. He grabbed hold of a hunter's leg, refusing to let go.

"Peleiko, mei gadon adad!" the boy cried. "My father...he is hurt! Badly! Peleiko, zze! Please, help!" The elder stepped forward to place a hand on the boy's shoulder, but the young boy pulled away and darted off. Hyko watched silently as the elder commanded that a few of the hunters go to see about the boy's father. Hyko knew that no one would really take the situation very seriously. They would all assume that the man had taken his son out on an expedition and the father ended up getting a few bruises.

The grip on her arm suddenly let up. Iatso released her from his hold, though he was still angry.

"I will go to help the boy," he hissed. "But, that does not mean you are excused from punishment." Hyko watched him storm off, her head hurting. Whatever happened to the Iatso who'd said she could always tell him anything?

For nearly an hour, Hyko quietly went around the village and delivered the letters. What more was there for her to do? She had no desire to return to the hovel and have Jaedon ask about her day. She didn't even feel like trying to warn the village anymore. She figured that if they wanted to ignore her warnings and get themselves killed, it was their choice. She'd done her part, and now, all that was left for her to do was deliver the packages.

It wasn't much longer before attention was once again focused on the North Gate. Iatso and the others returned with the little boy and his father. The father seemed to be hurt, though not quite as badly as the young boy had claimed. He had two men helping him walk while the other few muttered curiously to themselves. Elder Opi stepped out of his kytah, a worn-out expression on his worn-out face. He hobbled over to the father, ignoring the murmurs and discussions of the other villagers.

"That man looks just as he did when he went out this morning!" one woman near Hyko snapped. She was rinsing out dishes and dusting off shoes. "There is nothing wrong with him! His son simply made up stories!"

"Perhaps the boy was startled," another woman chimed in. "You know children. Sometimes they just cannot tell when something is bad enough to-"

"That boy is old enough to know not to fib!" the first woman interrupted. "He needs to learn to hold his tongue. Do you know what becomes of children who don't learn that lesson? They become just like that young woman from Tattao." At that, Hyko spun around to watch the women. Neither of them were paying attention to her presence less than fifty or so feet away.

"Aah, yes," the other woman said. "I do remember that outburst. Pretty girl she was...pretty name, too. Hyko, I believe it was?"

"Yes, yes, that was it," the first woman said with a nod. "I'll bet that girl got quite the beat-down when she returned home."

"Oh, goodness, yes," the other woman laughed. "I tell you, if my daughter, Hiyanto, ever acts like that, her father would not allow her back in the house." Biting her tongue, Hyko walked off. Had none of the villages forgotten her outburst at Samnba? Those women had ridiculed her. Laughed at her. For all she knew, they were probably on their knees, thanking the spirits that their daughters weren't like her. Tears sprang to her eyes as she bit down harder. It was all she could do to keep from lashing out at the two gossiping mothers.

"Hyko!" Iatso's voice startled her once more. As he walked towards her, Hyko noticed that he seemed even more exhausted than he had earlier. "There is a young boy whose father is hurt."

"You have a healer," she grumbled, not bothering to think of the consequences. "Go ask her to heal him."

"Hyko. Our healer is out gathering herbs and her apprentices are bimbos." Hyko rolled her eyes and complained, but followed Iatso anyway. At the village center, the rescue team of hunters and the boy crowded around the father. The man's body was covered in small puncture wounds. Most of them were bloody or caked with dry blood. Hyko started to remove the man's shirt, only to find that the gossipy women had been dead wrong. At least a hundred or so punctures were on his chest and stomach alone. Blood was smeared on his entire body, and his lips were blue and purple.

"What happened, Covi?" one of the apprentice healers snapped. "How did your father manage to hurt himself like this?"

"He...he fell," the boy sniffled. "He tripped over a rock, and he fell hard over a ledge." As the apprentice continued to question the troubled boy, Hyko worked quickly. She used the tools one of the hunters had brought her to remove what was causing the puncture wounds: the small metal rods. She was able to remove only a few before the man began to moan and twist away from her.

"You seem like you've removed these before," Iatso grumbled. Hyko glared at him quickly before going back to helping the man.

"These...these things have never been on our land before," one hunter mused aloud.

"They look a bit like splinters."

"Can they be removed like-"

"Shetteme!" Hyko hissed. "All of you-" A whack in the gut silenced her as well. The man suddenly lashed out, thrashing about on the ground. His eyes rolled to the back of head, and he was foaming at the mouth, making gagging and gargling noise as he began to choke. The hunters all stepped back, their eyes wide. Hyko panicked while going through the tools and herbs she had to use. Only once before had she ever seen a patient act that way, when a man had been bitten by a venomous insect while camping...

"He's been poisoned," Hyko gasped. "Those barb things must have poison in them."

"What can you do?" the boy cried. His face was red, his eyes wet with tears. "Can he be saved? Will he be alright?"

All she could do was turn to the boy and shake her head with a sigh of despair.

* * * * *

It was a dull, dry day for Jaedon. Compared to his condition the night before, he was much better, aside from the pain and slight numbness in his leg. Hyko had been gone when he woke up in the morning. With no one to talk to, all he could do was think or sleep some more.

Hyko's return would've been a relief to him, except that she appeared to be in a foul mood when she walked through the door. She even didn't bother with asking him if his leg was better. The instant she'd closed the door, she held up a small, thin piece of metal that looked a bit like an overgrown splinter.

"What are these?" she demanded, ferocity in her voice. Jaedon scooted back before plucking the thin piece of metal from her hand.

"What, no 'how are you' or anything?" he joked, flashing her a grin. He figured that teasing her would lighten the mood. But instead of returning the smile, she scowled and hit him on the arm.

"Koomo kaheil!" she shouted. "I mean it! What are these?" With a disheartened sigh, Jaedon gave up on his flirting idea.

"They're snares," he explained. "Or snags. They're used to hunt small animals. They get caught in a rabbit or a squirrel's foot and keeps it from running away. But..."

"But what?"

"My men haven't been around here...maybe...did Tristan...?" He began mumbling to himself, deep in thought. The desert and the woods were the two places Jaedon was almost positive had not been explored. If there were snares around Sasse, the men must've gone out farther than he'd originally thought.

"Can you rig them with poison?" Hyko asked, not quite as urgently as before. Jaedon nodded. It wasn't done often because the poison often times remained after the animal was cooked, but it could be done. "Ah mei vehaja..."

"What?"

"Your men are causing more trouble, is all," she murmured, making Jaedon shudder. Hyko raised an eyebrow at him. "Is something the matter? Your leg?"

"It's fine," he grumbled, refusing to go on about what he was really thinking. His men knew that hunting with rigged snares wasn't one hundred percent safe. Why would they be laying them out when they knew the risks? It was especially strange that they would do such a thing, considering that they were on new territory. It was then that a sickening thought crossed Jaedon's mind. Tristan wasn't stupid; he wouldn't have any of the men who'd been placed in charge use rigged snares to hunt for food. Could the men be laying the snags out to hunt or poison for something else? Jaedon gulped; he knew that the "something else" was not rabbits.

It took three more days for Jaedon's leg to get better and for the both of them to get on a regular sleeping schedule. During the day, the two would sleep while everyone was busy. When nightfall came, the two would wake up and talk or play games. A few times, Hyko told legends about things such as how bees made flowers their home, or why people build kytahs from different materials. Jaedon told a few stories of his own about his homeland. He talked about things such as toilets, showers and buses that took him to school. He spoke of video games and computers, none of which Hyko had ever heard of. It was hard for her to grasp the simple concept of shorts. For the most part, the two did their best to avoid speaking of the white men, the snares, or anything else involving the mysterious changes of Hyko's land.

"I'm going to teach you how to sleep in a tree," Hyko announced matter-of-factly about a week after their arrival in Sasse. Jaedon was still moving with a slight limp, but Hyko insisted that it would go away after a couple more weeks. It was dusk, earlier than the two would usually venture outside of the shack. The two were standing in front of one of the largest trees in all the land. Hyko claimed to have first climbed it when she was only ten or so years old. Jaedon was a little skeptical about that, but he kept the thought to himself.

"Huh." He kicked at some small rocks at his feet. "And how're you gonna do that?"

"Yeioy asanyu oopo dojei," she said with a rather chipper voice, forgetting to translate until Jaedon gave her an inquisitive look. "One learns by doing!" She swung her leg up over a branch, grasping tightly onto pieces of bark to keep from falling. Branch after branch, she continued up with ease. She was halfway up the tree before she realized that Jaedon hadn't even started.

"You scared?" Hyko teased, beaming down at him. "Come on up!" Jaedon shook his head and reluctantly made his way up the first few branches. He wanted to whine and ask why she was making him do this, like the kids in his math class who begged to know when they would use the skills in real life.

"You know, you're a jerk for making an injured man do this," he called up to her, and received an amused giggle in response. The whole way up, Jaedon concentrated solely on Hyko's chocolate-colored face. So long as he focused on that and that alone, he could more easily block out the thoughts of the pain in his leg. It took longer than fifteen minutes of climbing and coaxing for Jaedon to reach the same branch as Hyko. He was sure that Hyko would have a giggle fit when she got a good look at him. Twigs and dried up desert leaves were stuck all over him. His hair sticking out like the patches of arid grass so many feet below him, and his face was a deep red shade.

"I was beginning to think that you would never get up here," Hyko said, twisting her body so that she was sitting, her legs dangling in mid air. Jaedon was no more than a few feet away, though he looked a lot less comfortable than she did. He was gripping at the branch so tightly that his knuckles turned white.

"And I'm beginning to think I'll never get back down," he muttered under his breath. "Just climbing the tree was hell, and now you want me to *sleep in it?*"

"It's not as hard as it seems," Hyko insisted. "Watch me! Just make sure you have a sturdy branch that won't break under your weight. And once you-" The sound of a creaking branch and rustling leaves caused Hyko to clam up in an instant. She gazed around cautiously, only her eyes moving. Jaedon watched silently and flinched when he heard what sounded like a footstep. It was getting to be too dark to see much of anything, but he scanned the ground anyway. "Oh. Oops."

"Huh?"

"Mei gadon yuq." She wiggled the toes of her shoeless foot. "My shoe. That's what that was." Jaedon heaved a sigh of relief, only to become disappointed a moment later; if her shoe had fallen, that meant they had to go back down even sooner to get it. She seemed to sense his discontent and gently touched his shoulder. "If you want, you can wait here and I can go back down."

"Umm..." He bit his lip with a sigh. *Man up, Jaedon!* He thought to himself. *It's a stupid tree!* "Nah, it's okay. I'll...I'll be right behind you." To his pleasure, the trip back down to the ground was a heck of a lot easier than the way up; it was only a matter of back-tracking, going down exactly the way he'd gone up.

On the ground, everything was oddly quiet. There weren't very many trees, so all that could be heard was the calm, whispering wind as it whipped up some of the sand. He glanced over at Hyko, who was busy searching for her shoe. It wasn't the first time he'd ever thought it, but it truly occurred to him then that she was very pretty. In the moonlight, her light-colored skirt appeared almost transparent and contrasted completely with her skin. Her legs were long and lean, as if she'd spent a lifetime on the move. When she turned her face to his, her eyes were bright and shining, even in the dark. Her lips curled into a shy smile.

"Yes?" she said, placing a hand on her hip.

"What? Oh...uh...I just..." Jaedon stumbled over his own words. He couldn't flat out say that he'd been staring at her, thinking about how beautiful she looked. *That* he was *sure* he could not tell her. "I...I had a question for you...umm...how do you say...I forgot."

"Mei desuuque-kuai," she translated.

"No, that's not what I..." He let his words trail off into the night. Why bother with it? She was busy looking for her shoe once more, and he didn't have to explain what he'd really been thinking. In Jaedon's mind, it was a win-win situation.

He sauntered over in the opposite direction, gazing steadily at the ground. Half buried under the sand was something that appeared to be leather and brown; a shoe, perhaps? He bent down and brushed away some of the sand and pulled it out. Sure enough, it was a moccasin-style shoe, the same kind that Hyko had been wearing earlier. He opened his mouth to call Hyko over, but at that same time, he felt his leg give in beneath him. Rather ungracefully, he toppled over into the sand, knocking his head on something hard and covered in cloth. With a groan, he pushed himself up, startled by the boney feeling beneath his hands. He rubbed whatever was beneath him and realized with a jolt that he was, in fact, touching bone. Or something with bone. He leaned back, trying to let his eyes adjust to the darkness. Carefully, he brushed sand away from what he was perched on, and discovered the cloth was tattered. Beneath the cloth was a spine, icy cold and somewhat pale skin stretched over it.

A body.

"Hey, Jaedon, what's take-" Jaedon heard Hyko suck in a breath and her footsteps halted suddenly. There were several long moments of absolute silence before she took many slow steps forward. She reached out her hand and let her fingertips just barely graze the soft, tiny tufts of curls atop the body's head; chunks of his or her head had been either yanked out or shaved off. Frantically, Hyko brushed more sand from the body, revealing a dull green skirt that was just as tattered as the shirt.

"I don't believe it..." Jaedon growled quietly. He knew exactly who was to blame for the death of the young woman. He knew that the men of the villages were respectable and, though could be a bit harsh, genuinely cared about their wives and daughters. He knew that it was no man from Sasse or Tattao, or any of the other villages Hyko had told him about. Fury burned inside him, scorching his throat and making it dry. It was way beyond him why a man would sink so low.

Footsteps distracted his thoughts. In the distance, a group of at least three men from Sasse were walking steadily towards them. Immediately, Jaedon ducked behind a nearby boulder, concealing himself from sight before the men got any closer. Hyko crouched down at the dead girl's side, stroking her hair and trembling. Only when the men shouted something at her in her language did she even glance up.

As she and the men spoke, Jaedon tried his hardest to piece together the main points of the conversation. He caught on to the word for girl-he remembered that it was gliita from when Hyko had told him a few days ago-pretty quickly, and a few times, he thought he heard the words "ziolen rarroso," but they were speaking so fast that he wasn't entirely sure. It wasn't long before the men were enraged, kicking at the dust, words flying from their mouths so loudly that a few times, Hyko winced. Eventually, they calmed down so that they could lift the girl from the sand and carry her back to the village. Hyko did not move, did not speak to Jaedon, did not even turn towards the boulder until the men were no longer in view.

"Rossuko," she murmured. Her voice was so soft that it was almost carried away by the wind.

"What does that mean?"

"That was her name," Hyko clarified. "She was only a year or so older than Ohn-Tsung…" She dropped down to her knees, dirtying her light-colored skirt. A tear trickled down her cheek, but she swiftly swiped it away. "My mother…my mother taught her how to make cream filling using the Sakora flower…" Jaedon took a step towards her and hesitantly reached out his hand. He wanted to wipe away the tears she was crying. He wanted to tell her that things would be okay. He wanted to promise her that he would stand up to Bryce, London and Ashleigh and make them leave the women alone. He wanted to tell her that he would never let anything like that happen to her or her family ever. But instead, he let his hand fall back down at his side, and all of the words he'd wanted to say stayed in his dry, scratchy throat.

"We…we should head back," he sighed instead. He knew that staying out in the desert all night wasn't going to make her feel any better.

"No," she said firmly. "I'm staying here."

"You could get hurt by the wild dogs-"

"I said I am staying." She glowered up at him, her eyes moist from tears. "Do not try to tell me otherwise. I am not so stupid that I will get attacked by a dog, like you got bit by a snake." Jaedon dared to scowl at her.

"It could've happened to anyone," he snapped, but it didn't make a difference. She was no longer listening, and he started back to the hut.

* * * * *

The early morning heat shook Hyko from her light sleep. For hours on end, she'd sat in silence, praying to the spirits for Rossuko and her family. A few times, she felt guilt stab at her like a sewing needle whenever Jaedon crossed her mind. She tried not to dwell on thoughts of him, but it was hard to do, what with all the emptiness of the desert as her only company in the long night.

Her feet dragged the ground as she stood and started to make her way back to the hut. She dreaded facing Jaedon. She was sure that he'd be in less than a good mood when she returned. Although she didn't like it, the truth was that she was inconveniencing the boy with every step she took that he took with her. He could be back at Kainau in his hammock, snoozing away on the sunny beach shores. Instead, he was recovering from a snake bite in a shabby old hut that hadn't been used in decades.

"Have fun sulking?" Jaedon was sitting directly across from the door when she stepped inside, his back against the wall. His nose was buried in an old, dingy journal. Hyko exhaled a shaky breath.

"I was...praying," she told him quietly.

"Yeah, so was I." He set down the journal. "Praying that I would figure out how to read that thing." When Hyko gave him a curious look, he elaborated. "I found that old thing up on a shelf and I thought maybe it would have some interesting stories in it. All that's in it are a bunch of odd squiggly lines."

"What...I...koomo dasamundio?" she cried out, suppressing the urge to let her mouth hang wide open.

"Is something wrong?" Jaedon patted the spot on the floor next to him. Tentatively, Hyko trudged over and plopped down beside him. She turned to him with wide eyes.

"I...I thought that...well, I was mean to you and I thought you'd be...angry," she managed to get out. Never had a man ever reacted to her anger that way. It was as if Jaedon had completely forgotten what she'd said before he'd stormed off.

"It wasn't that big of a deal," he told her with a shrug, and Hyko saw that he truly was not angry with her; what she couldn't understand was why.

"...not at all?" she asked, timidly. Jaedon gave her a warm smile and chuckled softly. He placed his hand over hers and squeezed it.

"Hyko, it's okay," he reassured her. "Really. It's fine." Her mind could hardly understand how calm and collected he was. It made absolutely no sense to her.

"Umm...let me see the journal," Hyko said, eager to change the subject; she knew very little about white men and their reactions to anger, but she did know how to read the journal. She reached for the tattered book.

"So, what's in it?" Jaedon leaned over her shoulder, his breath tickling her ear.

"It's...the handwriting is terrible...it's just talking about d-" She swallowed back her words. Shutting her eyes tightly, she heaved a sigh and struggled on with the explanation. "Death."

"The death of what?" He asked the question hesitantly, his hand still covering hers. His thumb tenderly caressed her hand. She hoped that he couldn't feel her shaking, for even she could see how the paper shook from her trembling hands.

"The death of lovers, the death of women who...did not do as they were told, the death of..." She stopped suddenly. "A lot of dying, okay?" She shoved the book at Jaedon and slid away from him. For several hours, she sat in the corner of the hut, saying nothing. Her mind felt foggy, her stomach twisted into knots. There was a tugging at her heart. Too much was going on, and far too little of it was good. After a while, she dozed off again, her head pressed uncomfortably against the wall. It was Jaedon who shook her awake a little while later.

"Hyko...listen to that," he hissed, his mouth right at her ear. She shivered when she realized how close he was.

"Listen to what?" she groaned. Jaedon hastily placed a finger to her lips to quiet her.

"Listen!" he insisted. Outside the hut, the distinct sound of feet shuffling through the sand could be heard. More than just a few people, it seemed, were all headed out of the village; at one point, Hyko swore she heard women weeping.

"It's the vigil," she told him, laying back down, this time with her head on a pillow. "The village will go far out into the desert to bury her. We should be quiet...and sleep."

"I did; I'm not tired anymore," Jaedon said, his voice still hushed. "Will you teach me how to read these characters?" Reluctantly, Hyko rolled over onto her back, her face startlingly close to his. His nose was a mere few inches from hers as he leaned over her. Even in the darkness, his blue eyes seemed intense and beautiful.

"I...um..." She backed up, knocking her head against a nearby shelf. Dust and bits of debris showered down on them. There was a bit of a pause before a loud thud caused the two to jump. From the shelf, another old journal had tumbled, a few loose pages floating down after it. Hyko pulled the notebook to her and caught a glimpse of what was written on a few of the pages.

"What's it say?" Jaedon asked.

"Nothing...it's...nothing," she exhaled. In one swift movement, she shoved the notebook and the loose pieces of paper underneath her pillow.

"Can we please-"

"Peleiko, Jaedon!" Hyko groaned. "I don't want to be mean to you, but I am tired and my head is spinning and a girl that I knew just died...*and you want me to teach you the alphabet?*" Without waiting for him to respond, Hyko got to her feet clumsily. She stumbled towards the door. The footsteps beyond it had ceased, but she checked before opening the door anyway. Before stepping outside, she shot Jaedon a glare. When he gave her a sad frown in response, her expression softened. She shut the door with her head down and went over to Jaedon, trying to remember how her mother had taught her how to read the characters.

The noise began at nightfall. It was quiet at first, like the footsteps of the village had been that morning. As more moments passed, it grew louder. For a second, it sounded to Hyko like Samnba. Often times, when the villages were all together, the noise was great and could be heard from the forest. Perhaps it was the remembrance meal for Rossuko? Comforted by the thought, she started to doze once more when Jaedon shook her awake for the second time that day.

"Do you hear those screams?" he asked. Hyko blinked. His shirtless appearance was confusing her lethargic brain and groggy eyes; he'd been wearing a shirt when she'd fallen asleep. "Hyko!"

"Huh?" Disoriented, she pulled herself up and turned away from his shirtless chest. "Are you wearing clothes?"

"Wha-yes! I am wearing clothes!" He sounded serious, but she heard the smile in his voice as well. "I'm being serious, though. You hear that?" Pushing the thought of him with no shirt on to the back of her mind, she did as Jaedon had said and listened. Horrified cries filled the night air. They were continuous, growing louder and more shrill with each passing second. Hyko jumped up at once, digging through her things in desperate search of her throw. All the while, her stomach was as unsettled as she was. There had to be something very wrong for the cries of Sasse to be heard from the hut.

"I'll be back later," she said as she slipped on her shoes. She was so frantic to get out the door that she pulled it in and ran into the wall when she should've pushed it open. "Don't go anywhere...just wait right here."

Her feet hit the ground hard with every step, pounding the pavement, aching as they dared to run on. She had to keep running. She had to. The air-piercing shrieks and wails became almost deafening as she approached the North Gate, her feet throbbing and raw; she'd worn a hole into the sole of her shoe and tossed both of them to the side on the way.

She'd smelled the smoke before she'd reached the village, but the pungent smell burned at her nostrils once she entered. The ground scorched her aching soles, dark ashes mixed in with the golden sand. All around her, she saw nothing but thick, black smoke beginning to clear and burnt wood. The clothes the women had hung out to dry were no more than ashes. Dead desert grass was nowhere to be seen. The gate posts that marked each entrance to the village were scorched, and looked as though they could collapse at any given moment. Women stood with their sons and daughters, gawking at the seared remains of their once great village. A few groups of people were huddled together, muttering prayers as they choked back sobs. Most of the men shouted furiously at one another, trying urgently to get everything under control and put out whatever was still burning.

"Seven of the ill…gone." Elder Opi's voice turned a few heads here and there. He was standing in what was left of the village center. "Three of our village's elderly, including one of my fellow leaders…engulfed in flames. Two newborn babies perished before they could even recognize the face of their own mother." By then, Elder Opi had captured the attention of all of the villagers. Only a few of the men hung back, still grumbling crossly as the elder spoke. Despite this, Elder Opi continued on.

"It has been brought to my attention by three hunters that there are men with skin the color of the Sakora flower on our land!" he bellowed, his voice echoing through the empty, smoldering village. "Yet, even before then, I had been warned, and I did not believe what was being said to me…and for that, I am terribly sorry."

"Yeah, because now Sasse is nothing but a heap of ashes," Hyko muttered under her breath, earning a glower from a nearby mother. She kept her mouth shut after that.

"These white strangers…these ziolen rarroso…they are a danger to us!" Elder Opi continued. "They violate our women and leave them for dead. They burn down our villages. They have harmed our sister villages and threatened our way of life. Hyko of Tattao, are you present?" Hyko stepped forward from behind the families she'd been hiding behind. Whispers and murmurs followed her to the village center. She felt her face heat up and her throat burn. Still, she ignored the comments. Elder Opi placed one hand on her shoulder while raising the other in the air.

"Bring this message to our brothers and sisters of the village in the forest, otherwise known as Tattao; we *will* fight for our land, for the spirits' land! We will *not* let these white men get the best of us!" Cheers and applause erupted from the crowd. "And, due to the unfortunate circumstances, the matrimony of Hyko and Yonej will be postponed while we are facing hardships caused by these white strangers."

ODAYA
RETURN

Ohn-Tsung never realized how much she hated rooting until the day her sister had "run away." The process was long, repetitive and dull, taking away more of her free time than she liked. Normally, it was Hyko's job; she was a master at anything involving plants, herbs or roots on account of her training to become a healer. Ohn-Tsung had no skills in that area whatsoever, yet she was the one stuck with the job.

"Smaller pieces, Ohn-Tsung, smaller pieces!" Hanjeha snapped. "These will *never* dissolve into the soup, and if the pieces are too big, little Enna will choke on the broth!" The old woman continued to babble on about the difference between rooting for children and adults while Ohn-Tsung's mind wandered to thoughts of her sister.

Hyko had disappeared over two weeks ago. She'd claimed it was to carry out her job as a messenger. Adad still had it in his head that she had run away. He and Yonej had gone out to search for her several times with the idea that she needed some sense knocked into her. Eventually, Adad had started to lose hope and started to think the worse. Ohn-Tsung had overheard several arguments between Amam and Adad over Hyko and what would become of her. Her father insisted that she'd been taken by the strangers or was lying dead in the road; her mother believed that she'd be home any day now, or that she was visiting with distant cousins. It all made Ohn-Tsung's head hurt.

"You praying that your sister comes back so she can do this and not you?" Awa'hi teased in a hoarse voice. Ohn-Tsung paused and rolled up her sleeves with a groan the moment Hanjeha was gone.

"Ah mei vehaja, you have no idea!" the eight year old groaned. "I think I spent two hours on my knees yesterday, praying like crazy!" Awa'hi and Ohn-Tsung had grown close in the time Hyko had been away. It had taken some time for Awa'hi to get over what had happened with the white men. She still wasn't completely herself after what had happened. She stayed in the healer's hut to be away from everyone else, and to get over the cold she'd developed a few days after arriving in Tattao. When Ohn-Tsung had taken over her sister's job, the only other person there'd been to speak with, other than Hanjeha was a grumpy old man with a fever and Awa'hi.

Ohn-Tsung chose to converse with the more pleasant of the two.

"I'm sure she'll be back soon, Ohn-Tsung," Awa'hi said, her voice soft and comforting. Ohn-Tsung nodded slowly, mindlessly continuing to crush the roots into smaller pieces.

"I just hope nothing happened to her," she muttered. "I feel bad for her. She doesn't want to marry Yonej at all. And, Adad can be kind of mean sometimes. I understand why she left." Awa'hi sat up on her bed, coughing a few times as she did.

"It's a terrible thing that we sometimes get forced into things we don't want," Awa'hi hissed. Ohn-Tsung decided it was better to stay quiet. When Awa'hi was like that, it was best to leave her be. Hanjeha had said a couple of times that it would be best for Awa'hi not to dwell on the awful memories, but Ohn-Tsung didn't want to explain that to Awa'hi.

"I'm supposed to have a Whispering soon," Ohn-Tsung announced, anxious to change the subject and end the awkward silence. Awa'hi's face lit up when the girl mentioned a Whispering; they were generally very happy occasions when anyone nearing the years of young adulthood learned what they would be when they grew older.

"That's exciting." Awa'hi stood and walked over to a shelf filled with books. She skimmed through the first few; they were old plant indexes. "I remember my Whispering. I'd wanted nothing more than to be a teacher."

"What did you get?"

"Housewife." She rolled her eyes and groaned. "A housewife...*that's* what I'm going to be. At first, I hated it. I must've begged Elder Opi to let me have another Whispering for months on end. But as I got older, I learned that things have a way of working themselves out. Now, I'm okay with it, I guess."

"I want to be a freelance," Ohn-Tsung said. "I'd have all the time in the world to draw and draw!" Awa'hi laughed. It was the first time in nearly three days that Ohn-Tsung had heard her do so.

Hanjeha returned a few short moments later, her brow dripping with sweat. Her eyes, usually sparkling with youth, seemed dull and exhausted. In her hands was a basket of roots and herbs which she dropped right at Ohn-Tsung's feet.

"Girl, I will be thanking the spirits when your sister returns," the old woman squawked. "She is far better at being a healer than you and your ignorant eight-year-old self." Ohn-Tsung didn't dare open her mouth to talk smack back at Hanjeha, though she did make several irritated comments in her head. "Child, hurry up with that task! I gave it to you ages ago. As soon as you're done, you can go on to sorting herbs."

"Hanjeha, do you think a woman could be just as good a hunter as a man?" Awa'hi blurted out suddenly, and the entire room went quiet. Hanjeha glared at the girl, her mouth a tight, thin line. Ohn-Tsung stared in awe as Hanjeha watched Awa'hi. Ohn-Tsung was sure that Awa'hi knew the dangers of speaking out against the laws of their land, or to even question them. Only once had Ohn-Tsung ever heard a woman defy a man, and that woman had been her sister. The consequences of her actions continued daily; Ohn-Tsung heard the gossiping women of the village scorning Hyko and speaking of her disrespectfulness towards Elder Opi. Awa'hi knew of this as well. Why, then, was she bringing up a subject as dangerous as the roles of men and women?

"Child, not once in all my years have I seen a woman hunter," Hanjeha said, her voice low, almost disapprovingly. "And despite this, I have not a single doubt in my mind that a woman could be an exceptional hunter. Better than a man, even." Ohn-Tsung twirled around in an instant to gawk at the old woman. She wasn't even sure if she'd heard those words correctly.

"What?" she cried. "But...but that's not..."

"You have to wonder these things sometimes, Ohn-Tsung," Awa'hi said. "I mean, it's been done before, right? In the old days?"

"Yeah, and all of those women ended up dead!" Ohn-Tsung snapped. *That*, she thought, *or banished to the City in the Ruins, but it's a mystery if that place even exists.* After all, it was a place only heard of in legends. Therefore, all of the women who'd ever questioned their roles were killed. There was no way Ohn-Tsung would ever wonder about something that could possibly be the death of her.

"Do either of you remember that one family from Delfusio several years back?" Hanjeha asked after many long minutes of silence. Ohn-Tsung stared blankly at the healer, but Awa'hi looked thoughtfully off at the back wall of the hut.

"I...I think I do," she muttered, then more loudly added, "was it the family whose mother died?" Hanjeha nodded.

"Yes, that's the one," she said. "That mother's death left her husband with five little children under the age of seven to care for. You know, that man did a wonderful job with those children. He would scold them, but not too harshly. He managed to teach his oldest daughter how to sew a broken pair of shoes." When Hanjeha paused, the two girls grew curious.

"Whatever happened to them? I can't remember."

"The youngest child drowned in the fishing lake one summer," Hanjeha sighed, her voice shaky and laden with sadness. "After that, the father couldn't face his children any longer. He sent the remaining four to live with aunts and other relatives in different villages. Shortly after that, he left Delfusio, and the hunters found his body bruised, bloody and half frozen on a mountain path." Awa'hi merely nodded her head, but Ohn-Tsung felt utterly confused. Only moments ago, Hanjeha had claimed she believed a woman could do a man's job; then she'd contradicted herself with that heart-wrenching story and its tragic ending.

"So...what do you think?" Ohn-Tsung asked. The second the question escaped her mouth, her voice sounded too loud for the quiet room. Awa'hi and Hanjeha both pretended to ignore her at first, but Ohn-Tsung knew they'd heard. She'd seen the both of them flinch at the question. *"Well?"*

"Hush, girl, and finish rooting the herbs," Hanjeha hissed. For the rest of the afternoon, Ohn-Tsung bit back the urge to ask Hanjeha anymore questions. She finished rooting the herbs, her head aching from confusion. Awa'hi returned to her bed in the corner of the room for an afternoon rest. Hanjeha came and went, grumbling complaints about Ohn-Tsung's healer skills as she did.

It was hours before Ohn-Tsung was done with all her tasks. After the last herb had been sorted, she pulled a stool over to the window. She kept a sharp eye out for Gisipeh. She knew that he'd be coming in soon; he came almost every day, just as Hyko always said. The boy couldn't go a day without receiving some sort of injury that needed tending to. Mostly, he came to "exchange gossip" with Hanjeha. *No wonder the woman's got such a sharp tongue*, Ohn-Tsung thought with a slight smirk on her face.

"Ohn-Tsung!" The eight year old whipped around to see Gisipeh in the doorway. He was leaning his body against the frame of the door, sweat on his brow as he struggled to catch his breath.

"Is...is something the matter?"

"Noka. Ta ne Hyko...it's Hyko. She's returned!"

* * * * *

The whole idea behind entering Tattao through the west gate had been to avoid any and everyone. Barely anyone entered or exited the village through that gate, and she'd made the decision to enter that way to avoid any unwanted attention. Her plan had failed. Mothers gave her sideways glances as they sat in their yards washing dishes and clothes. Hunters and construction workers eyed her as they passed. When their eyes met hers, they looked away immediately. Hyko rolled her eyes at all of them. She'd doubted their behavior towards her would change once she returned. However, this was repulsively rude.

As she walked on, the dirty looks worsened. Old women sat in their yard chairs, staring right at her and whispering badly about her to her face. One woman was even less subtle than her companions when she loudly exclaimed "that young lady has the nerve to show her face here?" right as Hyko passed by. Only the children treated Hyko like an actual human being. They squealed when they saw her, bright smiles lighting up their faces.

"Hyko!" One small girl, her hair in desperate need of a comb, dashed over to her. She grabbed a hold of Hyko's leg and refused to release her grip, even as Hyko attempted to walk. "You came back! Why were you gone so long?" Hyko gave the child a forced smile and stopped so that the girl wouldn't hurt herself while clutching at her leg.

"I had some things to do," Hyko explained. "I had to deliver letters." The small girl tilted her head at an angle, furrowing her brow in deep thought.

"Isn't that a man's job?" she asked, and Hyko blinked. Even this little girl was "brainwashed" already, the delusional idea of men's and women's jobs in her head. "You won't get in trouble with the spirits, will you?"

"I-"

"Ha'lakea!" A woman in a nearby kytah called for the girl, sticking her head out the window. The woman's husband stood in the doorway of their home with his arms crossed. The tight scowl on his face made Hyko wary. "Ha'lakea, beinei te citon! Come here! Right now, young lady!"

"Bye, Hyko!" Hyko watched as the little girl scurried off to her home, her mother still in the window. The girl wore a smile on her face as she jumped up, trying to get her father to hold her. In response, the man slapped the girl in the face. At first, the child didn't know quite how to react. Her eyes grew wide and watery, her lip quivering. It took everything she had not to intervene, but Hyko managed to stand by and do nothing. The father's mouth was moving as if he were scolding the young girl. For the most part, Hyko couldn't make out what he was saying. It had to have been harsh, for the girl flinched at nearly every word he spat at her. Frustrated she couldn't help, Hyko started down the path to head home. As she moved closer to the house, Hyko could hear the father's words loud and clear, and they made her ears burn.

"You will *never* speak to that young woman again, unditiyo?" he growled, his tone low and scratchy. "If I ever hear you say so much as 'hiya' to that girl, you will be beat down, unditiyo? You will not be influenced by her, unditiyo? *Never!* Or, so help me spirits, *you will be beat raw.*"

* * * * *

Jaedon preferred eating his meals away from the rest of the men. However, on the evening of his return, he couldn't get his meal up to his room like he usually did. All thirty or so men occupying the beach town were to report to a mandatory dinner meeting out on one of the new tables that had been built. No exceptions. That meant that Jaedon had to throw something nice on, plaster a faux grin to his face, and laugh as men discussed their sexual conquests all evening.

The air was comfortably warm and breathable, contrasting completely with the air in Sasse. The light breeze tousled his neatly combed hair. Nearly all of the men were seated and conversing by the time he approached the table. A native woman timidly handed him a plate as soon as he sat down. Her hand shook as she poured him a drink that smelled of citrus. Jaedon felt his stomach twist when he saw what horrible shape she was in. She was so thin, the skin of her face looking like stretched wax paper. Her arms and legs were bruised up; several of them appeared to be new. She stepped back when she was finished pouring, watching him with dead-beat eyes. Jaedon cleared his throat, which suddenly felt unbearably dry.

“Sanaei,” he muttered. The “thank you” was barely audible so that none of the other men would hear. The woman shrieked, dropping the pitcher that was in her hands. The glass shattered against the table, the drink splashing onto four of the nearest men. The woman paid no attention to the mess she’d created, the swears flying from the men’s mouths or the threats being thrown at her. All she could do was stand there with her knees trembling and stare at Jaedon. One of the other native women came over and grabbed her by the shoulders, leading her away. She kept muttering in a calm, soothing voice as they left the beach.

“Stupid natives.” Bryce slid into the seat to the right of Jaedon, who inwardly groaned. “Too stupid to even pour a drink. I’m tellin’ you, man, it’s crazy. You just lucky you haven’t had to waste a whole buncha time around them.”

“Hmph.” Jaedon grunted in response, his eyes fixed on his food. He pushed it around his plate, his stomach churning.

“Where you been the past few days, man?” Bryce asked, stuffing some of whatever poultry was on his plate into his mouth. “It’s been like a mad house around here. We caught some of the younger girls tryin’ to escape.” He paused to chortle. “Boy, did we teach them.”

“What did you do to them?” Jaedon demanded, a bit too loudly. Bryce narrowed his eyes at him, but before he could speak, London rose to his feet and cleared his throat.

“So nice to see all of you men here!” he boomed. “It’s been busy these past few weeks, eh? Thanks to our construction crew, we’re all feasting at this wonderful table!” The table applauds, the crew raising their hands to claim their praise. “We have to get a move-on with our exploration of the remaining two villages-”

“We just sent men out there not too long ago!” one man grumbled.

"Yeah, we managed to scare that desert village real good," another man laughed. Jaedon dropped his fork and focused his eyes on the ground.

"Sure did!" A man on the opposite side of the table chimed in. "Burned down the entire thing while almost no one was there. No doubt they'll think twice about putting up a fight now, eh?" The men continued to cheer and add comments as Jaedon tried to hold his lunch in his stomach. At least half an hour went by before the subject changed and he was able to take a sip of his citrus drink.

"So, anyway...Jadey, you go out exploring these past few days?" Bryce asked, pulling away from a different conversation. "Haven't seen you."

"Here and there," Jaedon told him with a shrug. "Scouted out the area, took a look at some plants and whatever..."

"Aww, little Jadey's been out flower picking'," Bryce jeered. He punched Jaedon semi-playfully on the arm. "C'mon, man! Join the construction crew. Learn how to shoot a gun. That's why you're here, ain't it?"

"I don't have to do anything-"

"Unless it's an order from someone in charge," Bryce finished. "You lucky that Tristan, London and Ash have been goin' easy on you so far. Don't get too comfortable. If I was you, I'd watch out." The two glowered at each other while the men around them deliberately paid them little attention. Finally, Jaedon stood, slamming his glass down on the table. He couldn't stand listening to the men gleefully chatting about the innocent lives they'd taken any longer. Bryce yelled to him as he briskly made his way back towards his kytah, but Jaedon refused to so much as turn around.

*   *   *   *   *

The kytah was empty when Hyko made it back in the evening. Well, nearly so. Elder Agenee had turned in early for the night in the backroom. Her prayer book was still in her hand, and Hyko set it gently on the table beside her bed.

It felt strange to step inside her room again, to sit down on her own bed. Her blankets felt far too cold to the touch, as if they hadn't been used for days. She tried twice to curl up and drift off to sleep, but it seemed as though something was missing. As her mind began to wander, she thought of Jaedon and realized exactly what was missing. They'd slept curled up next to each other the entire time they'd traveled together. It seemed silly to her, but Hyko had found it soothing to wake up and see Jaedon sleeping peacefully a few inches away from her.

"You've been gone for ages." Gisipeh's voice was even more startling than his sudden presence in the doorway. She hadn't even heard him coming up the steps.

"Gisipeh!" she gasped, falling backwards off her bed. "Doh deshoney, you scared me half to death!" Gisipeh squeezed his eyes shut and shook his head.

"Please...don't say that word...I'm tired of hearing it," he said. Hyko bit her lip. She was tired of death as well. It had been everywhere in Sasse, even in the journals she'd been teaching Jaedon to read.

"More hunters died while I was gone?"

"No." Gisipeh took a few hesitant steps closer. "Children. You remember little Alindo? The little boy who never received his first haircut?" Hyko nodded, then felt a chill run through her body.

"H-h-he was only...was he even five yet...?" She clutched at her stomach. There was a great pain in her gut that wouldn't leave. "Ah mei vehaja...w-w-wha..."

"It's the white men," Gisipeh spat. "You know that as well as I do." It was then that Hyko remembered her encounter with Gisipeh in the woods several weeks ago. She'd completely forgotten that he and Jaedon had met and not exactly gotten off on the right foot. Gisipeh's sigh shook Hyko from her thoughts. He sat down at the foot of her bed and rubbed his forehead. "Look, Hyko...I need to speak with you about...that young man."

"Well...what is there to speak about?"

"Hyko, his men are destroying families!" Gisipeh cried, his eyes pleading. "What if he decides to turn on you? What if he hurts you?"

"He will *not* hurt me," Hyko insisted. Gisipeh cursed angrily.

"Doh deshoney!"

"How am I a fool?" Hyko snapped. "I am telling you good news, and you *refuse to listen!* You won't believe me and judge him because of something he isn't even doing!"

"No, you are a fool because you are being unreasonable," Gisipeh explained. "I am your oldest friend. You and I have been close since we were hardly old enough to speak. But, now...now you are willing to completely trust a man you haven't known for more than a summer." It was hardly appropriate, and despite the mood of the room, Hyko burst into an uncontrollable laughing fit.

"That's what this is about?" Hyko hooted. Her abdomen ached, she was laughing so hard. "You-you're jealous! That's what all of this is!"

"You are being ridiculous," Gisipeh hissed, though didn't deny her claim. He rose to his feet. "When these white men came, you started to change."

"Are you sure?" Hyko challenged. It was a weak one, for she was still giggling when she'd said it. Just before he left, Gisipeh gave her the one of the coldest glares she'd ever seen come across his face. That look shut her up instantly.

"*Yes*," he growled. "I am positive."

BASTANE
HORRIBLE

Hyko was home for less than twenty four hours before another child went missing. She'd finally managed to doze off, but had awoken to the sound of hysterical sobbing. In her sitting room was Elder Agenee and a young mother from a few kytahs over. Her son had gone out fishing earlier and never returned. The woman and Elder Agenee spent an hour praying before the woman left. Only then did Hyko descend down the stairs.

"Hyko, darling!" The elderly woman pulled her into a warm embrace, sniffling. "You had us all very worried."

"Could've fooled me," Hyko mumbled. "Sorry...that was rude." Elder Agenee pulled back, a dreary smile on her face. Dried tears stained her cheeks.

"I know it does not seem like it, but your family and friends care for you deeply and were upset when you left," the elder explained. Hyko was still a bit doubtful, but she nodded anyway. "Now. You must tell me. Why in Saiytah's name you were away for so long?" Hyko launched into her long, pre-rehearsed story on what had happened. Some of the parts were true-the dead girl, the burned village-yet, most of it was tweaked here and there to avoid explaining Jaedon. It had been hard to come up with a story completely excluding him. Half of what had occurred on her little adventure had been due to his curiosities, his fumbles, his injuries. In some parts, she replaced his name with Iatso's or Issiio's while in others, she made it seem like the fumble had been her own.

"...and so, I finally just decided to come back," Hyko finished. "Enough had already gone wrong. Plus, I'd already gotten the letters all delivered." She sat with her hands folded neatly in her lap. It took a little while for the awkward silence to set in, and Hyko knew then that the elder had not been fooled by her story.

"I do not appreciate it when sixteen year old young women lie straight to my face," Elder Agenee scolded. "Now, tell me, really. Who was the boy you went out to meet?"

"What?" Hyko scooted backwards, her throat going dry. "W-w-why...w-what would make you think-"

"I've been around a while," Elder Agenee said. She gave her a short, sharp laugh. "I can tell when a young woman is falling in love."

"B-but I-"

"You were angry with your father, with your friend and with your fiancée," she began, standing up. She glared into Hyko's eyes, and Hyko felt like she was looking through her. "You decided that becoming a messenger would allow you to leave the village with a valid excuse. You thought you would leave to clear your head and get away from everything. But while you were gone, you met someone." Hyko blinked. There was nothing to say; that was *exactly* what had happened. But, what she didn't understand was how Elder Agenee knew all of this and wasn't banishing her on the spot. "And if you're wondering how I know all this, that is all because of the spirits. They gave me dreams about you meeting with a young man you would not be wedding. Not only that, but Gisipeh's behavior has changed drastically since your absence, and Yonej...well, he was suspicious before. But now...?"

"So...you put two and two together is all," Hyko concluded, a bit relieved. Elder Agenee forced a smile that only lasted a few seconds. "And...and you're alright with all of this?" Elder Agenee fiddled with the tearing pages of her prayer book.

"I am not one to question the decisions of the spirits and who they say will be wed or not," she said. "Although, you are not the first to not wish to marry the one they were matched with." When Elder Agenee left it at that, Hyko managed to settle down. Even though she had gotten everything else correctly (besides the fact that she was in love, for Hyko was one hundred percent sure that she was not in love with anybody, Jaedon or otherwise), she was missing one very important detail; Elder Agenee did not know that the young man Hyko met was not a villager.

Even after Hyko went back up to her room exhausted, sleep would not come. There was still a commotion outside. Several families were gathered at the village center, praying and weeping. Hyko groaned. Was there no where she could go where there was no death? With an exasperated sigh, she reached her hand underneath her pillow and pulled out the old journals Jaedon and her had found in Sasse. She'd glanced at them a few times, but grown bored of them. Just as she'd told Jaedon, they were about nothing but death. *Whoever had written these journals must've had nothing but a depressing life,* Hyko thought. On only the second page of one, the author spoke of his only son, Covi, passing away in his sleep. On the thirteenth page, the writer wrote about a woman having an affair, then being stabbed to death by her husband. For pages and pages after that, the author went on and on about praying for change.

"What are you reading?" Hyko jumped up and shoved the journal under her bed. In the doorway stood Yonej. He was dressed in a dark, long-sleeved shirt and torn pants. His face was almost indistinguishable in the darkness, his expression unreadable.

"Yonej, you...nothing, it was-"

"Come with me," he commanded, grabbing a hold of her arm. Hyko was far too tired to put up a fight. He dragged her across the village and past the praying families until they reached his kytah. It seemed even larger and emptier than she remembered. The darkness of the night only made the eerie feel of the kytah worse.

"Sorry I left so suddenly after you were worried the first time, bu-"

"I was afraid you'd died!" he hissed. His tone was harsh, but she could tell that there was a hint of genuine worry in his voice. "I thought you'd been killed. We've been searching for you for days! Don't you know messengers must wait until they receive assignments before they leave?"

"I never got to finish my original task because I found Awa'hi and had to come back," Hyko explained. Yonej rubbed his forehead with his index finger and thumb, heaving a long sigh. "Yonej, I am sorry. I was only-"

"How was I supposed to know you weren't out looking for the white men, huh?" he interrupted. "Like when I found you in the woods during the floods. For all I knew, you could've been out looking for answers on those...those overgrown splinters and gotten yourself killed over it."

"Don't you think it's just a *little* weird that all this metal is around here, and yet we haven't even heard from anyone in Delfusio in months?" Hyko asked, struggling to keep her cool. "Delfusio is the *only* village that makes metal, and have you ever seen snares made by them, *ever?* Doesn't it make you even a *little* suspicious? A little bit curious to learn something more?" Yonej blinked, his eyes narrow and his brow furrowed.

"Snares?"

"Oh...that's...what I call the metal rods," Hyko said quickly. "Or snags. You know, because they snag...on stuff." She didn't dare look her future husband in the eyes. "Look, I am sorry for making you worry. I really am." Yonej took one too many steps closer to her. His dark eyes were a mere few inches from her face. She tried backing up only to find her back against the wall.

"You don't know what sorry is," he growled. Hyko sucked in an anxious breath, her eyes squeezed shut. "And trust me, you do not want me to show you what it is." He loomed over her, so close that she could feel his hot breath on her face.

"If you're going to hit me," she whimpered softly. "Just do it now...please." All of a sudden, he wasn't quite as close anymore. He took three large steps backwards, chuckling softly.

"Oh, no, I don't want to have to do that today," he told her, his tone softer. "This was just a stern warning. You're free to go now. Oh, and Hyko?" She turned to face her fiancée, whose gentle expression and tone changed suddenly. "It'd be a big help if you would stay in line and stay in the village from now on." Hyko bit her tongue to keep from saying anything that would make him change his mind about hitting her, and darted out into the night.

* * * * *

"Jadey, you're coming with us today," Bryce snapped when he walked in on Jaedon changing the day after the dinner meeting. "Be down by the caverns in fifteen minutes." On any other day, Jaedon would've refused or found a way out of it. But that day, there was something more menacing about Bryce that made Jaedon think twice about talking back. Dark bags remained under Bryce's eyes, despite the fact that it was almost midday. His clothes were sloppy and didn't match. To top it all off, he had the nastiest bruise on his left cheek. It was already discolored, turning dark blue with hints of green; there was no way Jaedon wanted to mess with Bryce and chance having his face busted up as well.

Kainau was unusually quiet that late morning. It seemed like every day, less and less natives roamed the streets of their home. Jaedon was positive that the men were taking them all somewhere, though he was a bit afraid to find out where. He had a feeling that once he saw where the natives were, it would make him sick.

The caverns were on the farthest side of the village. Towering above them were the sea cliffs, the ocean's waves crashing violently against them. Outside the caverns, a group of men in their mid thirties shifted impatiently. Only a few of them greeted Jaedon when he joined the group; most of them barely acknowledged his presence. Bryce and London were seven minutes late.

"Alright, everybody, listen up!" London's voice was loud and clear, even above the sound of the thrashing waves. "Ash's feeling under the weather, so Bryce will be standing in for him today." London lead them inside the cave. The men only took a few steps before they noticed the smell. The pungent odor was nauseating to the point where one of the men lost his lunch all over his shoes. For several endless minutes, Jaedon was torn between deeming the scent "rotting corpses on a late summer's day" or "37 days and still haven't showered."

London remained in the front while Bryce walked in the back; Jaedon tried to get as far up in the line as he could. In the back, Bryce kept grumbling curse words at one of the wimpiest men on the entire expedition.

"What's with him this morning?" One man with discolored eyes was mumbling to the guy ahead of him. "That bruise by his eye...who had the nerve to give him *that*?"

"One of the native women," the guy ahead of the man replied. "It was this big commotion last night. The girl wouldn't give him any, and smacked him in the face with a vase. Bryce was screaming and cussing for half the night!"

"Men, there are about to be big changes for us!" Bryce announced, moving up to the front of the line and ending any chatter. "While on this land, we have made a few major discoveries." The men paused at a fork in the road. One direction was better lit than the other. London motioned for the men to go down the path that had better lighting. Jaedon could make out distant chatter. Over and over again, he heard the words "ziolen rarroso" being said with much fervor.

It wasn't long before the path opened up to reveal a large, crowded room that stank even more than the entrance to the cave had. The room was dimly lit with candles, and at least seventy natives were packed into it. They were bunched up at tables, bent over and hard at work. All over the floors and tables were boxes and boxes of a dark green leafy plant.

"Is this...*what is this?*" a man behind Jaedon asked.

"This is the beginning of our wealth, gentlemen!" London cried with much gusto, a bright smile on his skinny face. "What you see before you isn't marijuana; it's even better, my comrades! This magnificent plant, I have learned, is called Jokpoh.

It induces a high without any major side effects. You come off it, you only feel like you have a little hangover." Murmurs moved furiously through the group. A new illegal drug that technically wasn't even illegal yet; it was the perfect idea. "These plants grow all over this land. In the forests, in the caves...even in a few select places in that frozen wasteland. You can get high off the smoke, or chew it to get the same effects."

London continued is explanation on the newfound drug, but Jaedon was extremely distracted. The natives working with drugs appeared to be engrossed in their work, but moved sluggishly. Dark circles outlined their eyes. Bruises marked each and every one of their faces and arms, as if they'd been beaten in order to get motivated. Most of them paid no mind to Jaedon or the others. A few did look up at Jaedon, eyes wide with fear, as if they'd seen him once before in a nightmare.

"Hopefully, but this time next year, we'll have every single one of their sorry black behinds growing, picking and packing these Jokpoh plants," Bryce chimed in with a laugh. Several other men joined in with Bryce's laughter as the men proceeded to the next room. The room the second path lead to was even more disgraceful than the first. Half-naked and malnourished women huddled in corners, shivering. On the floor were old, cracked plastic bowls half filled with some sort of mush that resembled wet dog food.

"Now, most of the women in here are a bit run down," London explained. It was as though he were talking about a car. "In the next room are the younger women that we all enjoy." Among the bunch of bruised up, underfed women was the one native who'd dropped the pitcher when Jaedon had said "thank you" in her language. She eyed him and only him as he walked through the room. He started to hang back as the group continued on. It was fairly easy to stay behind while the others kept going; none of the men paid much attention to Jaedon anyway, making it particularly easy for him to leave for a little bit.

He headed hesitantly over to the native who'd dropped the pitcher. She began fidgeting with her hair as soon as she'd seen him lag behind.

"You, boy...used my tongue," she said, her accent causing the words to sound heavy and sloppy. She had to repeat herself many times before Jaedon understood it, and at least four more times before he made sense of it.

"Umm, yes...I mean, shay," he said, deciding to use the word for yes in her language as opposed to his own. "Why did that upset you?"

"Ziolen rarroso," she started. "You do not use tongue of my people. Only for us to use. You use, you rob our freedom, what left of it. No secrets for us. No longer is it sacred." Her eyes started to tear up, her body shaking. "Already you take so much. This you don't. Tongue is ours. It is ours."

"But, I want to help," Jaedon hissed, trying to lean in closer to avoid being heard. The woman was frightened by his proximity and stumbled backwards. "Mei...um...zze."

"How you help us?" the woman shrieked. She fell to her knees. Terrible sobs shook her entire body as she rocked back and forth. A couple of other natives saw and darted over to their frenzied friend. One of the woman's friends began shouting at him in her language, drawing attention to Jaedon. The rest of the women shot cold scowls in his direction, murmuring amongst themselves, using mostly words Jaedon hadn't learned yet. He opened his mouth to explain, but the shouts and curses of the women did not cease.

He left the room feeling disheartened and rejoined the group silently at the back of the line. London was still explaining Jokpoh while Bryce marched wordlessly at his side. According to London, all they needed to put their drug plan in action was the word from Tristan.

"So long as he's okay with being ridiculously rich," London joked, earning a few laughs from the group. "We'll have all these natives working our Jokpoh fields in no time."

"What about the children?" Jaedon asked, the thought suddenly striking him. Aside from a couple of girls around the age of twelve, he hadn't seen any children in Kainau at all. He hadn't really paid attention to it at first, but after visiting Sasse and seeing dozens of children, it was oddly childless in Kainau.

"Where are they...? I haven't seen a room for them yet. Are they gonna-"

"Jaedon...come over here for a second," Bryce said, dropping his voice low. The green-eyed man put an arm around Jaedon's shoulder and pulled him close. "You see here, man, Tristan wants to run this excursion without any pests running around or getting in the way of anything we could find. London and Ash can't use the little boogers for harvesting drugs, either."

"So...where are they?"

"They are no use to us," Bryce continued. "They're like...they're like the mosquito that gets in your bedroom when you forget to close the window at night. The only way to get rid of a pest like that is to squash it." He let a short, sharp laugh escape his lips. "Kill it and that's all there is to it!" He gave Jaedon a hardy slap on the back and shoved him away. In all of his disorientation, Jaedon smacked into three or four people as the men made their way back to the entrance of the caverns. A throbbing in the back of his head would not let up, and he felt as if he were going to collapse on the ground. Bryce and London kept on talking until they dismissed the men back to their kytahs, but Jaedon hardly heard any of it. Only Bryce's words about the children continued to play through his head; *kill it and that's all there is to it!* Jaedon tried to imagine what he'd do if one of his sisters were killed like Bryce had said had happened to the kids of Kainau. It was a thought that he couldn't properly process.

For the rest of the day, Jaedon was in a funk. He was assigned several simple tasks and chores, all of which he completed at a pace that was shamefully slow due to his distracted mind. His brain would not focus on anything that he was doing. A few times, he thought he heard a child laughing, only to find that it was only someone's high pitched cough. By the time the other men were heading to bed, Jaedon was puking his dinner up onto his bedroom floor. He'd figured that maybe getting it all out would make him feel at least a little better, but it made him feel ten times worse. For twenty minutes, he sat staring at the chunky mess on his hardwood floor, his head throbbing. The smell of his regurgitated food wasn't helping him any, either.

"Hey man...whoa. What's up with *this?*" Bryce stepped through the door, eyeing the mess on the floor with disgust. "You feeling okay?"

"Had some bad fish, I think," Jaedon grunted, falling backwards onto his bed. "Ugh. I feel terrible."

"So I can see," Bryce said. He gave a short, dry laugh before reaching for an empty bucket. "Here. I'll help ya out." He began to clean up the room in silence, scooping up the vomit into the bucket and scrubbing down the floor.

"What do you want?" Jaedon sat up.

"Huh?"

"Come on, Bryce. I know you; what do you want from me?"

"Nothing, brah," Bryce laughed, tossing the bucket out the window. It struck the ground loudly, causing Jaedon to flinch. "I just wanted to help you out." When he paused, Jaedon raised a suspicious eyebrow. "Well, actually, I did come up here to talk to you. But, since you needed help, I figured I might as well, since I'm here and you look like a donkey's rear end." He leaned his body against the wall, putting a good ten feet between the two of them.

"Alright...go ahead."

"Okay, two things. You will have a new job," Bryce announced. "An official job. You also have a special assignment."

"You know that I don't need to take orde-"

"Don't mess with me today, Jaedon," Bryce snapped, and Jaedon shut his mouth. "Now, as I was saying. We're wanting to get this Jokpoh plan off the ground. So. This first order of business is straight from the big men in charge themselves. Since you've been spending so much time 'collecting flowers,' we figured you'd know the trails. We want you to get the news to Tristan. He's probably somewhere in the mountain village." Jaedon nodded, nibbling at his bottom lip. "This second one is pretty much all from me. You need to get your backside off this bed and help us out. This expedition is a punishment for you, not some beach vacation."

"I'm not-"

"Shut up and listen!" Bryce boomed. "You're officially in charge of 'motivating' the natives starting in three days. If they slip up, you put em' back in their place. If they're moving slowly, get em' to speed up. You get at what I'm saying?"

"Yeah, I hear ya," Jaedon grumbled. "How do I do this?" A cruel smile came across Bryce's face.

"That's the beauty of this all," he explained. "It doesn't matter. The punishments and motivations are all up to you, bro. But if I were you, I would choose a method that's more...*pleasurable* for the punisher, you know what I mean?"

"I'm not into-"

"Or, since you're a wuss, you could just take their food for a day and throw it off the sea cliffs as a punishment," he interrupted. "Hit them. Beat them. I dunno, something that'll make them regret stepping out of line." Bryce sauntered around the room, kicking away any clothes or shoes on the floor. "You have a few more days to keep on relaxing, but once that time is up, you'll be a working man."

PACALKENOU MEETING PLACE

The streets of Tattao were empty and quiet when he arrived. That was exactly the way he wanted to keep them; quiet and empty. It had taken him longer to reach the forest-surrounded village than he'd wanted it to, though he was glad he arrived so late. There would be little attention drawn to him so late at night, if any.

For the first several kytahs he passed, he peered inside each and every window. Every family was sleeping peacefully. No one had fires burning in their fireplaces. By the ninth kytah, he was tired of looking through every window and grunted, kicking at the dirt.

He grew impatient after a while. He couldn't find the person he was looking for, the village was unnervingly quiet, and he was exhausted and paranoid. It wasn't much longer before he realized that Tattao was far larger than he'd originally thought, which made him even more frustrated. It would take longer to find who he was searching for than he'd hoped.

A loud bang caught his attention and something induced a sharp pain in his leg. He cursed, falling to the ground. It wasn't long before he saw a light in a window of a nearby kytah. He scooted backwards, knocking into the same object that had caused the noise in the first place. He stayed hidden in the shadows, watching the light in the window move throughout the house until it reached the front door.

A tall, dark man holding a candle stormed out of his home. A scowl was on his face as he scanned the area, holding out the candle to shed more light on his yard. A woman joined him at the door, stroking his shoulders and arms while speaking in a low voice. His response seemed harsh, but the woman didn't flinch.

When the two headed back inside, he waited for several, long suspenseful minutes before daring to step out of the safety of the shadows. That man...he'd seen that man once before. Moving swiftly, he stayed low to the ground and made his way to the back of the kytah. There was a door that was cracked open with a shoe. He had to do a double take, for he could've sworn that he'd seen that exact shoe before as well. It was then that he knew he'd found the right place.

The door barely made a sound when he opened it wider and slipped inside. Twice on his way down the hall, he passed by rooms. A couple was sleeping peacefully in one, and an old woman was snoring in the other. Up the stairs he went, and found two more rooms. He passed by the first one; all that was in it were walls covered in drawings and a little girl, sleeping peacefully and clutching at a doll. Just as he was approaching the last room, he heard the frantic movement of feet. There was no time to check the room, and he dove into it without looking first. He'd half expected to find himself face to face with a furious native; instead, he found himself in a messy room with two windows, one of which was open. The sound of movement ceased after a few seconds, and he allowed himself to relax. A tree outside the kytah scraping the window was the only sound now.

There were things scattered all over the floor; clothes, shoes and even books appeared to have been thrown all around. The sheets on the bed couldn't have been used for more than a few nights. Next to the window, he noticed yet another familiar object: a messenger bag. Its handle had snapped in half.

Despite the bag, the shoe and the familiar man, the person he'd been searching for wasn't there. He slipped out of the home as quietly as he'd entered, the cool night air hitting him suddenly. The only movement was that of the trees as a breeze swept through. He took several steps away from the kytah, then found himself flat on the ground, cold and wet. He pulled himself up, kicking the side of the large bucket he'd knocked over. It was similar to the bucket he'd kicked earlier when he'd awoken the man, though that one hadn't been filled with a funny-smelling liquid.

He turned his head to the left to make sure the town was still asleep. He turned to the right and found himself face to face with a young woman. Her eyes were wide, standing out in the dark and contrasting with the color of her skin. She was breathing heavily, and he couldn't quite tell if she was surprised or angry. He tried to take a step towards her, but he slipped on the now muddy ground, knocking her to the ground.

"Jaedon!" she hissed, breathlessly. *"What are you doing here?"* He was lying on top of her, trying to scramble up onto his knees. He was soaking wet and muddy, his hair sticking to his forehead. "If my father sees you-"

"Relax!" Jaedon breathed. "He's not going to see me."

"I can't believe you were stupid enough to wake him up," she snapped. "Knocking your leg against the water bucket. Are you-"

"I need you to come with me," he said, more loudly than he should have. He lowered his voice before continuing. "I don't know...how to get there, and they're on my tail."

"Need me to go with you where?" she asked. "Who's on your *what?* Is someone chasing you?" He pulled himself off of her and took a deep breath. He was shivering now, trying to wipe the mud from his feet and arms.

"I-I-I need to g-go...need to g-go..." He struggled with each word that came out of his mouth. "It's really cold, H-Hyko...c-can we...?" She took his hand in hers and dragged him along. She continued on past the kytahs and past the farming fields until they reached dry, barren soil surrounded by boulders. Hyko then lifted her poncho-resembling sweater from around her shoulders.

"Take off your shirt," she instructed. Once he was shirtless and even colder than he'd been with the wet shirt on, she wrapped her sweater around him. “That better?” He wanted to nod and tell her thank you, but he was still chilled to the bone. When Jaedon gave no response, she pressed herself against him, hugging him tightly to her.

Her touch warmed him instantly, and within seconds, Jaedon felt a trickle of sweat make its way down his forehead. They sat in silence for the longest. Hyko ran her hands up and down Jaedon’s back, causing Jaedon’s mind to go crazy. He wondered what she was thinking. Was there more to her gestures than just wanting Jaedon to warm up and not catch cold? He sighed softly and Hyko leaned back.

“Are you warmer now?” she murmured. There was a certain playfulness in her voice. Jaedon felt his face grow hot, glad that the nighttime concealed his blush. He cleared his throat.

“Yeah…thanks, um, for that,” he said. “Sorry about…you know, waking up your folks.”

“And breaking into my house.”

“Right.” He pulled away just a little to free his arm from her embrace and swipe away the hair sticking to his forehead.

“Do you do that back on your homeland?” she teased. “Break into girls’ homes?” Jaedon smirked, trying to imagine what would happen if he’d done such a thing back at home.

“Nah,” he chuckled. “I’d get arrested on the spot, and my mom would…she’d…” His voice trailed off with each word. He thought of how his mother had actually reacted when he’d been arrested; the thought made his stomach twist. Hyko placed a hand on his chest.

“What?” she asked, but he shook his head.

“It’s a long story,” he grumbled, tugging at the sweater so that it was tighter around him. It wasn’t the time or place for him to reveal that story to her yet. “Some other time.”

“My mother is silent,” Hyko blurted out all of a sudden. Jaedon blinked and watched as she played with a curly lock of her hair. “She never says anything and doesn’t do anything. All she does is cook and clean and gather, sometimes, or tell my sister and I what to do. She never voices her opinion on anything. She’s like…like an ahro.” She paused to point to a nearby rock. “Just sits there and looks stupid. My father could tell her to jump off the highest ledge in Delfusio, and she'd do it."

When she was finished, Hyko was breathing hard. Her entire body was trembling. Her palms were white from squeezing her hands into fists. Jaedon moved a bit closer to her, closing the gap that had grown when she'd moved away after she'd warmed him up.

"That's a shame," he told her. "Really, it is. But, why are you telling me this *now?*" Hyko looked up at him, her brow furrowed.

"The things that hurt to speak about remain hidden behind our lips," she explained; Jaedon guessed he was quoting some old proverb of her people from the way she was talking. "There they stay until it is too much to hold and it all must come out. It's better to bear the pain of telling one hurt than try to keep peace of mind when they are all said at once."

Jaedon cast his gaze down at his feet. She was right; sooner or later, all of the stories he was putting off telling would have to be told if the two were to completely trust each other. Jaedon could sense that there were more of Hyko's hidden truths as well, and that she wanted to tell them. By telling of her mother's silence, Jaedon knew that Hyko had started the process of letting them out.

"Let's make a deal," he suggested. "Each time we see each other, we have to tell at least one of the secrets we've been keeping from the other until they've all been said. Starting today." Hyko smiled sheepishly and nodded. A part of him was relieved, but at the same time, he knew that the truth would be out.

"You know what?" Hyko jumped to her feet. "I think this could be our own little place. Como wei mei; come with me." Jaedon followed her as she headed in the direction of a large boulder pressed against a wall of rock. With all of her strength, she pushed the massive rock, moving it a few inches with every shove. It took some time, but eventually, there was enough of it pushed aside so that the small cavern behind it was visible. Hyko slipped inside, twisting her slender body so that she could fit through the space; Jaedon followed right behind her, inside the cavern, the only light was that of the moon as it came through the narrow entrance.

"This old cavern I found only months ago," she explained, excitedly. "No one ever uses it. I don't even think anyone knows it's here, so I started using it as a hideout. I used to bring snacks and things here in my spare time, but lately, I've been..."

"Yeah," Jaedon said when her voice trailed off. "I know. The ziolen rarroso put a halt to everything, right?" He slumped down, leaning his back against the wall. Though he could hardly see anything, he heard Hyko sit down next to him. He could feel the heat of her body, and it made every nerve in his body sensitive.

"Jaedon, didn't you need me to go with you somewhere?" she asked. Her voice was low and it made him shiver.

"Hmm...oh, yeah, right." He sat up just a little, suddenly remembering. "The men...they're making me go up to the mountains, to the village up there."

"Delfusio," she said. "I can take you there. But not right now. My family and friends are getting suspicious, especially my fian..." She bit her lip before she could say any more.

"Your what?" Jaedon asked, waiting expectantly. He heard shuffling and felt the heat from her body disappear. When she spoke again, her voice sounded farther away.

"It's a story for another day," she murmured, her voice trembling. Jaedon opened his mouth to speak, and then decided against it.

HYKO
MOON

"Sosii!" Ohn-Tsung cried. It had been years since she'd used that nickname for Hyko, but at that moment, she didn't care in the least. She dashed from the table, leaving her half-eaten breakfast, and made her way over to her sister. She wrapped her arms around Hyko so tightly that her older sister grunted in pain. "Sosii, you're back! Where were you last night? I needed help with my mathematics." Hyko didn't answer, and instead, walked over to the table. Her mother said nothing and neither did her father. They sat in silence, eating their creamed wheat. Ohn-Tsung's smile vanished in a heartbeat. "Well?"

"Keep your stupid questions to yourself," Hyko snapped, pouring milk into her breakfast. She hated seeing her little sister cringe at those harsh words, but Hyko couldn't have her asking questions that would make her father suspicious. Suddenly, Hyko's father slammed his bowl down on the table just as she set the milk container down. Creamed wheat and milk splashed onto both Ohn-Tsung and her mother.

"Noka, I do not deem my daughter's question stupid," he growled. "I, too, would like to know what it was you were doing last night. There was much noise, did you not hear?" Hyko bit her lip and set her breakfast bowl down on the table.

"I heard," she grumbled.

"Then you know that it woke both me and your mother up?"

"What, you think it was me outside crashing into water buckets?" she snapped. She was very close to crossing the line, and from the way her mother was shifting nervously in her seat, Hyko figured she might've already stepped halfway over it.

"You were the one who was out all night," he said with an intense glare. In her head, Hyko silently cursed Jaedon for unknowingly framing her.

"Adad, it was not I who was made noise last night," Hyko insisted. "Umm...maybe it was a dog...or something." Her father narrowed his eyes ad gritted his teeth.

"Dogs are not able to curse when they walk into a water bucket," he pointed out. The breakfast table was silent then. Hyko knew she'd lost. She watched her mother and sister eat as her father's glower stayed fixed on her. When she's grown tired of the noiselessness, she rose suddenly from the table. Once at the door, she turned to face her family, her stare icy cold.

"Think what you want, but it wasn't me who was out last night," she hissed sharply. As soon as she was out the door, she headed straight for the healer's hut. She noticed, but didn't bother confronting the villagers that stared and murmured as she passed by. It was oddly busy in the healer's hut when she arrived that morning. At least a dozen or so hunters were all crowded around an irritated, overworked Hanjeha. Blood dripped from the hands of most of the men, staining the ground. Hyko groaned inwardly; she knew that she'd be the one scrubbing it all up later.

"Awa'hi!" Hanjeha called out. "Awa'hi! Where is that girl...? Ah, Hyko! Thank the spirits, you're back!" Every single head turned as soon as the girl's name was mentioned. Aside from a little boy's cries as he had a cut cleaned, no one said a thing. All the hunters stared wordlessly, clutching at their injuries. Hyko took a step back, grabbing at the hem of her skirt uneasily.

"Umm...Hanjeha," she began. "I don't think that-"

"Girl, if you don't get your butt over here and help me, I swear to you, I will make you regret it," she threatened with more venom in her voice than Hyko had ever heard before. "I will remember this day for the rest of my years. When you have a broken bone, I kid you not when I tell you *I will make you set it yourself.* Girl, *I will not even help you when you birth your first child.*" As Hanjeha ended her tirade, a few of the men were snickering like gossiping old women. One of the younger men turned to his friend, smacking him playfully with his bloody hand.

"I hope the kid is by her husband," he jeered. "Cause if it's latso's, Yonej is gonna-"

"Whoa, wait, *what?*" Hyko interrupted. She went right up to the young hunter and gave him a small shove. "I am not going to having a-"

"Hey, hey, there," the young hunter jeered. He had a cocky grin on his dirty face. "I'm sorry. Is there some other lover? What about that one tall kid up in Sasse, eh? That dark one who kills scorpions? I'll bet you like em' real dark, huh?"

"Boy, shut up," Hanjeha squawked, gesturing for the next person to step up and have their wound looked at. "Hyko is not pregnant *now*. If she was, I'd have killed her already." The chatter in the hut settled down, and the men began to complain of their cuts and gashes once more. Hyko moved away from the young man and headed straight for the Nipperbree leaves.

"Thanks, Hanjeha," she muttered, preparing the roots to spread on the hunter's hand wounds. The old woman grunted in response. A hunter stepped up to Hyko, his clasped hand tightly around his arm. A series of small puncture wounds ran from his elbow to his wrist. He'd wrapped most of the injury in a ripped up cloth, but blood had soaked through and gotten his hands sticky and crimson. She reached her hands out to rub the herbs on his arm, and he pulled away, a scowl on his face.

"I do not wish to be treated by you," he growled, rather bluntly. A blood-curdling shriek pierced through the air. Even the eldest hunter in the room flinched at the sound that Hyko soon realized had come from Hanjeha.

"And *I* do not wish to treat *you*," she hissed. "So you have two choices; let Hyko help you, or get out. You're bleeding all over the floor." The two healers went on working like that for over an hour. Hanjeha tried to strike up some conversations with the wounded, but they were all too busy glaring at and complaining about Hyko. Once or twice, Hyko noticed Awa'hi cutting from one room to the next, not bothering to stop and help. She hadn't even bothered to take her eyes off the ground and say hi. What was with her? Surely she was better from her incident with the white men by then. The question stayed on Hyko's mind until the hut had cleared out and Hanjeha was preparing an herbal tea.

"Awa'hi hasn't gone home yet?" she asked. Hanjeha's focus remained on the tea. "Hanjeha...?"

"We're running low on Carabept spice," the old healer grumbled, tossing a few more spices into the tea. "Your sister should've brought me some by now-"

"Hanjeha!"

"*You young people these days!*" the old woman snapped. "Don't know how to treat adults! Being disrespectful and refusing to help. I swear, I plead with the spirits every night for the generations to come to act right, and instead, I get children like *you* and your little friend in there thrust upon me!" Hyko blinked. The old woman was mindlessly tossing spices and herbs into a pot of broth that wasn't even boiling yet as she grunted and grumbled with frustration. Her eyes were dull and the skin around them seemed even more worn and wrinkly than usual. Never before had Hyko seen her mentor look so...old. She scooted closer to the pot of broth and began to add the last of the Carabept more gently.

"Have things been alright here while I was gone?" Hyko asked, a bit less demanding than her previous question had been. Hanjeha heaved a sigh and let her hands fall to her sides. Her gaze was fixed on the tea, which was finally beginning to bubble and thicken.

"Not once in all my years have I been so tired," she explained. "Day in and day out, I have gotten few hours of rest. These white men have brought strange illness, strange injuries, and everyone is coming to me to heal them. They think I know everything. They think I can help. But in truth, I know not how to treat most of them." She paused to reach for her stirring spoon. "A little girl fell ill a couple of weeks ago. It seemed like nothing more than a cough at first. Then, she began to break out and swell up. She threw up enough blood to bathe in the day she died." Hanjeha's fingers were trembling as she readied the tea.

"I...I am sorry, Moro Hanjeha," Hyko muttered. What else was there for her to say? She chewed at her lip as a shaky sigh escaped Hanjeha's lips.

"All the while this was going on, Awa'hi just stood back and did nothing!" she snapped. She used her ladle to scoop the soupy, lumpy tea into a bowel. Most of the tea sloshed out of the ladle and onto the old healer's lap. "Can you believe that? *Nothing!* One day there were thirty men standing in here, bleeding from places I never knew existed on our bodies, and Awa'hi's butt stayed on that bed in the corner of the-"

"You know that Awa'hi isn't trained to be a healer," Hyko interrupted, attempting to defend her friend. "And besides, Awa'hi can sometimes be..." She let her voice trail off at the end of the sentence. What was she talking about? Awa'hi was never not doing anything. Before Hyko was even finished half-finishing her sentence, Hanjeha was gawking at her, her old and weary eyes wide.

"Does 'lazy and whiny' sound anything like Awa'hi to you?" She threw down the bowl of tea and dropped the ladle into the still boiling pot of broth. "Because that's what she's been like; whiny and lazy like a baby. 'Hanjeha, I need water from the stream to wash up! Hanjeha, get Ohn-Tsung to get me some more Carabept spice for my pain. Hanjeha, reach up to the shelf for me; I can't reach up that high because I have a pain in my-'"

"Give the girl a break," Hyko protested. "She was traumatized by what happened with the white men. It's a blessing that she's even still alive today."

"It'd be a blessing if the spirits would end her life now since the girl already walks around like the living dead," Hanjeha grumbled under her breath. Hyko's jaw dropped. The old woman opened her mouth to complain yet again, but was cut short when Awa'hi called for her from the doorway. She seemed to have put on some weight since the last time Hyko had seen her and her bruises had all vanished. Her hair was starting to grow back; it was still far shorter than Hyko was used to, but it had been trimmed and looked neater than the last time. Awa'hi's eyes were what struck Hyko the most; they were bloodshot, as if she'd been wasting the day away in bed, sobbing.

"There's no more Carabept," she moaned, her words almost completely slurred together. "Are all the men gone? Maybe Ohn-Tsung can go get some more."

"Or maybe *you*, young lady, can run out and get some more yourself!" Hanjeha stood as she spoke, spitting the words from her mouth as though they were hot embers. "You ought to know what they look like, what with how much you shove into that disgusting mouth of yours!"

"Hanjeha-"

"Do not speak, Hyko!" Hanjeha turned to Hyko with a fire in her eyes that she'd never seen before. "Awa'hi, it has been three days since you've last bathed. You have been lying around this hut for weeks on end. I understand that you were deeply hurt, and then fell ill with a cough. Nevertheless, this has gone on long enough!" Awa'hi stepped back, flinching at almost everything that came from Hanjeha's mouth. "If you are to stay here, you will help out around here. Starting this evening. Otherwise, one of the young men will escort you back to Sasse-"

"No!" Both Hyko and Awa'hi cried, then exchanged aghast glances. Hanjeha took a step back, folding her arms across her chest. She glared at the both of them with narrowed eyes.

"Matteo...wait a sec," Hyko murmured. She took a step away from Awa'hi, who looked close to breaking down. "Why don't *you* want to return to Sasse?" Hyko knew her reason, what with almost all of it burnt to a crisp; but there was no way that her friend could have any idea of what had gone on in the desert village.

Awa'hi's gaze fell to the ground and she fiddled with her thumbs. Hyko was beyond herself with disbelief! Whatever happened to the feisty spirit who always wanted to annoy the elders at Samnba just for laughs? Where was the girl who'd taken on Iatso and sent him home with a busted lip when he'd cracked a joke about her celebrations outfit? Where was the quick-witted sixteen year old girl who never let up about Gisipeh and Hyko being in love?

"I'm freaking out, okay?" she whimpered, her voice going up a couple of octaves. "I swear, if I run into another white man, I'll kill myself before they even get the chance to think of...of using me."

"Good," Hanjeha hissed under her breath. Awa'hi ignored the comment and went on.

"I can't trust a man after that. Any man, not just the white ones. I-I just can't, I mean...there've been men in our villages who have done that to their wives, right? Force them into...into *doing that?*"

"What about becoming a housewife?" Hyko asked, trying to use a gentle voice.

"House wife my apok!" Hanjeha hooted.

"Hanjeha!"

"Hush up, child, I'm seventy two years old. I can use whatever language I wish and the spirits will *still* bless me." She added on a few more cuss words just to get her point across. "But, Awa'hi, Hyko is correct; to be a housewife, you will need to be married. When you are married, you are going have children. And in order to have children, you have to-"

"I know how to have a baby!" Awa'hi yelled, lashing out and lunging at Hanjeha. "Why can't you be more understanding of what I went through?" She was sitting atop the old woman, grabbing at tufts of her hair and ripping some of it out. Hanjeha was squirming and cursing, her fingernails digging into Awa'hi's arm. Hyko stood and watched the ludicrous scene for a few moments. She knew it was wrong, but she was torn between ending the fight and bursting into laughter. Eventually, she found herself grabbing a hold of Awa'hi by her left leg and dragging her off the old healer.

"What is *wrong* with you?!" Hyko cried. Awa'hi's arm was bloody from Hanjeha's nails, some of it dripping onto Hyko's shoes. "The spirits are going to beat you *down!*"

"What more could they do to hurt me?" Awa'hi snapped, her tone fierce. "They took *everything* away from me when they did nothing as I was taken advantage of by those strangers!"

"Awa'hi, calm down," Hanjeha pleaded weakly. "You are acting foolish-"

"Tell Ohn-Tsung to get more Carabept," Awa'hi hissed, staggering towards the door. "I'll be washing my wounds." There was dead silence the moment Awa'hi was gone. Then, whimpers and sniffles. Heaving a sigh, Hanjeha got to her feet. Hyko watched as the old woman limped over to the wall where she covered her face and wept softly.

"I...I'll go and get some more Carabept and bring it by before sunset," Hyko said quietly, and stepped out into the cool evening air.

Jaedon was already at the meeting place when Hyko arrived just after sunset. She'd said she was going to bring Hanjeha more Carabept, but no part of her wished to return to the healer's hut that day. She needed some air and some time to think, away from Hanjeha and her squawking. Hyko had known that returning to Tattao wouldn't be easy, but things had gone far worse than she'd expected. At least with Jaedon, she felt that she could relax and talk about anything without being looked down upon.

"You know what would be nice right now?" Hyko asked. She and Jaedon were sitting side by side in their cave, watching the sky grow darker. Several times, Hyko nearly rested her head on his shoulder and stifled a yawn or two; she was dog-tired, yet didn't want Jaedon to think she was bored.

"Hmm? What's that?"

"Simplicity," she sighed. She gazed out at the moon. "Ehem da hyko; like the moon. It's so...simple. I wonder why *people* can't be that way." She could feel Jaedon's eyes on her, watching her become lost in thought.

"People make things more complicated than they need to be," Jaedon said. Hyko chortled, thinking of all the situations she'd made more complex than need be.

"I do that," she laughed. "A lot. Kind of strange how my name means 'moon' when I'm not simple like the moon at all."

"That's alright," Jaedon said, his voice low. "I like that about you. You're not simple. You're complex. Unique. Interesting...and I like it." He looked down at her and, despite the darkness, Hyko could tell that he was blushing. She began to play with a curly lock of her hair. "Hyko, tell me something."

"What?"

"Something. Anything. A story, a legend..." He scooted closer to her, and Hyko felt her entire body turn to fire. She hesitated at first, trying to ignore his how his proximity made her body react and recall a story for him.

"When I was born," she began. "I was very sick. I could barely breath. Our healer, Hanjeha, told my parents that there was no way I would survive the night. She'd done all she could, but since I was a newborn, there was only so much she could do. My parents prayed to the spirits for hours on end. They prayed that, somehow, I would make it.

"According to the spirits, we draw energy from the moon each night. That energy is what rejuvenates our bodies and allows us to go on to live another day. My father found his old prayer book and read da niiuqui so da hyko, the prayer of the moon. It is used for those who are ill and may not make it through the night. He repeated that prayer until his lips were numb. He said the prayer over and over until he was so exhausted that he fell asleep kneeling on the ground, his head in the open prayer book.

"In the morning, he awoke to a smiling, newborn daughter. I'd pulled through, despite what Hanjeha had said. Overjoyed, my parents decided to name me after what had saved me. And so...my name is Hyko." There were a few seconds of silence once Hyko had finished the story. And then, Jaedon started laughing. Hyko scooted away from him, trying to hide her disgust.

"Jaedon! I don't see anything funny about that story."

"No, it's not. I'm sorry. It's just...*you actually believe that stuff?*" he asked, still getting the last of his laughs out. "At first, I thought you were just telling stories from your culture. But I didn't know-"

"You didn't think that I believed in the spirits," Hyko finished. She furrowed her brow. "I still don't see any humor."

"Nothing. I just...well, I was taught something a little bit different," Jaedon said. "My family taught me that there's only one spirit. Except, we don't call Him a spirit, we call Him God."

"I don't know what you're talking about," Hyko snapped. She truly had never heard of such a thing before. "If I were you, I'd stop speaking like this, or the spirits will be sure to punish-"

"Hyko, there are no spirits," Jaedon murmured. "Not like your people taught you." Hyko's throat went dry. She pressed her hand to her temple.

"And what did *your* family teach you?" she hissed, crossly. Jaedon reached out to touch her, but she jerked away.

"Hyko, don't be angry with me-"

"Tell me, Jaedon." With a sigh, Jaedon began his explanation. He described the church he and his family would attend each Sunday. He told of the prayers, songs and sermon that made up each service. He talked about the Bible, comparing it to the prayer books of Hyko's people in any way that he could. He even elucidated on some of the stories and lessons that the Bible held. All the while, Hyko half listened, her head spinning. Only one spirit instead of many...it was a lot to take in after sixteen years of being told otherwise. It took ages for Jaedon to finish his explanation, but when he was finally through, Hyko was in tears.

"You're crying?" Jaedon asked softly. Her response was a quiet sniffle. "Hyko...I-"

"You're no different," she snapped. The tears on her cheeks felt hot and itchy. She tried to wipe them away, but more continued to fall. "You're no different from *any* of them. What makes you think you're right and I'm wrong?"

"I'm not saying-"

"What *are* you saying, then?"

"Just think about it!" Jaedon cried, but then lowered his voice. "It's not...I mean-"

"Exactly!" Hyko hissed. "If you think for one second that you can change *everything* my family has ever taught me, you are *wrong,* Jaedon. I don't want you controlling me as well." Jaedon groaned and rolled his eyes.

"Oh, will you *stop it?*" he shouted, jumping to his feet. He got right in Hyko's face, his nose only a few inches from hers. "You think everyone of the opposite sex wants to control you. You're all ticked off all the time because you say that the men are 'controlling' you. But, have you ever considered this? Maybe they do those things because they want to keep you safe. Maybe they're *worried* about you! Maybe *I'm* worried about you."

"Worried that I won't be in Heaven with you and your squeaky-clean white people?" Hyko spat. "From what I see, your white people aren't all that squeaky-clean, and neither are you. What have you done that's good this past summer, huh? Watch while my people are hurt, poisoned and killed? What a *wonderful* Christian man *you* are, Jaedon!"

"I try," he growled, his voice low.

"Didn't you say that you go to Heaven when you die?" she retorted. "I'm not dying yet, besho."

"You could die if you keep ignoring everything your family says." Jaedon took two steps back, grunting with annoyance. "And could you not cuss at me like that?" Hyko gave him a smug look. She narrowed her eyes and put her face so close to his that their sweat mixed.

"Besho." The word came out slowly and with great vehemence.

"Now you're acting stupid."

"Bastane besho!" Hyko jeered, taunting him and filling the air with more insults in both English and her own language. She could see the rage bubbling up inside him and it gave her a smug sort of satisfaction. His anger was especially obvious on his deep red face. His fists were clenched tight enough to turn his knuckles white.

"You're being ridiculous," he growled. "Get over yourself and think about what I'm saying to you." When she said nothing in response, he heaved a loud sigh. The quiet following all of their shouting was an awkward one. The tension in the cave had grown thick, suffocating the both of them. It was Jaedon who walked towards the entrance of the cave first. “Alright, fine. I’m sorry for caring *so much*, Hyko. Didn’t know it was too much for you to handle.”

“Just get out,” she hissed. She didn’t even watch as he disappeared off into the night.

SONMNONEN
APOLOGY

"Peleiko, ta ne hokey, meyé," a native woman moaned. She looked weak and fragile. Her hands were trembling and, if it weren't for the walking cane steadying her, she would most definitely have fallen over when she reached out for him. Her hair was in one braid that went just past her shoulders, though it looked as if it hadn't been redone in days. No matter how miserable she appeared to be, Jaedon had to turn away from her and get back to his job.

She's just hot, he thought to himself as he made his way towards the next room. *That's all she said. All she needs is some clean water. Give it to her, Jaedon! Just give her some water.*

"Hao!" Another woman nearby was crying out and clutching at her pregnant stomach. The older women in the room crowded around her and started chanting phrases over and over, using mostly words that Jaedon did not recognize.

"You!" The same woman who'd earlier scolded Jaedon for using their language and dropped the pitcher was standing several feet away, yelling for him. "Ziolen rarroso boy, come you here now." Hesitantly, he took a few steps so that he and the woman were a few paces apart.

"Umm...yes?"

"Life will enter world soon," she explained in broken English. "New baby is on way. We need things for baby." Jaedon blinked. He had no clue of what the natives gave their babies upon birth. He knew nothing about babies in general, except that they were cute and messy.

"Umm...you mean like bottles and diapers?" he asked, but the woman slapped him.

"You think I play game?" she cried. "You stand there, look stupid when we need bring life to world." The woman went through an extensive list of things, most of which Jaedon either couldn't get or didn't know what they were. He did manage to find quite a few blankets and some clean water. After that, the natives were pretty much on their own.

Eventually, the woman forced him to leave, and Jaedon passed the time by listening to their chanted prayers and doodling in the dirt while perched on a rock in the other room. The thought of prayers reminded Jaedon of the argument he and Hyko had had over a week ago. He hadn't contacted her at all since then. He'd told himself that he'd wait for her to come to him to apologize.

"Jii has birthed a son!" A native woman cried out joyously. The native men who'd been working with the Jokpoh all looked up, several of them stopping their work. At first, only a couple of men started towards the woman's quarters. Once it was apparent that Jaedon wasn't stopping them, nearly every man left his station to see the new baby.

Jaedon entered te woman's quarters slowly once all of the men had migrated from their workspaces. The natives had lined up, alternating between women and men, in front of the new mother and her baby. A woman planted a kiss on her index and pointer fingers, then stepped up to the mother. She pressed her two kissed fingers to the mother's temple, then to the baby's forehead. Once she'd done so, she exited the line, and the man behind her did the same as she had. Jaedon watched the process go on until every native had done the same.

Once each of the natives had gone through the ritual, they all turned to Jaedon. He didn't notice all the attention was on him until one of the women approached him. Jaedon stood uneasily when she came near him. Ever so slowly, she reached out her hand. Her fingers brushed against his upper arm just barely, her eyes wide.

"Ziolen rarroso boy," she said softly. "You do blessing." Jaedon blinked.

"Blessing...?" he asked. The native woman took Jaedon by the arm and led him up to the new mother. Sweat was dripping from her forehead and she appeared to be exhausted, yet she was beaming brightly down at her newborn baby boy. She glanced up at Jaedon when he walked up to her, her smile remaining.

"Mei gadon jyio," she said, her voice slightly hoarse. "My son...he name Somoson." She held out the baby boy for Jaedon to see. The child was asleep, a few of his soft curls falling in his light brown face. Jaedon couldn't help cracking a smile.

"Go on," the native woman urged. "Bless new life." She gave him a gentle push forward. Jaedon did just as he'd seen the others do, kissing his two fingers, then pressing them to the mother's temple and baby's forehead.

"What's all of this?" Jaedon jumped back, shielding the new mother and baby Somoson from sight. London and Bryce shoved women aside as they came storming in. Both of them had faces burning bright red, their lips curled into disgusted scowls. Bryce pulled Jaedon aside by the arm, yanking him so hard that there were red marks on his arm when the green-eyed man let go.

"Jaedon!" he shouted. "What is going on here? These stupid bastards should be *working* and they are all in here doing *who knows what* while you just stand here-"

"Bryce, will you *relax?*" Jaedon snapped. "She was going into labor, and I was-"

"There is a baby in here?" London bellowed. The natives cowered in the corners of the room, the men doing their best to comfort the women. Bryce made his way over to the mother, who was completely horrorstricken. She was trembling furiously and clutching at her son. A cruel sneer crept across London's dry and cracked lips. "Oh, a baby. How...revolting." In one swift motion,

London bent down and snatched up the baby boy. The newborn began to cry, his tiny wails bringing his mother to tears.

"Somoson!" she cried. "Somoson!"

"Shut up, woman!" London hissed. He held the child upside down by his foot, then turned to Jaedon. "Haven't you been told already? We have no need for children here around all this Jokpoh, Jaedon." Jaedon's blood boiled as he bit down hard on his tongue.

"London," he growled. "Leave that baby alone. Give him back to his mother-"

"You've no say in this, Jadey," Bryce said. "Step back."

"London, don't-" The sentence wasn't halfway out of Jaedon's mouth before the baby was dead. London had thrown the boy down on a rock. His head was smashed in on one side, blood pooling around his tiny body. The newborn's mother was hysterical, screaming and thrashing out. She dug her nails into the flesh of her cheeks. London pressed his foot down on the baby's body and kicked him to the side. Jaedon blinked back the tears that burned in his eyes.

"I give you one job to do," London growled. "One simple job is all you're assigned, and you manage to mess it all up."

"You didn't have to k-kill the baby, London," Jaedon croaked. The scrawny man narrowed his eyes and spat on the ground.

"You do your job, I'll do mine," he said. "Understood, boy? You keep *them* in line, and I'll keep *you* in line."

He and Bryce turned to leave, rendering the natives speechless. The child's mother continued to sob and injure herself. Her face was raw, and several of her self-inflicted cuts were bleeding. Jaedon couldn't feel anything except for the tears welling up in his eyes, his trembling bottom lip and the pain in his gut. He stood there for over an hour, saying nothing as the mother screamed and wailed. No one went to her; not even her husband, who'd been the first man to bless the her and his child, moved an inch as she mangled her face with her nails. Every one of the natives stood wordlessly in the women's quarters, their eyes fixed on baby Somoson, whose skin was now pale and bruised.

As Jaedon climbed into bed for the night, he found himself wiping tears from his eyes. It had been four days since baby Somoson had been slaughtered, and Jaedon was still so shaken by the traumatic experience. It seemed like anytime he closed his eyes, he saw the small child, sleeping peacefully in his mother's arms. Then, when he blinked, all he could see was the boy's dead body on the floor of the cavern.

"You're crying?" As soon as he heard her familiar voice, he sucked in a breath and turned around. Hyko was perched on the window sill, her wild curls pulled back just a little with a headband. In two quick strides, he'd made it over to her and pulled her into a tight embrace. "Jaedon...what's wrong?"

"Hyko, I...I'm sorry," he whispered into her hair. He could've sworn that he'd felt her shiver when he did. It was a while before she pulled away, but when she did, she was frowning with her eyes on the floor.

"No," she said. "Don't be sorry. I was being foolish. Besides, I...I did a lot of thinking about what you said." She turned her gaze towards him and smiled. "I think it makes a lot of sense, and I was thinking that...that maybe you could tell me more about it sometime?" Wiping his eyes, Jaedon let a gentle smile come across his face.

"Tell you what," he said, stepping away from her. He started gathering up piles of clothes on the floor and shoved them into an old duffle bag. "I'll tell you anything you wanna know on our way to the village in the mountains."

"Delfusio?" she asked. "Wh-why are we going there?"

"The men gave me a job to do," Jaedon explained. "If I don't, Bryce is gonna get on me." The green-eyed man's name left a sour taste in his mouth. "But, I don't know how to get there."

"Aww, and here I thought you just wanted to spend some time with me," Hyko teased.

"Oh, yeah. That too." Jaedon gave her a wink and threw his bag over his shoulder. "C'mon, you. Let's get going."

* * * * *

"You're pretty terrible at this," Hyko laughed as she watched her friend struggle. It was only their third day of traveling and, already, Jaedon had bandages on both his arms and his knee. He was sure to need another one if he didn't start watching where he put his foot as the two crossed the boulder field. Just past it was the curvy mountain pass that lead straight to Delfusio. Nevertheless, they had to make it past the boulder field first.

Jaedon stepped over one of the smaller rocks and leaped onto a larger one. He steadied himself, then prepared to jump up onto another one. Once she was sure that he would be able to catch up safely, Hyko continued on, a small grin on her face.

"You make all of this stuff look so easy!" Jaedon called out from several yards behind her. "Leaping on all these rocks, sleeping in the trees...not so simple for a guy who's used to cars and bathrooms!"

"Just try to keep up!" Hyko said. "Oh, and try to stay away from snake holes this time, okay?" She could hear Jaedon grumbling complaints from behind her, but all she did was giggle at them and keep pressing on.

It was midday when the two finally reached the pass. From the foot of the mountain, the path looked menacing. It was impossible to see the end of it, or even halfway up it. There was hardly any vegetation so high up in the mountains, and it was rather dark; ledges and ridges blocked the sun from view. Jaedon tightened the strap of his bag.

"This can't be safe," he muttered, shivering. Hyko ignored the comment and decided to be the one to take the first steps up the pass. Jaedon followed soon after. They traveled in a comfortable silence for several hours. Jaedon turned his head each time the wind howled as it blew through the mountains, but saw nothing more than rocks, crevasses and a few patches of grass here and there. Hyko took every path that she knew the hunters of Delfusio would not in order to avoid being seen, though found it odd that there was absolutely no one out at all.

"My people who live up here have been captured?" she asked. She felt sick to her stomach when Jaedon answered yes. "Is there anywhere they have not taken?"

"Tattao," he told her. "That's the only one."

"You know what?" She stopped suddenly and turned to face him. Plopping down to the ground, Hyko pulled her legs up to her chest and leaned in when Jaedon joined her. "I think that we could do something about this." Her idea was shot down when Jaedon had to stop himself from doubling over with laughter at her suggestion.

"You can't be serious," he hooted. Hyko watched him with an agitated scowl on her face. "*What?* You *really* think that's a good idea."

"We need to do something," Hyko insisted. "People are dying-"

"Yeah, and *we're* gonna die if we try to step in and say, 'hey! You guys are being jerks, wanna cut it out?'" Jaedon got to his feet and grabbed his duffle bag. "Let's concentrate on surviving through this pass first, and worry about the politics of our lives later, alright?"

"What? I don't even know what politics...ugh, never mind. Do you take this seriously or no?" Hyko cried as she caught up with him. "Because I've seen some bad things in my village that I don't want to ever happen again. You can't tell me that you've seen absolutely nothing you don't want to stop." Jaedon stopped in his tracks. His entire body tensed up, and he curled his hands into fists, but he said nothing for the longest of moments. Hyko watched the thoughtful look on his face turn into an intense grimace. Then, she saw his entire body relax as he let out a soft sigh.

"I still say we focus on getting up the mountain before we think about taking down a bunch of ticked off white men on a mission." Hyko poked out her lip dramatically, dragging her feet as she started to follow Jaedon. It wasn't long before Jaedon broke the silence and sighed. "I did see some bad things that my men did. They have this plan to use a Jokpoh plant, and they're abusing your people so that they'll plant it." Hyko frowned.

"Jokpoh is a plant not approved by the spirits," she muttered, then bit her tongue as she remembered her conversation from a couple of weeks ago. "Is…is it approved by…by *your* God?"

"I don't even know," Jaedon said, shaking his head. "But, I know that He wouldn't approve of how your people are being treated." Hyko gave him a thoughtful look, and he frowned at the ground. She placed a hand on his shoulder and he stopped walking.

"Maybe you could teach me how to pray to your God?" she asked, her voice soft. She felt out of place and awkward as Jaedon folded his hands and told her to do the same. What if Jaedon's God didn't hear her prayer because she and her people did not know He existed? What if she couldn't pray to his God because it wasn't allowed?

"Dear Lord," Jaedon began after closing his eyes. "Thank you for all that you give us that we need. Thank you for Hyko, and letting me meet her. Lord, I pray that…that we can find some way to make my men come to their senses. I pray that they'll see that what they're doing isn't right…please. I know everything happens for a reason, but I don't really know the reason for this. But, I know You do. In Jesus name I pray…amen." He opened his eyes and heaved a sigh while Hyko opened her eyes and smiled.

"You thanked Him for me," she laughed. "Why would you do that?" Jaedon shrugged as though it were no big deal, but she could see the blush in his cheeks and the smirk on his face.

"I was…you know…just being polite," he admitted sheepishly. "Besides, I am glad I met you. I was really lonely before, and you gave me someone to talk to. So, thanks, I guess."

"You know that word, Jaedon."

"What do you…oh, right. Umm, sanaei." When he said the word, it no longer sounded like a foreigner struggling to get the letters off his tongue. Hyko beamed brightly at him for the accomplishment, making him blush harder.

"It was nothing," she said, simply. "Now come on; we've got a pass to get through."

HATOYUMEN
AUTHORITY

Agreeing to join the expedition had been a last minute thing for Jaedon. The day he was headed to juvenile prison, the judge offered him the alternative punishment of joining three hundred and sixteen men on an voyage to uncharted land. Immediately, he'd accepted the alternative choice, and was told that the boat was to leave later on that afternoon. It was on that afternoon that Jaedon met Tristan for the first time.

When Jaedon had boarded the boat, a few of the men had gotten into a disagreement and were going at it. The three guys were pretty close to shedding blood when Tristan stepped in and yanked them off each other. Jaedon never forgot their punishments; one man was given no food until he was so weak that he couldn't speak without passing out. Another was told to bathe in the same water the men used to relieve themselves for the entire two week journey to the land. The other man was tossed off the boat two days into the expedition and had to swim beside the boat for an entire afternoon.

Jaedon couldn't help remembering that as he left a sleeping Hyko early one morning to meet Tristan in Delfusio. The autumn air in the mountains was too unnerving. Everything that made a sound echoed over and over, seeming closer than it actually was.

He clutched at his hoodie and trudged on. The soles of his feet were swollen and burning from all the walking he'd done the past several days. Seeing his destination at last should've given him a bit more energy; but after remembering his first encounter with the "big man in charge," the sight of the Delfusio village gate made him feel uneasy.

As soon as he entered the village, six of Tristan's right-hand men swarmed around him, digging in his pockets and duffle bag. None of them said a word to him until they were finished. Then, one of the men, a redhead named Justin, grunted and motioned for Jaedon to follow him.

Jaedon had always thought that London had no heart and Bryce had no soul.

Tristan had neither.

The man stood well over six feet tall with muscles on every inch of his body. His beady blue eyes were always narrowed and looking directly at you, yet his lips were always curled into a cruel sneer. That day was no different. As the six men lead him into one of the kytahs near the village center, Tristan looked just as menacing as ever. He took a sip of his ever present imported beer and smiled at Jaedon.

"Aah, Jaedon." Tristan set the beer bottle down on the table in front of him. "I heard that London and Ash were sending you up here. You look...like you took a beating." As he chuckled, Jaedon shifted uncomfortably. Tristan waved the men away and motioned for Jaedon to take a seat. "Come on, man! I'm joking. Sit down. Have a drink."

"I'm good," Jaedon grumbled. He opted for leaning against the wall with his arms folded across his chest. Tristan shrugged and sipped from his beer again. The last droplet slid down his throat, and he set the bottle down on the floor next to him.

"So then," he said. "I haven't got all day, Jadey. Let me know what's up, or I'm going to have to have Justin escort you out of the village."

"Umm." Jaedon shifted again, clearing his throat. "Two things, actually. Uh, I never really knew...why are we here, and, what are we going to do...?" Tristan's narrow blue eyes stared

Jaedon down. The grin disappeared from his face for the shortest of moments. When he got to his feet, the smile was back again. He shoved his hands in the pockets of his deep navy blue jeans and started to pace.

"I've heard you were a little dense," he chuckled. He cracked his knuckles as he walked. "I always figured that you were using this trip as a 'get out of jail free card' from what I've seen of you."

"Hey, man, I just want to-"

"None of this is about you, *boy*," Tristan growled. "All of this is about *me* and what *I* have planned. Originally, I only expected to find some marijuana or something over here. Maybe some extra land for housing or workers and factories. Imagine my surprise when I find all these *blackies* here!" Jaedon unfolded his arms and began fidgeting with a bandage on his wrist.

"I…know *I* sure was surprised," he muttered, trying to sound interested. Tristan made his way over by Jaedon and slapped him on the shoulder with a laugh.

"Hundreds of them!" he laughed. "Thousands of them, even. An entire civilization of blackies that we never knew about."

"If you don't mind me asking…um, if you didn't find what you thought was here, why are we still here?" Jaedon asked, earning a glare from Tristan as soon as the question had escaped his mouth. The narrow-eyed man grabbed a hold of Jaedon, and pulled him to the table. He leaned in so close that Jaedon could smell the beer and stale bread on his breath.

"Boy, are you stupid?" he hissed. All Jaedon could do was blink and let his lip quiver. "Do you know how much free sex I've had since I've gotten here?"

"Okay, that's just…come on, man." Jaedon jumped up. "I don't need to hear about that."

"Oh, but you do," Tristan objected. "Because that's only one of the free things these natives can give us. Free labor is another thing to add to the list. The construction crews up here have had a steady supply of blackies helping them update these shabby huts these animals call 'home' since we got here." Tristan paused to raise an eyebrow at Jaedon, who was trembling with rage. "What's the matter with you?"

"I...nothing, I guess."

"Then let me finish, you son-"

"Tristan!" Justin the Redhead barged in, sweat dripping from his brow. A team of seven or eight other men were lined up behind him, shouting heatedly at each other and the few natives standing behind them. "There's some kind of commotion going on out here, man. Something about some blackie burning the side of Jacob's face." With a loud exasperated sigh, Tristan shook his head and stepped away from Jaedon.

"It's so hard to keep these animals in check," he groaned. "Come on, Jadey. You could benefit from watching this."

Upon stepping outside, Jaedon saw that Justin hadn't been kidding. In fact, "commotion" was an understatement. In the village center, at least a dozen natives were circled around one native man who was shouting at the top of his lungs. The entire population of white men occupying the village of Delfusio was swarming around the natives. The words flying from their mouths didn't seem to faze the natives at all.

Tristan situated himself between two of his right hand men and folded his arms across his chest, watching the scene unfold. Jaedon stayed back, paying attention to the enraged expressions on the men's faces. The fury burning in Tristan's eyes intensified with every moment he spent observing. Eventually, he stepped forward. He pushed aside anyone who stood between him and the natives, barking orders to the few men who followed him into the mob of people.

"Everyone *shut up!*" Tristan's bellow echoed through the mountains, ricocheting off each kytah. Jaedon flinched. "You understand me? *Shut up!*" Any chatter that had continued after the first "shut up" ceased immediately after the second.

"What's all this about, anyway?" A man behind Jaedon leaned in and hissed in his ear. He was a large man who breathed heavily, and smelled like Tristan's breath. Jaedon hesitated before answering.

"I-"

"Who is still speaking?" Tristan shouted, whipped his head around to see who had dared to defy his orders. "The next man, woman or otherwise to even whisper will be punished. *Severely*." He turned back to the circle of natives. "Now. I hear one of you savages assaulted one of my men." The man in the center of all the natives went forward.

"It was I," he growled fearlessly. "The man kill my wife with cold heart." Jaedon felt a pain in his gut as the man spoke, but Tristan busted up laughing.

"Do you have any idea how stupid you sound right now?" he hooted. "Your wife. So find a new one! That's what I did! It's nothing to get upset about. You can still have babies and junk with another woman."

"I love no one but my wife," the native man managed to get out. He was trembling, both from anger and heartbreak, Jaedon figured.

"Oh, what a shame," Tristan said in a monotone. "That's why you don't get so emotionally attached to things in life. Justin?" The redhead made his way through the crowd. In his hands was a branding iron. The entire crowd began to murmur, but the natives stood firm. The man in the middle curled his hands into fists and heaved a shaky sigh. Tristan took the iron from Justin and held it out to the native's face. The native man reeled back, a painfully petrified look on his countenance.

"You white men," he gasped. The heat was so close to his face that he was sweating. "You think world around you."

"Well, I know it ain't around you," Tristan growled, and pressed the branding iron to the man's face."

* * * * *

Jaedon has been gone for too long, Hyko thought as she frantically scrambled up the rocky path to Delfusio. She tripped several times over her long skirt as she climbed up and over boulders in her hurry. She'd heard Jaedon leave early in the morning, before she'd even gotten up herself. He'd whispered in her ear that what he needed to get done wouldn't take too long, and that he'd be back in a couple of hours at most. Now, the sun was getting low. The sky was an array of colors, from a deep blood red to a bright yellow.

"I know Tristan wouldn't put up with that." The voice seemed to come from nowhere. As soon as she heard it, Hyko threw herself to the ground, using the brush and boulders as cover. "Tristan doesn't tolerate that kind of-"

"Hey, you hear that?" Another voice joined the original one. Peering out from behind the patch of thick shrubbery, Hyko saw two white men not more than fifteen feet away. They were young; not as young as Jaedon, though not as old as the green-eyed man that Jaedon often times complained about.

"Bro, you're hearing stuff," the first man said. "Come on, let's get back before Tristan gets mad."

"No, for real," the second man insisted. As he started to get closer to her hiding place, Hyko ducked down as far as she could . She knew that he was going to find her even before he grabbed her by the front of her top. Even so, it was no less frightening when he actually did.

"Peleiko...please don't-"

"Aah, a lucky catch right here!" the first man jeered, pulling her up to him. He eyed her with an amused look in his gleaming hazel eyes. "How'd you get out of the storage?"

"I-"

"You're a smart little one, ain't ya?" he said, giving her a sideways grin. Hyko knew she should kick him, or struggle, or try to get away somehow. Nevertheless, she stood frozen, her eyes wide as the white man held her in place. His hands stroked her arms and sides, making her shudder.

"Please, I just-"

"Your English is pretty good, baby," he murmured. "Where'd you learn to speak like that?"

"I only want to go-"

"Go where?" he asked, chuckling. "You should be in storage, you know that? You remember what happens to the women who don't stay in storage, hmm?" The man reached around to touch her, but Hyko pulled away. She scowled at him while the other ziolen rarroso let out a deep, throaty laugh.

"Whoa, man!" he hooted. "Watch out! You got a wild animal right there!" The first man gave an amused grunt and turned to face his friend. Hyko used his distraction to her advantage and tore away from him, breaking into a sprint back down the mountain. She only glanced back once, keeping her eyes ahead of her no matter how much the men's cuss words burned her ears. The path was treacherous, mountains lying dead ahead as well as on every side of her. A few times, she stumbled, tripping over a rock or two. She had several cuts on her knees from her falls. She noticed droplets of blood on the ground when she looked down from one of her worse injuries.

"You aren't gonna like the consequences of this!" Tuning out the voices of the white men, she squeezed her eyes shut and ran on. When she opened them once more, she came to a sudden halt. Right in front of her was a ledge. Looking down it, she couldn't see to the bottom of the ravine. If she'd continued on even a few more steps, she'd have tumbled to her death in the chasm.

"You were stupid to think that running like that would work." The men grabbed her by the shoulders, shoving her down to her bloody knees. Hyko cried out in pain and bit her lip. "You really think you were the first one to try and make a run for it?"

"I didn't do anything wrong!" Hyko spat, wriggling out of their grasp. The hazel-eyed man kicked her shin just as she was starting to get to her feet.

"You *did* do something wrong," he explained. The two pushed her up against a boulder so that she was laying flat on her back, their hands tight around her wrists. Her breathing was ragged as she glared up at them. Hazel-eyed man let a smug grin come across his face. "You escaped storage. There are some serious consequences for doing that, and you know it." The man leaned in closer to her, his hand hovering over her stomach. He was lifting her shirt up slowly when the ground beneath them began to tremble. He paused, glancing down at the ground. Beneath his feet, the earth cracked once. When he shifted his position, a second crack appeared. Then a third.

"Hey, man." The hazel-eyed man's comrade lessened his grip on Hyko's arms, glancing around for anything unordinary. When he saw nothing, he took a small step forward to tighten his grip around her arms once more. Another crack. Hazel-eyed man glowered at his comrade. Behind the man, another split in the ground appeared.

"We need to move," Hyko murmured with a trembling voice. For that, she earned a strike on the cheek from the hazel-eyed man.

"Shut up, do you hear me?" he hissed. "Just *shut up*." She bit her lip and nodded feebly, watching more cracks appear in the ground beneath them.

"John!" The other man yelled. "Maybe we should take this little thing back before we give her a puni-"

"Don't go against me on this one, man!" Hazel-eyed John spat. "This girl will receive her punishment here and-"

Before all of the words had made it out of his mouth, the man was tumbling down into the depths of the chasm. Hyko felt her body dropping before long as well. The ground beneath her feet broke off from the ledge just like the large piece of earth had crumbled right underneath the two men. Thinking quickly, she stretched out her hand and grabbed a hold of a rag root; the green weed, she'd been told once before, was strong enough to hold the weight of two full grown men.

She listened as the screams and yells of the men grew fainter and farther away, and after a while, she could no longer hear them. Hyko wondered if they'd hit the bottom yet, if there even was a bottom. She was holding onto the root for what felt like a lifetime, dangling with the gaping chasm directly under her feet, until the ground stopped crumbling and breaking off. Slowly, she eased herself back up onto the ledge, rolling over onto her back and scooting backwards once she was up. All of the wind was completely knocked out of her, so much so that she almost felt as if she would pass out. Her brain seemed frozen in her state of exhaustion.

"Those men...they were going to...they would've..." Her throat suddenly felt constricted as it all sank in. Lightly, Hyko let the tips of her fingers brush against her tender wrists.

And then, she was up and running, focused only on what was ahead of her and when Jaedon would be returning.

* * * * *

"That was *such* a waste of my time!" Jaedon was still fuming even as nightfall crept up on the two of them. He'd talked with Tristan hours ago, but could not seem to get all of the rage that had built up during their conversation out of his system. The two had managed to get back down the mountain and were nearly past the boulder field by then, but Jaedon was still grumbling and groaning about the man under his breath. "He didn't answer *any* of my questions *at all!* He freakin' burned a man in the face! *That's inhumane!* That guy is-I swear, if I ever have to even say *'hi'* to him again-"

"Relax! Nidtho!" Hyko grabbed him gently by the shoulders and spun him around to face her. She ran her hands up and down his arms once then let them drop. "This Tristan guy has got you so worked up."

"And I thought Bryce and them were bad," Jaedon grumbled, shaking his head. "Hyko, this guy thinks he runs it all. He doesn't care about anything at all- "

"Which is why I think we should do something." She raised an eyebrow at him. Jaedon sighed and ran a hand through his hair. "Please...? Jaedon, I really don't want to see any more of my people get hurt."

"Alright, *alright!*" He groaned and dropped down to the ground. "You're lucky you're so convincing. If I promise you that from here on out we'll do everything we can to stop my men, will it make you happy?" His gaze remained on her as her lips curled up into a smile. Then, she wrapped her arms around him, pulling him into a tight embrace. Jaedon hesitated for a few moments before hugging her back.

"More than you could ever know," she murmured, her lips at his neck. With a shiver, Jaedon had to force himself to pull away. "Thank you so much."

"Of course, Hyko," he said, laughing softly. When he looked at her again, she was still grinning.

It seemed like nothing as Jaedon and Hyko made their way back to Kainau. Jaedon passed most of the time telling Hyko stories and lessons from the Bible. For a change, it was Hyko who was listening wide-eyed as he told her colorful and vivid stories. In fact, Jaedon started to surprise himself, for it was as if he never ran out of stories. Their second night of travel, the two grew quiet earlier than usual. They had neared the part of the Kainau forest that opened up to the beach by the caverns. Cracked plastic bowls were scattered in the grass. Jaedon could see from the corner of his eye that they were catching Hyko's attention, but hoped to himself that she wouldn't ask about them.

"What are these?" she asked, her voice soft.

Jaedon cursed under his breath.

"Jaedon." Hyko murmured his name as she bent down to pick one up. A large piece of the cracked bowl fell off and onto Hyko's foot. "How can your men eat with these shabby things?"

"We, um...don't." Jaedon's eyes remained on the ground as the muttered words escaped his mouth. Hyko dropped the bowl and kicked it to the side.

"That why your men threw them way out here?" she asked, continuing on. Jaedon followed behind her, biting his lip. He opened his mouth to begin the explanation he'd been dreading for a long while, but he heard an excited giggle come from Hyko's mouth before he could say anything. "Oh, Jaedon, come look!" Up ahead, the forest cleared, revealing the beautiful Kainau beach and the caverns. Jaedon froze, his palms beginning to sweat. "The Kainau Caverns! I used to play here when I-"

"Hyko, I don't think-"

"Come on, I wanna show you!" she laughed, dashing off to the entrance. He jogged to catch up with her, the stench of the caves hitting him before he even entered; he'd almost forgotten about that pungent odor in the time he'd been away. The only dim light source for the gloomy place was provided by the moon. Hyko was nowhere in sight, so he proceeded on to the next room. Most of the women were huddled together under their raggedy blankets. A few were coughing, bent over on their knees. But no Hyko.

"You, ziolen rarroso boy, know not when to stop." The woman who'd dropped the pitcher stepped forward on weak, shaky legs. "When you go and leave us be?"

"I'm just looking for a friend of mine," Jaedon hissed. "Please, just go back to sleep-"

"I not slept in four days," she snapped back. Jaedon gritted his teeth.

"Well, I am so sorry about your insomnia," Jaedon growled. Then, his face was in the dirt. He looked up to see who'd shoved him; his eyes widened and his jaw fell when he saw that it had been Hyko. She stood over him, tears of rage streaming down her cheeks.

"How dare you speak to Pata like that!" Hyko snapped. Jaedon groaned, pulling himself up to his knees.

"I'm sorry, Hyko, really-"

"Shut up! You lied to me!" she cried.

"How did I-"

"This is what's happening to my people?" she shouted. "This is what's going on? You...you besho! How come you never told me?" She hugged herself and hung her head, her body shaking as she wept. Jaedon heaved a sigh and got to his feet, wrapping his arms around Hyko's shoulders. Several of the natives flinched when they saw him touch her, but Jaedon paid them no mind.

"I...I couldn't," he murmured. "But believe me, watching this happen hurt me as much as it did...er, does you."

"But why didn't you do anything to stop it?" she whispered. "I don't understand. Jaedon, you need to tell me what's going on."

"And I will," he promised. "I'll tell you the whole story, I promise. But, here isn't the place." He glanced around at all of the apprehensive women, their dull eyes wide with anticipation. He hugged her even tighter. "Come on. Let's get out of here."

The fresh air was a huge relief, and Jaedon savored every breath of it as he stepped back outside. Off in the distance, he noticed a few shadowy figures milling about near the kytahs on the far side of the village. He took Hyko by the hand and swiftly pulled her into the bushes. She was still wiping tears from her eyes when Jaedon was able to settle down and get a good look at her.

"Will you tell me now?" she asked, heaving a shaky sigh. Jaedon leaned back. Closing his eyes and exhaling, he started his story.

"I was arrested for a serious crime that I didn't even commit," Jaedon began. "I had nothing to do with it. I mean, sure, I was with the wrong guys some of the time, but I didn't even know it was being planned when it was. All I'd done was try to help my friend who sounded like he was in trouble on the phone, and I ended up getting arrested for murder. After they ran tests on the body, though, they found out that it wasn't actually me, so the terms of my arrest were changed, and I was arrested for assisting with a murder. My family pretty much shunned me from the time they found out what happened up until I came here. My dad told me not to do anything with my sisters and my mom. I couldn't even eat with them; I had to bring my meals to my room and sit and pray all day. To make everything worse, I still I had to go to jail, and the thought of that was terrifying to me. Then, about a week before my sentence was to be carried out, the judge gave me an alternative punish; this trip.

"That's why I'm here. The other men came here to find out if there were any resources they could used. Instead, they found your people." Once finished with his explanation, he felt weak. His head was spinning from all the heartrending memories. Hyko scooted closer to him, placing her hand over his trembling one. "I never thought anyone would get hurt when I first came. I hate seeing all these innocent people being taken captive and used and k...killed. But, I can't do anything. I have no power because I'm the youngest one here. Bryce has already threatened me countless times, and he's not the kind of guy who'll reason with you and take them all back." Hyko caressed his cream-colored hand with her thumb.

"Jaedon...I never knew..."

"It's fine." He shifted uncomfortably.

"No, it isn't," she insisted. "This whole time, I've been complaining about how my people have been wronged and abused. But, you've been suffering too, and I never really realized it. For that I apologize." She gave him a weary yet genuine smile. The silence following their talk was a comfortable one, relaxing, even. Jaedon felt as though he could've dozed off peacefully there next to her. Nonetheless, the silence was broken abruptly, causing the two to jump up. Lights flickered brightly through the trees, shouts and curse words filling the air. Jaedon reached for Hyko's arm.

"Go," he hissed, pushing her away from him. "Go home, quickly! I'll meet you at the meeting place in about a week. At dusk!" She was hesitant to leave at first, but he was insistent about it. Hyko had just barely managed to break into a sprint deep into the woods when two white men appeared. One of them looked disappointed.

"Aw, Jadey, it's just *you?*" he groaned. "Man, I was hoping I would get me some...uh, well I guess since you're here, I might as well tell you; Bryce wants to speak with you." Jaedon rolled his eyes and the man snorted. "Don't look so excited."

"Can't it wait?" he grumbled.

"Um, knowing Bryce? Probably not," the man mumbled. "It's most likely got something to do with...oh crap."

"What?"

"You see, there's been...it's...just go talk to the man, okay?" The man slapped at his knee and growled. "I'm getting eaten alive by bugs out here. Quit wasting my evening. Bryce'll get ticked if you don't show up."

As soon as he entered Bryce's kytah, Jaedon could tell that something wasn't right. Two of the three men Bryce shared the kytah with were not themselves. Their faces were far too solemn; London's face was buried in his hands and Cole-Ashleigh's older and tougher looking brother-was staring off at the wall. Jaedon felt out of place in the kytah that the men often referred to as the "power house." He felt even more awkward when he cleared his throat to get someone's attention.

"If you're going to ask one of these deadbeat fools 'what's going on' or 'where's Bryce,' don't waste your breath." The green-eyed man stepped forward, dressed in a suit. Jaedon blinked, rubbed his eyes, and almost did a double take; the suit was too tight, the pants were flooding, and it was anything but regular beach attire.

"Umm...okay." Jaedon stepped forward, his eyes darting from London to Cole back to Bryce. "Is everything okay here?" Bryce lowered his head. For a second, Jaedon thought that the man might actually shed a tear. *Nah, that's not humanly possible,* he thought to himself after reconsidering the previous thought when Bryce lifted his head up again; his eyes weren't even moist.

"I don't know if you've heard, but..." He paused to sniffle, and Jaedon let his jaw drop. "Something very...very tragic has happened to Ash. You see, Ashleigh, he...he must've caught some sort of weird, new disease while he was here and he has..." Jaedon stood deathly still, his gaze unfocused.

"No..." he murmured.

"And in the event of such an occurrence, Tristan made it so that the third man of power would step up and take his place. So, Jadey? Say hello to the new man in charge." Jaedon blinked.

"Umm...hello, Cole," he croaked, his throat dry. Cole gave him a pained expression and shook his head. Bryce busted up laughing.

"You're funny, you know that, Jadey?" he hooted. He reached out and pulled Jaedon into a tight, awkward embrace by putting his arm around his shoulders. "I just know that you and me are going to bond much, much more, don't you think?"

SAKORLEJIA
DISCOVERY

Awa'hi was hunched over a bucket when Hyko arrived at the healer's hut. Terrible retching sounds were coming from her, and her body was trembling. This was the sixth straight day she'd done so since Hyko had returned from Delfusio with Jaedon.

Awa'hi glanced up when she noticed Hyko, but her face was back in the bucket before too long. Hyko sighed. Her heart truly ached for the girl. Everyone else in the village had grown frustrated with her, and couldn't figure out why she was still staying in Tattao. Only Hyko knew that even if she wanted to, Awa'hi couldn't return to her smoldered home. Hanjeha had tried suggesting to Awa'hi that she should get someone to escort her back before the winter months, but Awa'hi stubbornly refused each time. She continued to claim that she wasn't yet over what had happened with the white men. Most everyone else didn't buy it, but Hyko believed her friend, no matter how annoying she could be in the hut sometimes.

"Awa'hi...are you alright?" Hyko asked gently. Her friend lifted up her head and coughed. She wiped her chin and groaned.

"Yeah...I'm fine," Awa'hi answered. "This will all be over by midday." Hyko eyed her suspiciously, then grabbed an empty bucket.

"You've been saying that for just about a week now," Hyko pointed out.

"It always ends by then, does it not?"

"Yeah, but you shouldn't be sick everyday like this-"

"Haven't *you* ever had a stomach pain for a week?" Awa'hi snapped, turning to glare at Hyko with a fierce yet worn-out look in her eyes, "It'll go away, I just need more pain-relief herbs. Do we have more Carabept?"

"*We* don't have *anything*," Hyko hissed. "But I might be able to find some...if I feel like it. Why do you eat so much of this stuff? It doesn't even taste good." Awa'hi said nothing. As she got to her feet, she accidentally knocked over the bucket she'd thrown up into. Its contents spilled out onto the floor, but all she did was watch as it formed a puddle.

Her blood boiling, Hyko let out an enraged scream. She kicked the bucket even further to the side. Awa'hi flinched at the sound it made as it hit the wall, but did nothing when Hyko put her face so close to hers that the two could feel the hostility radiating off each other.

"*What is wrong with you?*" Hyko shrieked. The sound of her own voice her in ears startled her. "You...you fat, lazy heifer! Get off your big *ookom* and do something around here since I guess you're never going to leave!"

"You can't understand what I'm going through," Awa'hi grumbled.

"What you *went* through," Hyko corrected, crossly. "*Months ago*." Awa'hi's lip quivered, and she gritted her teeth. Before Awa'hi could retort, Hyko turned away.

"You know, I hear what they say about you," Awa'hi hissed. "The other villagers? They think you're stubborn, and rude, and ignorant. I used to correct them and tell them that you had just been scared, and hadn't meant to slip up like that. Now...? I'm not sure I was right about you." Hyko winced and bit her lip before turning around.

"Are you so naive that you don't think people don't talk about *you?*" she jeered. "They're mad that you haven't yet left Tattao. Little kids poke fun at how much 'rounder' you've gotten since you've been here. They tell jokes about how you're a lazy, whiny-"

"Stop this, the both of you!" Hanjeha grabbed hold of the front of Hyko's blouse, and shoved her away from Awa'hi. The old woman's force surprised Hyko so much that she tripped over her own feet and stumbled, landing flat on her rear end. " Tessa ne catahou ; this is ridiculous! You two are friends! And Hyko! Yelling at Awa'hi and getting her all worked up when she's in such a delicate state."

"Delicate state...?" Hyko asked, eyeing Awa'hi up and down. "She's flabby. That's not what I would call 'delicate.'"

"Watch your tongue, Hyko!" the old woman snapped.

"Hanjeha, koomo dasamundio? What is wrong with you?" Hyko pushed herself up and gave the old healer a curious look. "You yourself have been complaining about Awa'hi this whole time." Hanjeha exhaled loudly and closed her eyes. All anger quickly vanished from Hyko, and was replaced with curiosity and, even more so, confusion. Hanjeha took Awa'hi's hand and squeezed it, and the girl's eyes grew wide.

"That was before I knew what was going on," Hanjeha sighed. "There's a reason as to why she has been so indolent and tired...why she has had so many aches and feels so sick before midday. By the spirits, I don't understand how I never realized it sooner-"

"Hanjeha, *what is wrong with me?*" Awa'hi demanded. By then, terror was spilling from her eyes in the form of salty tears. The longer no one spoke, the more Hyko became afraid as well. Finally, Hanjeha opened her mouth and spit it out.

"Awa'hi, my dear...you're with child," she said so softly that at first, Hyko didn't think she'd heard correctly. She looked over at Awa'hi, whose bottom lip was trembling along with the rest of her body. The old woman then turned to scowl at Hyko, who took one step backwards. "Therefore, she is not a 'fat, lazy heifer,' as you put earlier, Hyko. She is pregnant."

"I...I had no idea, I..."

"None of us did," Hanjeha muttered, frustrated. "Or perhaps we did, but overlooked it because of what had happened to her with the ziolen rarroso…" All of a sudden, Awa'hi violently broke away from Hanjeha, a disgusted look on her face. She kept backing up, stumbling over buckets and baskets of roots, muttering to herself. She only stopped once her back was pressed against a shelf.

"So, you're telling me," she managed to get out. "That the reason as to why I've been feeling like the dirt beneath our feet…is because inside of me…is the child of a…white man?"

"My dear, it will be-"

"*I cannot have a ziolen rarroso's baby!*" Awa'hi snapped, raising her voice. "That's…it's…what is it even going to look like? I'll be reminded every day for the rest of my life what happened to me!"

"Awa'hi, nidtho! Calm down, it's not-"

"*Shut up, Hyko!*" Hyko blinked and frowned after Awa'hi yelled, interrupting her. "Don't say *anything!* You can't understand this!" Awa'hi paused, trying to wipe the tears from her eyes. "I'm sorry, but…you just…can't." Neither Hanjeha nor Hyko tried to speak with Awa'hi after that. She retreated back to her bed in the other room, shoved her head in her pillow and sobbed. The old healer heaved a sigh and took a seat on a floor pillow, pressing her hands to her temples.

"I should have paid more attention and not been so hard on her," she groaned. "The poor girl…she knows not what to do."

Ohn-Tsung was laying on her stomach on the floor in her sitting room, her head buried in a lesson book when Hyko arrived home. The girl looked up with a smile when she heard her older sister come in. The pleasant look on her face didn't stay for long.

"Where's Adad?" Hyko didn't even bother to greet her sister, and she passed her by.

"So, I suppose I won't receive a greeting?" Ohn-Tsung pouted, poking out her bottom lip. Hyko paused on the bottom step, rolled her eyes and laced her words with sarcasm.

"Hiya," Hyko said, greeting her in their language. Ohn-Tsung growled.

"You're *mean!*" she whined. Hyko laughed.

"That's the best insult you can come up with?" she sneered. She didn't wait for Ohn-Tsung to respond before retreating to her room. She collapsed onto her bed, a tear, trickling down her cheek. Her mind was completely blank except for one thing; Awa'hi's pregnant belly. How had no one figured it out before?

Bewildered and exhausted, she rolled over onto her stomach, letting her arms hang over the side of the bed. She traced the lines and scuff marks on the wooden floor with a sigh. Then, one of her fingers brushed against something just under her bed; the journals from Sasse. Hyko grabbed the one she'd started reading upon her return to Tattao. She'd only gotten about halfway through it. It wasn't terribly exciting, and she only read it by candle light when she couldn't sleep at night. Mostly, the author wrote about everyone who had died and how depressing life had become for them. With a sigh, she skimmed through a handful of pages before shoving that journal back under her bed; she had no desire to read about a dead son here, or a seriously ill uncle there. Instead, Hyko reached her hand under and pulled out another journal.

When she and Jaedon had visited Sasse and stayed in the hut, this journal Hyko had only gotten a chance to glance at. She'd hidden it from Jaedon only for selfish reasons; she'd wanted to read it without any interruptions later on. That, and she'd been feeling pretty irritated and hadn't been in the mood for "story time."

As soon as she opened it to the first page, she knew that something was very different from the other journals. This one was more than complaining and sob stories. Some of it would start of like the others; the author would complain of unreasonable punishments, but then go off on a tangent and describe long day trips to unnamed places. Curiosity got the best of her, and before long, Hyko had read more than fifty pages. Twice within those pages, the author mentioned friends of hers from other villages either journeying to "places only told of in legends," or young people going to do their jobs for the day and not returning, leaving behind nothing more than a short goodbye note. Hyko flipped the page, and there was nothing but notes from an old school lesson. Confused, she slapped herself on the forehead with the notebook, a few pages falling out from the binding.

"By the spirits, what the..." she growled, annoyed. She set the journal down at the foot of her bed, and leaned her head against the wall. In her hands were the six or so pages that had come out from the journal. Casually, she started skimming over the one with the earliest date which read:

Banna left Sasse today. He is the seventeenth to have left within the past two months. Where could they all possibly have gone? Why would they leave so suddenly? Mostly, it's the young people, though a couple middle-aged villagers have up and gone as well. They are the ones who have heard the legends and focused on them for far too long. Most of the villages think they have lost their minds and are trying to find them in the wrong places.

She let her eyes rest on the one paragraph for the longest of moments before jumping down to the next one:

My brothers thought Heeimn was crazy when he said he was leaving. They just laughed and continued gathering their weapons for hunting. By then, I had grown much too curious about the disappearing villagers to sit by and do nothing. I hopped up and demanded some answers from Heeimn, why he was going, where it was he was going. He said that his little sister tagged along with her close friend weeks ago up to the mountains, the unexplored parts that were past the Delfusio boundaries. He said that at first, he couldn't understand it. But, in the time his sister had been gone, Heeimn had done some thinking and observing. Maybe, he'd said, there could be a different way to live. Maybe the places in legends are real, better, even, than Sasse and the other villages. When he left our kytah that morning, I felt angry, confused, and even more curious than I had been before. It's been less than fifteen minutes that I've been sitting here feeling jumpy. How far has Heeimn gotten?

She flipped ahead; the next few paragraphs were smeared and illegible:

Heeimn had been right. The other seventeen were right. I've never seen anywhere like this. How had none of us ever realized this before?

The few paragraphs following that were also smeared and torn. Hyko cursed the journal under her breath, then started reading the next decipherable entry.

Heeimn and I returned. We got back earlier this afternoon. I'd thought my parents would be thrilled when I came home and told them they'd be grandparents. They were furious that I hadn't gone through a proper marriage ceremony, even when I explained to them over and over that Heeimn and I were wed in the mountains before I ever discovered I was with child. They haven't been speaking to us since I left home midday. Heeimn said that one of the elders is seriously considering banishing the both of us. Heeimn said not to worry, that we'd be okay no matter what. I guess it's hard not to trust the man who's been with me for more than a year. Maybe I shouldn't worry. I knew that things wouldn't be the same when we returned. Still, are they really going to make this so much of an issue?

Hyko glanced outside; if she didn't finish reading, the sun would go down, and she'd have no light. She went on ahead to the next entry.

Before this baby is born and has to deal with the primitive lifestyle and culture of my village and people, Heeimn and I are leaving. We are returning to da laimoht en da oazai for good. We've been banished, anyway. It's not so bad of a thing, because Heeimn and I wanted to leave. After living with so much freedom and so many choices, coming back to Sasse seems more and more like a big mistake. I'm leaving this journal here, in hopes that anyone who finds it will know the truth, and know that there is a better way to live.

After that entry, the rest of the pages were blank and tattered. Of all the pages she'd read, only five words truly stuck out to her; da laimoht en da oazai, or as it was more commonly called, the City in the Ruins. It actually existed. People actually lived past the sealed-off Delfusio boundaries. Everything that had ever been told in that legend was true. Hyko closed her eyes. When she reopened them, the room was spinning. She had to tell Jaedon. She couldn't wait until they met again at their meeting place, she had to go-

"Hey. I've been wondering if you were still alive." Spinning around, she found herself looking at a worn-out Gisipeh in the doorway. Her jaw dropped, then closed, her mouth curling down into a frown.

"Gisi!" she hissed. "Not now, I was-"

"You just can't stay in one place for more than a week, can you?" He chuckled softly and shook his head. "Have you even seen your fiancée in the past month?" Hyko opened her mouth to snap at him, then clamped it shut. She let her gaze fall on the floor.

"I…no," she admitted. "Is he…mad?"

"Mad? No," Gisipeh said. "Annoyed? Yes, very." Hyko's stomach lurched. "Annoyed" in public for Yonej meant "furious beyond reason" for Hyko. She found herself fiddling with her fingers.

"I completely forgot," she grumbled.

"Does it have anything to do with that white boy?" Gisipeh asked. Hyko kept quiet. "You're not continuing to see him, are you?"

"You make it sound so horrible," she retorted.

"It *is* so horrible!" he snapped. "This will only stay hidden for so long, Hyko. What will you do when everyone discovers the truth?"

"Would you please leave now?" Hyko hissed, her tone ice cold. "Elder Agenee is going to think things if you don't leave soon." She moved to the doorway, shoving Gisipeh forward and away from her room. He stared at her, a slightly pained look in his eyes. Hyko bit her lip and furrowed her brow, letting out a quiet sigh. "Please go…"

"You're going to end up hurting yourself," he told her, quietly, starting down the hall.

"You can't tell me what to do," she countered. He turned his head to scowl at her, then shook his head and continued on down the hall to the stairs. Hyko held her breath until she heard the front door click shut, and his footsteps as he headed down the dirt path. She sank down, her knees pulled up to her chest. Her earlier discovery suddenly came to mind once she could no longer hear Gisipeh's footsteps outside. From what the journal's author had said about the place, people seemed to be far more understanding of opinions and in favor of free will in the City in the Ruins. *There is a better way to live,* the journal had said. Hyko snorted; what wasn't better than how she was currently living?

TANNAHMO
ESCAPE

The night was quiet.

Well, almost.

Jaedon could hear noises from the room downstairs. Bryce had tried to take advantage of another native girl that night, one of the younger and feistier girls. All evening, Jaedon had heard harsh language coming from the girl as she cursed at Bryce in both English and her own language. Bryce was finally releasing her, calling her every name he could possibly think of that weren't her own; half of them didn't even make sense.

Shaking his head, Jaedon threw another shirt into his bag. Tomorrow, he'd have to make his way to the meeting place, as he'd promised Hyko about a week before. This time, he had a plan to present to her. He was done asking Hyko for help; this time, he would return the favor.

A tapping sound coming from outside caught Jaedon's attention. He started to ignore it after a moment; he figured it was probably one of the men dong something stupid, as usual. Eventually the tapping ceased, but it wasn't long before a rustling and thumping sound started up. Now inquisitive, Jaedon casually walked to the window to peer out into the night. As a result, he got two feet in his face, and ended up flat on his back, groaning. On top of him was a surprised and excited Hyko.

"You really should stop crashing into me like this," he said, struggling to get the words out with her sitting on his chest. "This is the second time. Maybe third."

"Jaedon! I learned something!" she exclaimed breathlessly, still sitting atop him. "I had to get here and let you know. And I...I, umm..." Jaedon sat up, his face coming closer to hers. Hyko's voice trailed off and a small smirk came across her face.

"Want to get off me now?" Jaedon whispered, a playful tone in his voice. Hyko could only nod, and she climbed off him quickly and ungracefully. "Thanks."

"Uh-huh," she managed to get out.

"Now, I was planning this whole big thi-" Jaedon closed his mouth abruptly, and moved closer to her, placing his hands on her arms quickly but gently. Outside, the men were shouting and laughing. From the sounds of it, Jaedon guessed there was a beating going on out there, for he could also hear the screams of native women. He gritted his teeth and frowned.

"Are things getting really bad here?" Hyko asked, quietly. Jaedon took his hands off her and nodded his head. He was serious for only a moment, but then let an excited smile come across his face.

"Do you remember when I told you we'd do something about it?" he asked, and Hyko nodded grimly. "I've got a plan. We're freeing the village of Kainau."

* * * * *

Running through the woods, Hyko was sure that Jaedon was crazy. The late fall temperatures were setting in, and the air she breathed in burned her nostrils. *How are we going to pull this off?* She thought to herself to block out the feeling of the cold. It was twenty minutes, maybe more, before Hyko finally made it in one piece to the back entrance to the caverns. Village elders had sealed off the entrance so long ago that most no one in the villages had any idea that there even was a back entrance.

"I noticed a couple of little kids playing with rocks out in the woods one night after I left the caverns at moonrise," Jaedon had explained earlier. "I tried calling to them in your language, but they ran away. I followed them, curious to see where they'd come from-I wasn't so sure if there were any little kids left around here until seeing those ones-and when I did, I discovered the rear entrance of these caves. There's only a few small cracks and holes in the barrier sealing off the caves, so I don't think that's how they got out. There's probably a hidden tunnel big enough for a person to fit through. Try to find that tunnel, and I'll distract the men so that we can get your people out."

Hyko kicked at the dirt in frustration.

"Alright, Jaedon," she grumbled. "It won't be any trouble to find this hidden tunnel." She kept kicking around at the ground, finding nothing helpful. Heaving a sigh, she leaned against the sealed off entrance and closed her eyes. Suddenly, the ground beneath her gave in, and her left foot fell down, the rest of her body collapsing into an awkward heap on the ground. Before she could even clutch at her bruised knee, the rest of her body fell into the now very visible sinkhole that seemed to have come from nowhere. Groaning, she tried picking herself back up, only to find a face two inches from her own.

"Hyko-jete?" The person gasped, and an uproarious noise erupted from a crowd. The person scooted back and held out a hand, helping her up as all the noise died down. Hyko blinked, trying to make out the faces of her people; nearly everyone had the face of death, grim expressions and weary eyes.

"Um...hiya," she said quietly.

"How on earth did you get here...? Why did you come?" the woman asked, her voice trembling. "You must leave at once! Before they realize you are here. Do you know what they would do if they-"

"Forgive me for cutting you short, but I understand the risks," Hyko interrupted. "That's why I'm here to get you all out. This was all planned with Ja...with a friend." She motioned for everyone to begin climbing out of the hidden tunnel-or pitfall, as Hyko had discovered. As more and more people crowded in clusters closer to the exit, the room became stuffy and unbearably malodorous. Hyko found herself gagging a she helped lift children up and out of the cavern. One little boy with a mess of tangled curls atop his head made Hyko's eyes water.

"I not take bath in long time, Hyko-jete," he exclaimed cheerfully, and Hyko tried to fake a smile, but it came out much more like a scared and anxious grin.

Hyko lead the first group of thirty two villagers through the woods until they reached the charted forest paths she knew they'd recognize. She then left a distant relative of hers in charge of leading the group back to Tattao so that she could sprint back to the caverns, and do the same for the second group of people. She slowed up halfway to the hidden pitfall, when she noticed bright lights flickering through the trees and heard distant chattering. Hyko cursed Jaedon silently; how hard was it to distract a few of the fat, lazy night scouts?

"Hyko!" A small voice startled Hyko enough to make her drop to her already bruised knees and shriek obnoxiously. When she whirled around, she noticed a little girl giggling wildly.

"Illi!" Hyko hissed. "Keep quiet!"

"But my sisters and I want to gather moon berries-"

"Shut up and wait here!" Hyko hissed harshly. "I need to go get the others."

"We are all right here." A middle aged woman stepped out of the shadows. Behind her stood the remaining Kainau villagers. "We followed Illi up the tunnel, assuming you had called for her." Hyko gritted her teeth and said nothing in annoyance, and turned to keep walking.

Jaedon smacked into her. Blood immediately started to drip from her nose. She tried to wipe up the blood that was dribbling down her bottom lip.

"*Jaedon!*" she growled. "*What the-*"

"Run," he said, shoving her forward. "They're coming. Right now, Hurry, go!"

"But I-"

"Take the villagers!" He pushed her forward even more, and right as he did, the sound of a gunshot pierced the air. The noise sent the natives into a frenzy. Many of them ran off in all different directions, straying from the path leading to Tattao. More gunshots rang out and Jaedon dropped to the ground. He pulled at Hyko but she didn't budge.

"What *is* that?"

"A gun! Get *down!*" Jaedon urged. Hyko hesitated and while she did, another gunshot rang out. Less than two seconds following the sound of the fired weapon, Hyko's eyes clamped shut and she let out a sharp, high-pitched cry. Her body crashed to the ground and she clutched at her midsection, moaning.

"*What happened?*" she wailed, gritting her teeth. Her entire body was shaking. She managed to open her eyes just slightly, and noticed that Jaedon had grown pale when she did.

"I...I think you just got shot," Jaedon managed to get out, his voice trembling. A dark liquid was smearing against her stomach and her arms, some dripping down into the dirt. Panicking at the sight of so much of her own blood, Hyko began taking in short, shallow breaths, muttering in her language. Tears spilled from her eyes, mixing with her blood.

"Jaedon!" she cried. "Zze! Help, please! Oww, haowo!"

"Hyko, just...calm down," he croaked, bending down. He gently pried her hands away from her stomach and tried to lift the fabric of her top from the wound. When she flinched and moaned, he pulled away quickly.

"It hurts," she gasped. "Please, help me."

"I-I'm trying," Jaedon groaned. "I'm sorr-" Before he could get his words out, he was knocked to the ground by a native man who bellowed at him in his native language. Hyko tried opening her mouth to explain what was going on, but her mind was fuzzy. Her thoughts were unclear and her throat was so dry. There was so much shouting and guns firing, and the pungent smell of blood would not go away. Everything was suddenly happening in slow motion, and Hyko could not see Jaedon at all. Her eyes darted back and forth, but it was becoming harder and harder to make sense of things. The noise faded away, and the world started becoming darker and darker...

* * * * *

"Hey...hey...you awake?" He watched as she stirred in her sleep, turning towards him ever so slightly. Someone had tied her hair back and wrapped a bandage around her mid section. He bit his lip and reached out his hand, smoothing down a few loose strands of her hair. She groaned ever so softly, and he sucked in a breath.

"Mmm...Jae...is it you?" Her voice was hoarse and barely audible, but the sound of it made him heave a sigh of relief.

"Yes, it's me," he replied softly. "Hyko, I'm so sorry this happened to you." She chuckled weakly.

"Guess that's what I get for letting...letting the white boy plan the rescue," she said. "Jaedon...how did that gun hurt me?"

"Guns shoot bullets," he explained, pressing something into her hand. She opened it and saw a piece of metal. It wasn't a snare, but it was something she'd seen before in the woods. "The bullet didn't go into you; it grazed you bad enough to leave a pretty serious wound though."

"I've seen these before," Hyko told him. "In the woods, with a bunch of snares." She paused and took a few concentrated breaths. "There were a lot of people who died from these. I think the men are upset because...because some of them lost their wives and..." She winced suddenly and sucked in a breath, arching her back just barely. Jaedon put a hand on her shoulder.

"We can talk more about this later," he told her. "You rest, and we can meet at our meeting place soon. Alright?" She gave him a weak but genuine smile, and reached up to touch his cheek. His entire body turned to mush.

"You're good to me," she whispered so softly that it made Jaedon shiver.

"Nearly one hundred natives...*completely gone!*" Bryce bellowed, the spit from his foul-smelling mouth flying onto the first several people in the crowd; but, of course, one of those people was Jaedon. "You idiots can't keep a few blackies in line? How did they all even manage to escape?"

"Well, sir, we did manage to shoot some of them," one of the four gunmen who'd been shooting at the escaped natives said, daring to stand up as he addressed Bryce. Bryce narrowed his eyes at the man, his face burning bright red from anger. Suddenly timid, the gunman sat back down.

"Tell me, Mr. Wentingjones," Bryce hissed. "How are we supposed to grow Jokpoh *if there are no natives to do it?!*" No one had an answer. "This is it. I have had it was these...these natives. I swear, if I find the blackie...or man who has done this..." He paused to rub his temples and exhale. "Get out of my sight. All of you. Except *you.*"

The entire group swiftly cleared out of the meeting except for the one young man Bryce had pointed to and commanded to stay put. London paced back and forth while Bryce came closer to the young man and glared directly into his eyes. Jaedon shifted uncomfortably in the now empty room.

"Umm...any reason as to why I'm still here?" he asked quietly, trying to scoot back away from a furious Bryce.

"*You,*" Bryce growled. "I know there's something up with you. There *always* has been."

"I don't know what you're talking about."

"Oh, but I think you do," Bryce countered, taking a step back and pulling a cigarette out of his pocket. "You got something you wanna let me in on, Jadey?" Jaedon stood defiantly, taking broad steps over to Bryce until the two were so close that the smoke from the green-eyed man's cigarette made Jaedon's eyes water.

"I...have...*nothing* to say to you," he growled, more ferocity in his voice than he'd ever used before when speaking with the ruthless leader. To Jaedon's surprise, the man did not laugh or scoff at him; instead, Bryce's eye twitched and he exhaled loudly through gritted teeth. He backed away, and let out a puff of smoke, his fingers trembling.

"If I ever find out you've been up to something," Bryce warned. "Someone is going to suffer." His glare lingered on Jaedon for the longest of moments before he turned away from him, and dismissed the young man from the room.

* * * * *

"Is she going to be okay?"

"She was up walking earlier today."

"She shouldn't have been."

"No excuses! She is well enough to come to this meeting."

Hyko grunted and tried to ignore each comment that the village elders and Hanjeha made in the other room. She was content enough resting in the healers hut, though one of the more irritable elders kept insisting that she join the other villagers at the village center just after moonrise. Hanjeha was fighting on Hyko's side, but it was doubtful that her voice would count; as respected as she was, Hanjeha was still a woman.

"You think they'll make you go?" Awa'hi asked, slumping in her seat. Now that Hyko knew she was with child, her pregnant belly was very obvious, especially when she was hunched over or sitting down. Hyko shrugged and leaned back against the wall her bed was pressed against.

"I don't care," Hyko grumbled. "They can do what they want." She sank down into her bed, pulling the covers up over her head. "I don't understand why it's so important that I'm present at this meeting." Awa'hi opened her mouth to respond, but right as she was about to speak, three of the four village elders stepped into the room with Hanjeha following behind them. Elder Agenee was among them. Awa'hi sat up straighter, silently urging for Hyko to do the same.

"I bid you good evening, young ladies," one of the male elders said, dipping his head to the two girls. "It has been decided, Hyko, daughter of Peoto, that you are well enough to attend the village meeting just after moonrise tonight."

"Says who?" Hyko mumbled from under the blankets.

"Young lady, watch your tongue," the elder snapped before continuing on. "You will do as you are told. We have come to escort you to the village center. It would do us good to make haste, for the others are beginning to assemble as we speak."

Sure enough, a crowd had gathered at the village center, murmuring furiously as they noticed Hyko and her escorts. As she neared the bulk of the crowd, she started to hear her name being whispered. At each comment, she simply rolled her eyes and limped on. Mixed in with the people of Tattao were the escaped refugees from the beach village. Several of them smiled at Hyko as she passed by them, though many of them scowled fiercely.

"Tattao villagers!" Elder Banna, one of the oldest men in the village, boomed. All hushed conversations started to die down. "Brothers and sisters of Kainau! We welcome you with open arms, and will provide for you a place to stay and eat until these white men have left."

"These men aren't planning on leaving," one man from Kainau muttered under his breath. "They're planning on using us! Every last one of us." The man's comments started up more conversations and worried whispers. Hyko bit her lip and kept silent.

"I beg you, my brothers, keep quiet while I carry out this meeting," Elder Banna exclaimed, and once again, all talking ceased. "Now, as you all know, these white men have been causing problems for us. I am hoping that you, brothers and sisters from Kainau, have heard something from their foul mouths that might help us gain insight on their plans or motives." Everyone started to murmur furiously, and Hyko shifted uncomfortably in her seat, clutching at her sore middle.

"Our sincere apologies," one man said. "We would be more than willing to help get these white men out, but we do not know much of what they plan to do. Close to nothing." Elder Banna's eyes widened and his shoulders slumped.

"How can you know nothing?" he gasped, appalled.

"They were very careful about explaining their plans around us," another man explained. "They threw us into caverns, and forced us to work with Jokpoh plants and barely fed us." Elder Banna shut his eyes and rubbed his temple with his index and middle fingers.

"Why are you just now deciding to do something about the ziolen rarroso?" Another man cried out disrespectfully, jumping to his feet. "They have been killing your own, have they not? Why have you not stood on your own two feet, and done something about them?"

"We have been preparing for battle against these strangers for weeks," Elder Agenee snapped, joining in on the conversation. "It is not as easy as you would think. Their technologies and weapons are far greater than-"

"We know all about their weapons first hand," one of the younger men spat. "We lost far too many of our own during our escape from the caverns thanks to those cursed weapons."

"That's what occurs, I suppose, when one lets an impudent woman head a rescue," another young man hissed, his voice loud enough for just about the entire front half of the crowd to hear. Hyko's throat grew dry as the crowd began murmuring again. The people of Kainau raised their voices and turned to glare in Hyko's direction. The elders standing by and guarding her scooted to the side, shooting the young woman a curious look. Hyko bit her lip, and tried to slump down and hide her face from the rest of the crowd.

"*Woman?*" Elder Banna hissed, pushing Elder Agenee aside to get a good view of the crowd. "What woman dared leave Tattao to carry out such a mission?" Her legs precarious, Hyko got to her feet and stood as tall and firm as she could without causing herself too much pain.

"For the love of all things good, I was doing it because I knew how I could help, you *ingrates!*" she snapped. The women in the crowd gasped and reeled back at the girl's tone. The elders furrowed their brows and cringed, but said nothing as she continued on. "I discovered countless things while serving as a messenger. I knew where the people were, I knew how to get them out, and I knew how to get past the white men."

"You lie!" One man shouted. "More than a dozen women, men and children were killed because we did *not* get past the white men, and your feeble plan failed."

"It was *not* feeble, it just..."Hyko stopped herself and clenched her fists. She had no real explanation that she could give. The plan's failure was really Jaedon's fault; he hadn't kept the gunmen distracted for long enough, which resulted in their plan failing. Nevertheless, how was she to explain to her people that her escape plan had been planned with a young white man?

"See here? The girl has no answer," the man said. "This is why we should not allow women to get in the way of a man's responsibility."

"I saved your life!" Hyko spat.

"And killed my son!" he countered. Hyko had nothing to say to that. "How is it that you knew so much, anyway? Were you out wandering? Any responsible, mature, smart woman would have stayed home and helped her neighbors with laundry or some such chore." Hyko scowled at the man's smug countenance.

"I-"

"Please, the two of you!" Elder Agenee stepped in. "We will get nowhere with all of us bickering about the rolls of men and women!" The crowd started to settle down, and the young man backed off, but Hyko's blood was still boiling. Her lip trembled as she slowly lowered herself back down to her seat. "Now, this nonsense with the strangers has gone on long enough. We need to get them out immediately-"

"Let us wait until after the winter months," one man suggested. "The harsh weather is sure to kill them all within a few weeks time."

"They've made it this long, have they not?" Elder Banna said. "I'm not so sure a winter is going to do much."

"I say we kill them all!" a rowdy member of the crowd shouted, a fire in his eyes. "If we simply chase them off, they will only run home and send more. Possibly even more than they did this time."

More men started tossing around ideas, though Hyko tuned it all out. Her mind was on the City in the Ruins, Jaedon, and just about everything except how to get the white men out. All she really wanted to do was lie down and...and...

Be with Jaedon?

The thought crossed her mind and made her shiver.

"Daughter of Peoto, are you alright?" one of her escorts asked, leaning in towards her. She shook her head and got to her feet.

"I think I need to walk off a cramp, if I may," she told him. She managed to muster up the most pathetic face she could, and the escort excused her from the meeting. The chatter from the village center died down as Hyko got farther away from it. She pulled her throw up higher on her shoulders and hugged herself. As she walked on, she noticed that there were soft footsteps behind her. All of a sudden, a harsh hand was on her shoulder turning her around. Hyko cried out in pain, and dropped down to her knees. Above her, his hand clasped tightly around her upper arm, was the man whom she'd forgotten to speak to for weeks on end.

"How difficult," he growled, dragging her along. "Tell me, girl, how *hard* could it be for you to stick around, and *stay in the village?*"

"But I have been in-"

"Everyone knows of your stupid rescue," Yonej snapped. "How could you have gotten yourself and others hurt or killed? What were you trying to pull?"

"I only want to help!" she whispered. By then, Yonej had pulled her up off her knees, dragged her all the way back to his kytah and slammed the door shut. "Yonej, I'm sorry-"

"Sorry doesn't cut it!" he bellowed. "If you are to be my wife, I suggest you learn your roll. How are you to raise our children if you still act like a child yourself?"

"Our wedding is postponed," she muttered. Her voice was shaky. "I...I went to Sasse several weeks back, and...Elder Opi told me that...our wedding is postponed." Her eyes were on the ground, but she knew that the look on his face was not a pleased one.

"You...went...*where?*"

"I was a messenger" she cried in her defense. "I-"

"You disgrace me!" he yelled. "I suppose I cannot do much about what you have done in past months and weeks. But, I swear to you, if I hear of you leaving the village to carry out any more outlandish plans, schemes, or even *meet someone else*, I swear..." He backed away from her, though he was no less intimidating. "I will have to teach you some respect myself." He stepped into the sitting room of his home, and took a sip of some water.

"I...I was only trying to help," she croaked, starting to get to her feet. Yonej set the cup down, but did not turn around.

"You will help when I say you will help," he growled. "No sooner, no later."

JETISAHATN'A COMMUNICATION

The bitter cold came to the villages suddenly and brutally. The first time he'd had to go out in it, he'd thought to himself that he could make it. The second time, he'd been a little less than thrilled. Now that this was his fourth time trudging down the now frostbitten path to Tattao, his own angry blood boiling wasn't enough to keep him half warm.

It hadn't yet snowed, but from the feel of the wind and weather, Jaedon knew that it would be coming soon. *God forbid there's some sort of blizzard while I'm out here by myself,* Jaedon thought to himself. He continued on for several more minutes before reaching the east village gate. The homes looked very different from the last time he'd been. Windows were covered with thick pelt blankets. No clothes were hanging out to dry in yards, and there were no toys or supplies outside. In the heart of the night, it felt almost like a ghost town.

"Jaedon!" Her whisper was harsh and urgent. She pulled him back into the shadows, grabbing onto his shoulders. "You need to be more careful!"

"*This* is the *fourth time* I have come up here!" he hissed. "I am cold, and sore, and…sorry, I'm just really, really not understanding why all of a sudden you've stopped meeting me like we used to. You keep leaving me notes and blowing me off." The more he explained his frustration, the more he noticed that she seemed exhausted and upset. There were dark bags under her eyes. "Umm...what's up with you?"

"This isn't a good place to talk," she muttered. She took him by the hand and lead him into the woods, saying nothing until they'd walked a good fifteen minutes. He spoke up several times to mumble and complain about her silence, or groan after hitting his toe on the root of a tree, but received no response.

"Will you cut out all the silence and tell me, Hyko?" Jaedon snapped. He tore away from her, snatching back his hand and making her flinch. "I hate to say it, but I'm pretty ticked off-"

"I can explain," she whispered, her head down. "It's not my fault, and I am very sorry." She inhaled slowly, her breath curling in the air in front of her as she exhaled.

"Can you explain it quickly?" Jaedon hissed, his teeth chattering. His lips were chapped and bleeding as he spoke. "I swear-"

"Please, just hear me out!" Hyko interrupted harshly. "It wasn't me, it was Yonej!" Jaedon blinked and shoved his hands in his pockets.

"...Yonej. Oh, it aaall makes sense now!" Jaedon cried, an obnoxious smile on his face. "*It was Yonej!*" Hyko started to relax and smile until the grin on Jaedon's face vanished, and his angry tone returned. "Hyko, who is Yonej?"

"I never told you," Hyko murmured, kneeling down in the dirt. "I was too afraid to tell you..." She covered her face with her hands, shaking her head. Jaedon sucked in a breath to try and cool himself down. He looked over at her and really saw for the first time that night how distressed she seemed.

"Hyko, you can tell me now," he told her, his tone not quite as harsh and angry.

"I have a fiancée," Hyko spit out. "He's almost ten years older than me. He's threatening and doesn't trust me. I've been staying with him, in the extra room in his house, and he won't let me leave. I can only get away for a little bit of time at night, if he's not still awake." The look on Hyko's face was one of anger and hurt.

Judging by her attitude towards the man and the way she'd never mentioned him before, Jaedon could tell that Hyko felt absolutely nothing for the man.

"So...that really *does* explain everything," Jaedon muttered under his breath. Hyko glanced up at him, giving an apologetic look. "Don't look at me like that."

"I don't know what to do, Jaedon," she said. He reached out his hand and helped pull up her to her feet. "I'm miserable." Still hand in hand, the two continued on once again.

"If you hate living here so much, why not just leave?" Jaedon asked as the two stepped over a fallen tree. It felt oddly nice to be talking to her for the first time in so long, despite the heavy topic.

"As of recently, I haven't been able to do much more than heal from my gunshot wound," she sighed, pulling her scarf up over her mouth. "Other than that, there's not really anywhere else to go. This is an island. And anyways, no one knows how safe it is past the village boundaries."

"Well...are you sure there's nowhere else at *all?*" He looked at her, and when she lifted her head, she had a thoughtful look on her face.

"I...think there might be one place!" Hyko excitedly dropped down to her knees once more and reached for a stick. In the dirt, she drew a map of the five villages. "These are the five villages: Kainau, Tattao, Sasse, Delfusio and Fayune. Right here...between the snow-capped mountains and the Delfusio boundaries is a cave said to hold many dangers. It is also said to be the entrance to the City in the Ruins." She launched into the many legends and stories of the Great City of Stone that had fallen when the spirits had found that the people no longer obeyed their superior laws. She explained that it was rumored that those who were banished from the villages would seek refuge in the City, though no one knew if they had ever made it that far. She also told him of the journal she'd read that had deemed all of the legends true. With each word Hyko spoke, the more her words were laced with excitement. By the time she'd explained it all, she was bouncing on her knees, and a bright look was in her eyes.

"You think you might want to travel there one day?" Jaedon laughed. "You sound as though you're ready to take off right now."

"It just sounds so great!" Hyko exclaimed. "A place where everyone is treated the same? It almost sounds unreal! Maybe..." She paused and bit her lip, still smiling.

"Maybe what?"

"Maybe they'd be accepting of us being...friends." Jaedon raised his eyebrows at Hyko's word choice, and how she'd hesitated, as if trying to decide if it was fitting.

"*Friends?*" He repeated, and noticed Hyko growing shy. He then felt himself blushing as a smile crept across her face.

"I, um..." She bit her lip. Jaedon stepped closer to her, patiently awaiting her next statement when a heavy wind sent an intense chill coursing through his entire body. Hyko wrapped her arms around herself and clamped her eyes shut, shivering.

"Guess the winter winds are really taking a toll on you," Jaedon chuckled. He reached out and pulled her into his arms. The sudden heat from her body made him let out a contented, slightly surprised sigh. He looked down at the girl he'd come to think of as beautiful and smiled. "Is that better?"

"Much," she whispered, her voice so soft and gentle that it was almost carried away on the wind. The two stood like that for the longest of moments, Jaedon's mind going through so many things all at once. If what Hyko was saying about a city far up in the mountains, he knew undoubtedly that she would be up and ready to go there the very next time a man ticked her off, be it her fiancée, or anyone else. Jaedon rolled his eyes and chuckled at the thought of him trying to tell her to calm down, how it probably wouldn't work, and he'd end up going along with it.

"Jae," Hyko said suddenly. Jaedon looked up, his eyes wide; she'd only called him that once before. "Would I be accepted where you come from?"

"Umm..." Jaedon had no idea.

"Or would they treat me like the other ziolen rarroso?"

"No...no, they wouldn't," he told her, his voice gentle. "Not all the people where I come from are like that. You and your people encountered some of the most heartless fools on the face of this Earth."

"But, despite all that, I got to meet you," Hyko said, smiling up at him. "There's good in everything, they say."

"If we're lucky, sometimes it even outweighs the bad," Jaedon added, and winked at her.

All of a sudden, she was tense again. She flinched and broke out of his embrace. When Jaedon opened his mouth to ask her what was wrong, Hyko held a finger to his lips to silence him. As he listened, he could hear distant shouting.

"Too many of our encounters end like this," he whispered as quietly as he could. She nodded and looked at him, an intense look in her eyes. Then, she leaned forward and pressed her lips to his cheek. The feel of the kiss made Jaedon blush furiously. When Hyko pulled back, she gave him a sad smile.

"He's looking for me," Hyko whispered. The shouts were getting closer. "I need to go."

"Will you be ok?" he asked, but she shook her head. Hyko was sprinting back towards the village before Jaedon could protest, or even more importantly, comment on the kiss.

* * * * *

She stumbled twice in the dark as she raced back towards Tattao, panting and huffing. She hadn't run that hard since before being hurt by the bullet. The cold bit mercilessly at her face and the other exposed parts of her body. Each time she had to use her hands to push herself up after falling, it became more painful. She could hear the venom and pure fury in Yonej's voice as his calls for her grew louder and louder.

"I'm right here!" Hyko replied, her voice hoarse and dry. Her lips were cracked, but she still managed to smile as she thought suddenly of how they'd felt on Jaedon's cheek. She fell once more, and when she looked up, she saw Yonej looming over her. His eyes seemed to glow red in the dark night, and Hyko cringed.

"Are you so dim-witted that you didn't think I saw you?" he roared. "I saw you sneak out of the house. Who is he?" Hyko clutched at her middle, which was sore and throbbing from the running she'd done. She followed slowly behind Yonej, not answering either of his questions.

"Yonej, I need to sit," she moaned.

"Shut up!" he snapped. "Walk faster, and answer me. Who was he? Was it Gisipeh?"

"No!" Hyko answered immediately. Upon entering his house again, Yonej pinned Hyko up against the wall. "Yonej, I swear it wasn't him! Ow, I need to sit! My gunshot wound-"

"Was it a white man?" he growled, and Hyko bit her lip. "You have been sneaking around and leaving the village, perhaps...*to be with a white man?"*

"I-"

"Shut up!" The command was reinforced with a blow to the face. Hyko cried out in pain, whimpering. *"Is it a white boy? Tell me!"* She closed her eyes, her body trembling. "Is it one of them? One of the killers? *Are you plotting with him?"*

"No! No, no!" she cried, tears streaming down her cheeks. "I'm not, I'm not-"

"Then what have you been up to?" His roar was followed by another slap even more painful than the first had been. *"Why have you been going out?* What could possibly be more important than what your fiancée-the man with whom you will wed!-commands you to do?" Hyko bit her lip, deep in thought, and tried to conjure up some sort of believable excuse, but none came to her.

"I have no answer for that," Hyko admitted, desolately. For the third time, the man struck her in the face. The forceful blow knocked Hyko's head against the wall in an unnatural way, and her body slumped to the ground. Her head hung loosely, blood welling up in the one spot of her head that had banged against the wall. The same sticky crimson dripped from her nose as she moaned and struggled to lift her head up.

"You shame me, girl," he spat. "Get on your feet." He yanked on her arm unrelentingly, and pulled her battered body up, stepping back to look at his handy work. Glaring into his eyes as best as she could, Hyko opened her mouth and spoke with a trembling voice.

"You are worth less than dirt to me," she croaked. Yonej reeled back to slap her again, but restrained himself at the last moment, and punched the wall instead. She didn't wait for him to wave her away that night; no part of her wanted to end up looking like the wall he'd just smashed in. Hyko bolted out of the kytah, Yonej's angry shouts and bellows still ringing in her ears. She ran at top speed until her legs were sore and her healing gunshot wound was burning and irritated. Falling to her knees, sobs began to shake her entire body as she cried in the middle of the woods.

"What did he do to you?"

"Jaedon!" Hyko whispered. She glanced up and saw his comforting face only an inch away from hers. "Where did you come from?"

"I didn't leave," he told her, his eyes sweeping over her entire body; Hyko was sure that it looked like blood was coming from everywhere from the way it was smeared all over her face, hands and clothing. "What did that man..." He stopped himself, chocking on the last words of his sentence. "Did he hit you?" When she nodded, Jaedon took her hand and helped her to her feet, then started walking.

"Jae, where are we going?" she sniffled.

"To The City," came his short, gruff reply.

"The...City," Hyko repeated. "In the Ruins?" He took a quick, sharp turn, and when the forest cleared, Hyko saw the entrance to their secret meeting place.

"That's the one!" He bent down and started gathering the clothes, snacks and journals they kept in their hiding spot for entertainment, and shoved them all into a duffle bag. Hyko stood back and watched him for a while until he glanced up at her."Can I have some help?"

"Don't do this for me," she told him quietly, putting a hand on his arm. Jaedon slowed up and turned to face her.

"If you stay here," he began. "You're going to get hurt. Look at yourself." He touched her face gently, and she winced just a little. “You can’t keep living with a man that does this to you.” There was no more disputing the matter after that for more than one reason; for one, Hyko was very curious and anxious to see what was past the Delfusio and Fayune boundaries, and had hoped to travel there one day anyway. Not only that, but after feeling Jaedon’s hand on her cheek, all tangible thoughts had completely escaped her mind. It was well into the night by the time the two had finished packing and were heading out of their meeting place. Neither of them made any attempts to strike up conversation until they’d made it out of Tattao, and were well on their way to the mountains.

“Communication,” Jaedon said simply after probably over an hour of silence.

“Huh?”

“Communication,” he repeated. “We’ve been lacking it, you know.” Hyko thought about it for a second before nodding her head in agreement.

“My fault,” she admitted. “I’m sorry.”

“You’ve cleared part of it up,” he went on. “The part about your fiancée, and why you haven’t been able to meet up with me until tonight. But, there’s something else I’d like explained.” He stopped walking, and turned to look her in the eyes. “That kiss.” Hyko felt like her face was on fire.

“I, um...what?” She danced around the question, looking at everything except him. “We should, um, keep moving. It’s really late-”

“Hyko,” Jaedon laughed gently. “There’s no way you’re avoiding this question.” He stepped closer to her and held her hands. “Had you wanted to do that sooner?”

A wave of emotions came flooding over Hyko, and she bit her lip due to the simple fact that she didn’t know what to say first. Had she wanted to do such a thing earlier? The thought had never truly occurred to her until then.

“Yes,” she told him, and then the words all just came to her. “Many times. I don’t know why I didn’t do it sooner.” A smile crept across Jaedon’s face, and he nodded his head.

"Can I tell you a secret?" he whispered. When Hyko leaned in to hear what he had to say, Jaedon pressed a gentle kiss to her lips. When he pulled back to look at her, a look of pure surprise was on her face. "I've wanted to, too."

LAIMOHT EN DA OAZAI
CITY IN THE RUINS

It had started as mere flurries, floating peacefully down from the heavens onto the harsh terrain below. The tiny white flakes hadn't been sticking, only lightly powdering the grass, the boulders, and the dirt paths. However, as the days went on, the flurries evolved into something more. By their fourth day of traveling, Hyko and Jaedon were trudging through thick snow so cold that it burned their shins and the soles of their feet as it seeped in through their shoes.

"How do people live up here?" Jaedon managed to get out of his chapped and bleeding lips. He ran his tongue over them, but didn't receive much relief. Hyko looked back and took his hand in hers.

"Years of experience," she told him just as she slipped on a slick, icy rock. When she started to fall, she realized that she was taking Jaedon with her, and the boy tumbled on top of her. As she struggled underneath him, she grumbled, "years of experience that I don't have." Jaedon laughed and climbed off of her.

"It's fine," he said. "There's nothing wrong with the fact that you don't live in an environment of constant ice and snow and...ice." He sniffled, ad Hyko could feel him shivering when he held out his hand to help her up.

"It will not take much longer," she said, pressing on. "Pretty soon, we will have reached the path directly between Delfusio and Fayune. It will not snow up there as much, so I hope." All of a sudden, Hyko looked over and saw a scowling Jaedon, his eyes on the frost-bitten path beneath their feet.

"This is where we first discovered your people," he mumbled. "We landed on the icy shores of Fayune, and saw a little boy playing. I can't believe things have gotten so bad since then."

"Yeah...well, it's not our concern any longer," Hyko spat, her voice as cold as the air that was burning her lungs. "They deserve it. Maybe it's God's way of punishing them for-"

"I don't think that's it, Hyko," Jaedon interrupted. "God is not like that. Your people had no way of learning about Him. He would not punish them for that." Hyko's sudden burst of anger subsided, and she shrugged, then continued on.

"Well...maybe He's punishing them for being jerks," she grumbled. "Not even the spirits approve of jerkiness." Even though she was not watching him, she knew that his eyes were on her. A disapproving frown marked his face when Hyko glanced up.

"What's wrong with you?" he asked. "You used to be so fired up and avid about protecting your people. Now, you're acting like you'd be happy if lightning came down and struck them."

"I'm just...angry," she sighed. "I hate it, though. Being angry and mad all the time. That's why I liked you right away; you didn't make me feel like that." Jaedon said nothing, but Hyko could see the corners of his mouth turning up into a small grin. Suddenly, Hyko stopped and gasped, pointing straight in front of them. An evergreen that had to be several stories tall cast a shadow over almost everything within a two mile radius. The two stepped into its shadow, shivering; the temperature dropped drastically out of the sun.

"Does this mean we're close?" Jaedon asked, his teeth chattering.

"No," she answered. "It's means we're here." It didn't look like much at first. But, when he squinted his eyes and looked farther off, closer to the tree trunk, he noticed large slabs of stone. Each slab was shaped artfully and decorated with the same types of symbols and characters Hyko had shown Jaedon how to read earlier on. Hyko watched as he tilted his head in an attempt to read the characters written upside down and sideways.

"This is the City in the Ruins?" Jaedon asked incredulously. "It sounded more like a city in the journals."

"No, you!" Hyko slapped him playfully on the arm. "It is further ahead. Right now, we are directly between Delfusio and Fayune." She pressed all of her body weight against one of the bigger stone slabs, grunting and pushing so hard that her body trembled. With tremendous effort and a helpful push from Jaedon, the slab budged. Eventually, the two had moved it to the side just enough for the both of them to fit behind it. Jaedon slipped through into the space behind the stone right away. He called excitedly for Hyko once on the other side, though the girl was hesitant before entering. She turned around to face the treacherous mountain path they'd just sojourned. With an angry grunt, she kicked a rock and watched it tumble back down the mountain, and crawled behind the slab, sealing off the opening once she had crossed to the other side.

* * * * *

Jaedon's first impression of what he believed to be "The City" was not much. The place looked almost exactly like the mountain paths of Fayune had, only there were boulders everywhere. Sure, it had been cool to see the writings carved into all the rocks at first. But, by the time they were setting up camp for the night, Jaedon never wanted to see another one of those strange characters again.

"I don't see how this is a city," he yawned, pulling his blanket up to his chin. "I don't see any ruins, either." Hyko shook her head, and settled into her sleeping mat next to him.

"We haven't reached the City yet," Hyko explained. "And these *are* ruins. According to legend, when this was once the Great City of Stone, these rocks we've been seeing along the way marked the path to the city. A proverb was carved into each stone. Trust me, we're getting there."

"How are you so sure of this place?" he asked, and Hyko gave him a playful shove.

"You were the one who'd insisted on coming up here!" she teased. "Now, you just need to trust that I know where I'm going."

Their journey continued the next morning as soon as the sun was up. The air was becoming harder to breathe as the altitude increased. Snowfall picked up again in the early afternoon, and Jaedon stayed close to Hyko for warmth. As it turned out, Hyko had been right about them being on the correct path; before long, the two found themselves climbing over fallen columns and smashed remains of brick walls that peeked out from under the snow.

"*Look!*" Hyko's eyes widened with horror as she pointed straight ahead of them. Through the blinding snow, Jaedon could see almost nothing.

"At *what?*" he cried, squinting.

"At *that!*" This time, when she pointed, Jaedon saw exactly what she was seeing. Dead ahead of them was half of an ancient structure; the other half had tumbled over and was lying in a pile of brick and stone. Standing atop all of the rubble was a small boy wearing a scarf around his neck and heavy coat for the winter months. Hyko gasped, her hands covering her mouth.

"Where did he-"

"Hey! Beinei te citon!" Hyko shouted, her voice echoing through the mountains. The boy looked up. To Jaedon's surprise, he waved and laughed.

"What did you say to him?"

"I told him to get down!" She pushed past Jaedon and dashed out towards the structure as fast as her legs would take her in the snow. Jaedon stood back and watched as she started to make her way up the pile of the demolished structure. The further up Hyko climbed, the further up the boy went as well. He was laughing hysterically, as if it were all a game. His laughing ceased abruptly when the edge of his scarf wrapped around a sharp object in the snow, and the slick surface beneath him caused him to slip. The scarf tightened around his neck as he hung in midair. Hyko clasped her hands around her mouth and gasped, willing her body to move even faster. Just as she reached him, she noticed he was writhing around and twirling in a circle, loosening the hold his scarf had on his neck. Before she could reach out and grab him, he dropped, sliding down the slippery slope on his knees, giggling wildly the whole way.

He swayed unsteadily once he reached the ground, still getting out the last of his laughs. Jaedon rushed over to him, dropping to his own knees when he finally reached the boy. The kid didn't seem to be frazzled in the least after what most would consider a sort of traumatic experience. He looked more like he'd just been in a tickle fight.

"What were you thinking?" Jaedon exclaimed, glaring down at the boy. He wasn't that old, but he was old enough to know better than to try to pull a stunt like that. The boy shrugged, completely unaffected by the color of Jaedon's skin. "Don't you know that you could have been seriously hurt?"

"Yes, mister, I know that," the boy said. "But, dad said it was okay, and my kead said that if I tried it, he'd give me a new toy!"

"Kay-ahd?" Jaedon tried to pronounce the word, but it fell sloppily off his tongue.

"That means uncle." Hyko came trudging over. "Why on earth would your uncle tell you that?"

"I dunno," he replied sarcastically. "Maybe because pretty much every other man in the City has done it before and no one's ever died from it?" At the mention of the City, Jaedon's eyes widened. However, the boy turned and started to skip away, moving surprisingly quickly though the snow.

"Wait, wait!" Hyko cried. "Hassah matteo! Where are you going? Why are you out here by yourself?" The look the boy gave the two of them when he spun around was one of disbelief.

"Where did you two come from?" he asked. "You're awfully weird, if you don't mind me saying so. How old do you think I am, six?" Hyko and Jaedon exchanged bewildered glances.

"Umm, let's start with a different question," Hyko said, following after the boy. "What is your name?"

"Dantelo," he answered, happily. "But, everyone calls me Dante." Jaedon recognized the name, but judging from the confused look on Hyko's face, he could tell that it was completely foreign to her.

"We're Hyko and Jaedon," Jaedon replied. "If it's alright, can we come with you to the City?" Dantelo nodded, and started to skip away once more. He moved through the snow as swiftly and skillfully as Jaedon had seen Hyko make her way through the woods. The boy paused every now and then to wait for them to catch up, but most of the time, he was several yards ahead of them. As they walked on, the heavy snowfall came to a stop.

"You should come in the summer!" Dantelo said cheerfully. They were walking on a snowless stone path with elaborate patterns Jaedon had never seen before. "There's no snow, of course, and all the kids go rock climbing..." As the boy was describing his summer adventures, Jaedon was too busy having his mind blown to be paying attention. There was no doubt that they'd arrived at the City now. They stepped down into what appeared to be an old temple. Its dramatic architecture and details were astounding.

"*This* is where you *live?*" Hyko gasped. Dantelo shot her another "you're crazy" look.

"No," he answered. "We just come here for prayer on the first day of the week." He continued on, walking through the temple to another part of the city. It appeared that they'd crossed over to the City Center. At least one hundred people were milling about, stopping at shops, stands and carts for produce and other goods.

"It's actually real," Hyko breathed. "The City...I...I can't-"

"Come on, I'll take you to my mother!" Dantelo cried, rushing off across the City Center through the crowds of people. At the far end of the Center was a flight of stairs embellished with gold. A young woman dressed in all royal blue robes and a purple head piece stood at the top of the stairs. As Dantelo neared her, a bright smile spread across her face, and she stretched out her arms for the boy to run into. Hyko and Jaedon approached the stairs slowly, almost hesitantly. The woman came over to them with Dantelo in her arms. She smiled warmly, though there was something strikingly powerful about her demeanor.

"My son tells me that he found the two of you while he was out playing," she said. "It has been so long since we've had people travel up here."

"That's because all of my people believe that this place is nothing more than a legend," Hyko explained. "It is so amazing to finally be here. Um, could you tell me if there is someone leading this City? Like an elder?" The woman set Dantelo down, watched him dash off into the City Center, and then she smiled happily.

"That would be I," she answered. "I am Sauda, and I am the chief of the City."

KANAKUWASS ATTACK

Ohn-Tsung knew that she should be excited. Nevertheless, the farther they walked, the more miserable she became. As she and seven of her friends were sent off for their Whispering, Hyko should've been with her parents at the blessing in the village center earlier that afternoon to send her off; it had felt kind of empty standing up there all dressed up in her anneta with no sister to do the blessing along with her mother and father. Sighing, she kicked at the dirt.

"You feeling alright, kiddo?" Gisipeh came up to the girl's side. He was one of the escorts leading the youth through the woods along with three other young men. "You've seemed pretty down today."

"I just miss my sister," she mumbled. A boy about her age looked up with a grimace on his face.

"Ugh, you mean *Hyko?*" He said Ohn-Tsung's sister's name as if it were a curse word. "Why would you even say her name here?" Gritting her teeth, Ohn-Tsung turned away from Gisipeh to glare at the boy.

"Because she is my sister," she growled.

"If I were you, I wouldn't admit that to anyone," the boy went on. "I mean, aren't you embarrassed? She insulted soooo many people; Elder Opi, her father, her fiancée, men in general, not to mention the spiri-"

He gagged and dropped to the ground, blood pouring from a small hole in his chest. The rest of the youth erupted into a chorus of mortified screams and started glancing around frantically. This time, they heard it before someone went down. It sounded like thunder ringing out through the woods, yet there was not a cloud in the sky. After the third shot and the third person dropped dead on the ground, Ohn-Tsung and the others found themselves completely surrounded by strange white men with strange weapons they'd never seen before.

"So, *this* is what Jaedon has been sneaking out of the city for." A tall, green-eyed man stepped out from behind the trees, a smug grin on his awkwardly shaped face. For a moment, Ohn-Tsung thought he was a demon; never in her life had she seen someone with eyes any color other than brown. "Well then. I told him someone would be hurt if he was hiding something." He held out the silver weapon and aimed it at the center of Gisipeh's chest, his hand on the trigger. Frozen with fear and confusion, Gisipeh stood silently, his entire body shaking. Ohn-Tsung watched from several feel away, her bottom lip trembling.

"Move, Gisi," she hissed under her breath. Just as the words escaped her mouth, she heard the thunder, and Gisipeh cried out as he fell to the ground. The tears began to spill from Ohn-Tsung's eyes and she bit back a loud sob. She prayed to the spirits that the white men would leave her and the other survivors alone. She prayed that she wouldn't need to see anymore of her friends murdered. She prayed that Gisipeh wouldn't have to die right there in front of her.

"Bryce!" Another man burst out from the bushes, a look of terror on his face. "There's at least two or three dozen blackies heading this way. We'll be slaughtered if we don't move now!" The green-eyed man nodded, but said nothing. He gestured towards the other white men, and just as quickly as they'd emerged from behind the trees, they slipped back into the shadows. They left behind nothing but a confused, terrified group of kids, their remaining two escorts and a pile of dead bodies.

Ohn-Tsung looked down at Gisipeh, and touched his face. His lips were turning blue, and his skin had already become cool to the touch.

DESUYISO
DESTRUCTION

Each time Hyko woke up in the City, she couldn't help but smile. For one, her room was beautifully decorated with gold and other refined minerals. Two, Jaedon was laying right next to her. She laughed to herself as she thought of Elder Agenee nodding disapprovingly at the idea of her sharing a bed with a man, and a white man at that! She had a legitimate excuse; there was only one spare room in the chief's house, and Dantelo had gotten the extra sleeping pad dirty and ripped when he'd used it to sled down a hill covered in mud.

The third reason was the chief. A woman in charge of an entire secret society! It was almost unreal! Not only was she the chief; she was the granddaughter of the woman who'd written the journal that had ended with "there is a better way to live." One night at dinner, Chief Sauda described how she'd only ever heard stories of life in the villages. Nevertheless, she'd developed a hatred for their lifestyle and how the women living such lives were treated over time. She'd also gone on to say that she didn't know why the villagers were so afraid to stand up for themselves against the white men.

"Although I do not agree with how they live, I do know that the five villages have always been a proud people," Chief Sauda had said. "They should be standing up and fighting instead of putting all of this off for so long. The men shouldn't be telling the women to sit back and do nothing, while women shouldn't be so submissive to the point where they are getting themselves and their children killed. You were wise to take matters into your own hands."

Jaedon rolled over and moaned, interrupting her thoughts. She smiled and slid out of bed, stretching.

"Jaedon, you know what?" Hyko said excitedly, leaning in towards Jaedon's face. His eyes fluttered open, but she could tell that he wasn't awake. "Jaedon, listen! I think I know how we can help my people!" He sat up, almost knocking heads with her.

"I thought you were done helping them," he yawned, his voice quiet as he tried waking himself up. Hyko glanced down at the floor, slightly ashamed.

"I've had another change of heart," she explained. "It was wrong of me to say those things before. But, that's beside the point, Jae! We can show my people that there's a better way to live! We can have Chief Sauda come back down with us and-"

"What is it you would like my mom to do?" Dantelo came bursting in. He had half a shaved head; the other half was a massive ball of wild curls.

"Dante!" Jaedon cried. "What're you-"

"Sshhh! Not so loud!" He pressed his pointer finger to his lips. "I'm trying to hide from my mother!"

"Nice try, my son, but your mother could find you anywhere." Chief Sauda stepped into the room and gathered up her son into her arms. "Will you let me finish cutting your hair or what?"

"Umm....Mom! They have something to tell you!" Dantelo pointed at the two and Hyko bit her lip. *Well played, Dante*, she thought to herself, amused. Chief Sauda raised her eyebrows at them..

"Well, umm...Chief Sauda," Hyko began hesitantly. "Jaedon and I greatly admire your city and the way you live your lives." The chief smiled and nodded her head in thanks. "And...I was really wanting to, maybe, have your help...umm, maybe you could help us get rid of these white men and...and then introduce my people to a life of peace and equality. De noyev mossodela; a fresh start." A scowl came across Chief Sauda's face, and she set Dantelo down, telling him to go out of the room. She shut the door behind him and heaved a sigh.

"Why would I be willing to risk the lives of my men and women by sending them out to fight or help a people who do not help themselves?" she snapped, and Jaedon sunk back under the covers. Hyko fiddled with her fingers. "I will never put my people in danger for such a cause."

"But, there are so many people dying-"

"Because they sit back, do nothing, and that is the reason why they are dying left and right." She opened the door, starting to step out. "I will not leave my son and my people for something so petty and foolish." The door slammed shut, and Hyko collapsed onto the bed, her hands over her eyes. Jaedon sat up and exhaled loudly.

"It's fine, Hyko," he soothed, smoothing down her hair.

"No, it isn't, Jae," she groaned. "Why did I ever abandon my people...?" She jumped to her feet, scurrying around the room and collecting up her things. "We need to go back." As soon as she said it, Jaedon's eyes grew big.

"All the way back down the mountain?" he complained. When Hyko shot him a look, he clamped his mouth shut.

"Yes," she snapped. *"All the way back down."*

"But, what about living a better life and all that?"

"If we bring the better life to my people, we won't have to run away!" Hyko exclaimed. "It'll be best for everyone, and...what?" She slowed down with her packing, and dropped the pair of shoes in her hand. Jaedon looked truly crushed by the news she'd just given him. She crossed to the other side of the room and placed her hand on his.

"Nothing important," he grumbled, snatching his hand away. As he got to his feet and hastily threw his clothes into his bag, Hyko stood back and watched him, perplexed.

"Why won't you tell me?" she asked softly, and saw him tense up at her words. When he refused to even turn around and face her, she growled and threw a shoe at him. "Fine, then just keep packing. We've been here long enough as it is." Suddenly, his lips were pressed to hers before she even realized he'd moved over to her. She pushed him away gently and searched his face for answers.

"It's been, what, almost three months now?" he said softly. "Not worrying about Bryce or London or your fiancée or your father…it's been just the two of us up here. Hasn't it been nice?" Her eyes widened and she bit her lip. With trembling fingers, Hyko reached up and pushed some of her wild curls away from her eyes.

"You wanted to stay here with just me," she gasped, talking mostly to herself. He nodded at her realization. "You don't want to go…but, Jae-"

"I know it's not right, and it's pretty selfish," he said. "But, I guess…I mean, winter is going to be over soon enough, and my men will have the courage to move again. We should go now, since there won't be so much-"

"We'll come back!" Hyko cried, excitedly. "If things don't go over well in the villages, we'll come back." Jaedon ran his hand though his hair, which was growing out and almost covering his eyes. When he pushed his long locks back, she was able to see his bright blue eyes.

"Only if you promise me that you'll let me beat the crap out of that guy you're supposed to marry," he teased, a playful look on his face.

Gone. Absolutely everything she'd ever known to be home was almost completely in shambles. The kytahs were torn down and lying in piles of wood and brick. The east, west and south village gate markers appeared to have been set on fire. Small tents made out of animal skins and furs were scattered throughout the village, pots and pans sitting out in front of them with laundry sitting atop the pots and pans. For several long moments, Hyko stood back and stared at her demolished home, her hand over her mouth. The only thing that was even partially standing and not under construction was the healer's hut.

"Hyko." Ohn-Tsung climbed over the remains of an old table, a thick throw adorning her tiny body; had she been eating in the time she and Jaedon had been away?

"Ohn-Tsung!" Hyko cried. She rushed forward and grabbed onto her sister's arm. It had become thin and boney. "What the... Whatta ifite? What happened here? Everything is...is..."

"The white men," the girl explained. "They tormented us. They destroyed everything. Hyko, they ki...ki..." She bit the inside of her cheek. "Sosii, they killed Gisipeh." The news made Hyko physically sick, her body weakening so suddenly that she dropped down to her knees. Greif hit her like a collapsing stone wall, and her throat felt constricted. "They held his vigil and buried him in the Field of Spirits almost a month ago."

"Please, Ohn-Tsung...don't say anything else," Hyko croaked. Her mind was completely blank as she tried to make sense of what her little sister had said.

"I just thought you'd want to know what happened," Ohn-Tsung said. "He was killed right in front of me, you know. We were on our way to my Whispering. The spirits never assigned to me anything. Hanjeha says it's because they were grieving the death of Gisipeh right along with us and-"

"Ohn-Tsung, *stop*." Getting to her feet, she made her voice firm and serious. "Stop with all of this 'spirits' nonsense, and lying to me about Gisi." Ohn-Tsung reeled back in pure shock.

"But, I-"

"Noka. Shetteme; *shut up*."

"Hyko, I'm not lying!" Ohn-Tsung cried. "And what do you mean 'spirits' nonsense? Hyko, did where you go change you?"

"No," she replied. "I changed me."

"Hyko-jete!" A little girl came dashing across the village, moving as fast as her little legs would carry her; it was the same girl whose father had told her months ago to never speak with Hyko or he would beat her raw. She looked even more underfed and sickly than Ohn-Tsung. "Hyko-jete, come quick!"

"What is it?" Hyko stepped forward.

"It's Awa'hi!" the girl panted. "I was at the healer's hut to get medicines, but Hanjeha was not there, and Awa'hi was screaming like something was breaking out of her."

The baby. It had to be.

Hyko broke into a sprint towards the still standing healer's hit. Inside, Awa'hi was shrieking and crying as if something was killing her from the inside. Then, Hyko saw the blood. It was all over the front of her skirt, spilling down onto the floor beneath her. All of the words that Hyko could've said stayed trapped in her throat.

"Hyko!" Awa'hi screamed. The sound was almost not human. *"Get it out of me! it needs to come out of me!"* Tears began to fall from the young healer's eyes. She'd only ever delivered two other babies. However, it had all been under the watchful eye and harsh criticism and instruction of Hanjeha, and there hadn't been nearly that much blood. *"Hyko, do it now, this thing is going to kill me!"* After that, Hyko hesitated no more. She fetched as many rags and buckets of water as she could, throwing up into one of them before starting the delivery process.

It was almost two hours before the baby girl came. Two hours of ear-piercing screams and blood. Two hours of a migraine and a stench that made Hyko want to pass out. But, when the girl finally came out, all Hyko could do was hold her in her arms and stare. Never in her life had she seen such a thing. The infant's skin was almost as fair as Jaedon's. Atop her head were thick, downy curls, bigger and fuller than any she'd ever seen on any of her people. She was, in a few words, a thing of unspeakable beauty.

"Mei gadon eneh," Awa'hi muttered in their language. "My daughter." Her breaths were shallow and raspy. Gently, Hyko washed off the baby girl with a wet rag as Awa'hi chanted prayers and blessings for her newborn daughter.

"I've been wondering for weeks what my new baby would look like," she managed to get out. "She...she's more beautiful than I could even imagine." Her eyes began to flutter shut, and her breathing quickened. Hyko held out the little girl to her mother, but Awa'hi was too weak to hold the baby properly.

"Awa'hi, how are you feeling?" Hyko asked softly. The girl gave no reply. She just sat there, her mouth slightly open.

"Gisipeh can take me back to Sasse now," she murmured. Her voice was barely audible. "I've had...had my...my baby..." Hyko felt a pang in her heart, and held the baby close.

"Gisipeh...I don't think he's...you need your rest," she said quietly. Thinking as quickly as she could, she grabbed a few thick blankets and threw them sloppily over Awa'hi. She felt a deep sense of relief with the infant in her arms. All of Awa'hi's struggles and physical pain was finally over. Nevertheless, as her old friend drifted off to sleep, Hyko could tell by her breathing that something was wrong, though tried not to think of what it might be.

* * * * *

The beach as warm once more since winter was ending. Still, the atmosphere in Kainau felt colder than ever when Jaedon returned. Everywhere he went, cold glares followed him. The afternoon that he came back, there was a meeting held at the power house; Jaedon was the only one not invited. The next morning, he was dragged out of bed before sunrise down to the beach.

"What is this all about?" Jaedon groaned, dusting the sand from his hair.

"Shut up, Jadey, or I will drown you in the ocean right now without feeling any bit of remorse." Bryce stormed down the beach dressed in one of Ash's old suits that had to be at least three or four sizes too small. "Who is she?" Instead of letting his true temper show, Jaedon laughed.

"Bryce, you have lost your mind," he chuckled. "Is that suit cutting off your brain circulation or something? I mean, what are you-"

"I know about your little lady friend," he bellowed. His face resembled that of the devil. "The suspicion had been there all along, though it wasn't until a few months ago that I saw you with her." Jaedon's eyes grew wide with confusion; how could he have possibly seen the two of them together? *What does it matter?* He thought to himself after a moment. *If he hurts Hyko...*

"Bryce I swear, if you even think about touching her-"

"You know, at first, I thought you had finally come to your senses and decided to *get some,*" he said. "But then, I connected the dots. All those times you've gone out 'collecting flowers,' how you hadn't wanted to become a punisher in the caverns..." All of the color vanished from Jaedon's face. "I laughed at the thought, but after a while, it started to dawn on me; this is something serious! Jaedon is in love with a blackie! That blackie probably has him brainwashed, and *that's* why he is so nice to these animals." Jaedon fought against the men's hold as Bryce went on.

"You touch her *at all* Bryce, and I will-"

"What, kill me? You've got it backwards, Jadey." He stepped closer to him, and Jaedon grimaced at the man's ever-present bad breath. "I told *you* that someone would get hurt if I ever found out you were away doing who knows what, and your behavior today has stirred up a fire in me. I don't think I've seen enough bloodshed just yet." Jaedon quit his struggling just to gawk at the man; he really had lost his mind.

He took the very next moment that he could to get away, kneeing the men holding him down in the sand and breaking free while Bryce was in the middle of his rant. He raced down the beach, through the village and into the forest. He'd never run so fast in his entire life; but, then again, he'd never felt so strongly about something or someone in his life, either. *I don't think I've seen enough bloodshed yet.* Each time those words echoed through his head, he willed his body to move faster. He was a pro at getting through the forest by then; no longer did he trip on tree roots, or twist his ankle in snake holes.

He didn't stop running until he reached the east village gate, or whatever was left of it. Stopping to catch his breath and gape in absolute horror at Tattao, Jaedon gasped. It was completely destroyed. There was much activity in the demolished village as the men worked to rebuild and the women worked to keep the children from getting in the way. All of a sudden, the sense of urgency returned to Jaedon. Bryce would be there soon, raring and ready to kill.

Jaedon's gaze darted from a little girl to an old woman to a group of preteens chanting rhythms, dancing and laughing. He groaned, knowing that Bryce wouldn't spare any of them. Without thinking, he staggered breathlessly into the village on numb legs. At first, no one paid him much attention; they were engrossed in their work, yelling for more materials or at kids to move away from dangerous tools. Little by little, Jaedon started to hear the words "ziolen rarroso" being whispered as he stumbled through the village.

He stopped when he got to the only structure that was still standing, staring at the entrance for several seconds before deciding to enter. Inside it was dim, cool, and not nearly as noisy as it had been outside. There were three rooms, and he entered the room to the right of him. When he stepped inside, he sucked in a breath. Sitting on a bed a few feet away was Hyko. In her arms was something small and moving wrapped in rags. She was singing to it in her language, but the tune was that of one of the church songs Jaedon had taught her while in the City.

"Hyko." His voice startled her, and she stopped singing suddenly to turn around. On her face was one of the brightest smiles he had ever seen. She came over to him and held out the tiny newborn in her arms. The baby was wide awake, gazing up at Jaedon with sparkling hazel eyes.

"She's only a day old," she told him, still grinning. "Isn't she beautiful? I didn't know how she would look because her father is..." She paused, holding the baby close to her. Hyko then looked up at Jaedon with a curious look on her face. "What's a name for a girl where you come from?"

"Huh?"

"I want to give her a name that is unique and reflects on both sides of her." She softly pressed a few downy curls away from her face. "I was thinking Enna for her first name. It means cutie." Jaedon closed his eyes and thought. He thought of his little sisters, and how much they'd looked up to him, especially Johannah.

"Leah," he said. "It's my youngest sister's middle name." Hyko fixed her eyes on the baby girl once again.

"Enna Leah," she said. "Daughter of Awa'hi, and daughter of a ziolen rarroso." At the mention of the strangers, Jaedon noticed an uproarious noise coming from outside. Hyko held onto Enna Leah tightly and glanced out the window. Over thirty white men had charged into the village, tearing down some of what the men had just reconstructed, knocking over children and firing off guns. Hyko cursed under her breath. Jaedon frowned immensely.

"Bryce," he growled. "I told him not to hurt anyone. Hyko, stay here."

"*What?* No!" She pushed past him, but Jaedon grabbed her by the waist. "Let go! Jaedon!"

"No," he insisted. "You need to stay here with the baby. She needs you. I'll take care of this." He didn't waste any time waiting for her to protest. By the time he reached Bryce at the village center, dead bodies were laying in the streets. Bryce grinned as Jaedon approached him.

"Where is she?" he shouted. "If you get her out here, I will not kill anyone else." Jaedon stood with his chest puffed out and his face blazing red.

"Just get out of here!" Jaedon yelled back. He was sure that the entire village was gawking. A white boy defending a bunch of natives? That was definitely new.

"Jadey, you are being incredibly stupid," Bryce chuckled. "I swear, everyone here will die if you do not give her to me." Jaedon stood firm, listening to the terrified murmurs around him. Over and over, he heard the people asking, "hopin sok yeioy?" which translated to "who is he" in English.

"I-"

"I'm right here!" Whirling around, he saw Hyko walking slowly towards him. His heart sunk while a cruel sneer spread across Bryce's countenance.

"Ah, the girl turns herself in," the man laughed. London and two other men rushed forward. In their hands were metal shackles that looked at least two sizes too small. They clamped them around Hyko's wrists, smirking as she cried out in sheer pain once they were fastened. "You, girl, have been causing me a great deal of pain."

"Good," she spat.

"A sense of humor," Bryce grumbled. "We'll have to break that. Take a look around you girl; there is nothing humorous going on here. Look at all the people you've hurt because you decided to bend all the rules to their breaking points." Hyko did look around, and Jaedon was sure that all she could see was death and destruction.

"Come on, Jaedon," London growled, smacking him on the arm. "You've done enough today. We're heading back. You can even keep your little girlfriend company." The whole way back, Jaedon didn't even look up at her.

SABATEL
REVENGE

Hyko curled up into a ball, shivering and sniffling. It had been two and a half weeks of pure torture. Two and a half weeks of being whipped, overworked, abused, and underfed. Two and a half weeks of bruising, bleeding, crying and hurting. Finally, after all that time, there was a glimmer of light entering the cave; the entrance was unsealed at last.

She stumbled drunkenly towards the light, her entire body screaming. The light at the entrance was blinding, and the early spring warmth felt more like blistering heat. There was someone standing there; a white man who was much younger than any of the other men who'd come beat her. His facial expression was soft, and he seemed kind. Hyko racked her brain trying to remember who he was.

"Move quickly!" he hissed, taking her by the arm. She flinched when he touched her. "Hyko, it's just me." As her eyes adjusted to the light, she realized who it was.

"Jaedon," she breathed, wrapping her arms around him. "I'm sorry, I...I don't feel-"

"You'll feel better soon, I promise, but you need to hurry," he murmured in her ear. He gave her a gently push forward, and this time, she moved hastily. She had to limp for the first few minutes but once they reached Jaedon's kytah, she'd gathered her bearings and could walk properly up the stairs and to his room. Once inside, Jaedon closed the door and pushed a chest against it.

"This might sound greedy, but do you have any food at all?" she asked, curling up under the blankets on Jaedon's bed. Her eyes fluttered shut before he gave her an answer.

"Sure, anything you need to feel better," he said softly. "I'm sorry I couldn't get you out sooner. Bryce has been watching me like-" There was banging on the bedroom door, and Hyko jumped up. She tumbled out of the bed and dove underneath it, shoving dirty clothes in front of her face to keep hidden. Bryce's voice came from the other side of the door, cussing and name-calling at the top of his lungs. Jaedon did nothing until the man barged in, knocking the chest to the side.

"You went and got her," he bellowed. His face had turned purple, and a blood vessel had burst in his eye. "The cave is unsealed, and she's gone; *where is she?*" Jaedon shrugged and took a step backwards, stumbling over a pair of shoes. "Boy, what is it with this room of yours?"

"Get out of here," Jaedon snapped. "I'm not telling you anything. And shut up about my room." Bryce reached into his pocket and pulled out a hammer. Hyko sucked in a breath and bit her lip; how had he managed to sneak that in?

"You never get the point, do you?" he growled, taking a few threatening steps forward. "I try to run a tight ship, and you keep managing to screw it all I up. You're lucky I've let you go on this long without doing some serious damage." With every menacing step he took forward, Jaedon took one terrified one backwards. Bryce was now holding the hammer above his head, his trembling fingers wrapped around the handle.

"Bryce-"

"*NO!*" He swung at him, missing Jaedon's head by a few inches. "I'm done giving you second chances! *This is it!*" He tried again, and missed once more. He only missed by a couple of inches this time. Biting her lip and saying a prayer, Hyko burst out from her hiding spot, shoving Bryce with a loud cry. The man cursed and stumbled backwards, stepping on one of Jaedon's shoes. The hammer fell on top of a pile of dirty socks just as Bryce slid back towards the chest. His head hit the edge of it, and his neck made a terrible crunching noise as it bent forward. He was deathly still and the room went silent. Hyko clutched at her middle.

"I...I just didn't want him to hurt you," she whimpered. Jaedon wrapped his arms around her just briefly. Then, the urgency returned; he was dragging her out the door without saying anything after a short moment. "*Jaedon!* I just killed a man, and now you're-"

"If the other men find out, you're not going to leave this city alive," Jaedon said. "I know it was an accident, but none of the men will believe that."

"But-"

"Don't say anything, Hyko,!" Jaedon cried. His voice was overwrought with pain. "I can't watch you get hurt again. Just trust me. *We need to keep moving!*" Hyko bit her lip and kept running.

* * * * *

London gathered all of the men at the power house. There was absolutely no talking or movement. It was questionable whether or not there was even any breathing. They could all hear the other men coming. From the sound of it, there had to be close to one hundred of them, and they knew that their leader would show no compassion or mercy once he arrived. He entered with great composure and a disgusted scowl. He pushed past London, saying nothing as he made his way to the podium at the front of the room.

"How stupid could one group of fools possibly be?" he growled. His glare wasn't fixed on one person, but swept over each man in the room. "I entrust you with a few simple tasks, and you manage to mess them all up. You even managed to mess up your own idea! One of your leaders died. His step-in dies. *What's next?*" He pounded the podium once for emphasis, and the entire room flinched. "I have half a mind to kill you all."

"It was none of us!" one cowardly man with a pale face and ugly freckles whimpered. "We never did anything wrong, Tristan!" Tristan narrowed his eyes and drummed his fingers on the edge of the podium.

"Unless someone speaks up and tells me who the culprit here is, there will be enough punishments to go around," he threatened. London cleared his throat.

"It's the young boy," he explained. "Jaedon. His...*relationship* with the natives has been interfering with our missions. It had to have been him who killed Bryce. I know none of us would be bold enough to do it." Men began to shout and cry out crossly, cursing Jaedon's name. London's gaze remained fixed on Tristan, who was watching the men while deep in thought.

"Who here," he bellowed after a few moments, his voice immediately silencing the other men. "Who here thinks that we should get out there and avenge our favorite green-eyed leader?" Many of the men voiced their approval of the idea; surprisingly, London was not one of them, which made Tristan raise his eyebrows. "London?"

"He's just a boy," he sighed.

"A boy who needs to learn to stick to the plan and do as he is told!" This time, when Tristan smacked the podium for emphasis, most of the crowd cheered. "If he wanted to live, he wouldn't have risked so much by messing around with the blackies." With a sigh, London's shoulders slumped. He couldn't bring himself to be happy with the plan. He'd never had that hatred for Jaedon that Bryce had. He'd actually felt sorry for the boy once he'd learned how he'd gotten stuck on such a mission in the first place. No part of him felt that Jaedon should die, even if he had done such a thing to Bryce.

"We move out tomorrow." A man patted London on the shoulder. When he blinked, the man gave him a look. "Didn't you hear what Tristan just said about Jaedon? Those who are for killing the boy are moving out tomorrow. We figure he went off with his blackie again, so he's probably in that village in the woods. We're going to kill him. Oh, and the girl too."

* * * * *

"Hyko, he and his people are bringing changes to our land. Bad changes. Did you know that two other soldiers in Fayune have been seriously injured?"

"Jaedon has done nothing but kind things to me since I have met him," she argued. "Why won't you see my side in all of this? Why can't you trust me and my decisions?"

"Because your choices have been nothing but stupid and rash." He kicked up dirt as he spoke. He still wouldn't look her in the eyes, either. "You haven't thought anything through. You've been speaking when you shouldn't and stepping out of line."

"Alright, so I've been making some mistakes," she admitted, exasperated. "But you need to believe me when I say that Jaedon isn't an enemy of ours. If you don't, I know that Tattao and the other villages won't listen either. Until they will, I need you to keep Jaedon a secret. "

"Hyko-"

"Please. Peleiko, Gisi. Don't tell anyone about him and me speaking. Please."

Her eyes flew open as she woke up covered in cold sweat. Hot, salty tears were streaming down her face, and Jaedon was gone. Scrambling quickly, she pushed herself up and used the stone wall to guide her to the sealed entrance of their meeting place. As she reached out to touch it, someone grabbed her by the collar of her torn-up top and pulled her away from the door. A hand clamped her mouth shut, rendering all of her attempts to scream useless.

"You lied straight to my face." Yonej's voice was menacing. His mouth was right at her ear, and his hot breath made Hyko cringe. Light filled the small cavern suddenly as the boulder blocking the entrance was removed. Her eyes adjusted instantly, and it was then that Hyko saw Jaedon; he was unconscious, a bloody cut on his bottom lip. His limp body had been thrown in the corner of the cavern carelessly.

"So...it's true," said a low voice filled with pain and sadness. Hyko's watery gaze tore away from Jaedon and shifted to the entrance. Her father stood on unsteady legs, watching Yonej handle his daughter roughly. He exhaled loudly, his breath shaky. "I had prayed that Yonej was wrong."

"Adad, I am so sorry," Hyko sobbed. "I couldn't tell you, or anyone, I...he's not a bad man, Adad, trust me." Her father looked away and spat on the ground.

"How can I trust your words when so many of his kind have destroyed everything we hold dear?" he snapped. "The white men killed your mother, Hyko."

"Noka...don't say that," she cried. "That's not true."

"My daughter, I wish it were not," he grunted.

"But..."

"This is nothing that concerns us right now!" Yonej snapped, jerking Hyko by the arm and shoving her forward. When he released her, she landed on her hands and knees in the dirt. "You have disobeyed your father, late your mother, your late friend Gisipeh, the elders and the spirits by becoming involved with this boy. You have betrayed your entire people." Hyko whipped her head around to glower at her fiancée.

"No!" she spat. "I didn't do any of those things! You never had any power over me; all you wanted was a wife and a dozen kids to boss around. By being with Jaedon, I've learned more than any of our sister villages have combined in the past several months, and have saved more lives than any of our men ever will."

"That's enough!" Yonej bellowed. His voice caused Jaedon to stir in his sleep. Hyko's father stepped back when he noticed the white boy moving. Hyko dashed over to Jaedon and pushed his long brown hair out of his eyes, revealing a bruise on his forehead. She leaned in closer to him and pressed a gentle kiss to his head. Her father choked on a sob.

"Hey," she whispered as he opened his brilliant blue eyes. "Careful sitting up; you were hit on the head." He groaned, trying his best to get to his feet. Yonej helped him in the end, but it was in no way gentle. He threw the white boy to the ground just as he had done to Hyko once he was stable on his feet.

"Get away from her," he growled.

"Yonej, stop-"

"Hyko, it's time that you confess this great secret to the entire village," her fiancée interrupted. He was pushing both her and Jaedon along by then. Hyko's father was several yards ahead of them and his head was down. "Then, we'll decide on what to do with the both of you."

The village center was crowded, and the people were fuming. Mothers and children expressed their views using vulgar language. Hyko and Jaedon were thrown into the middle of the violent mob, clinging tightly to one another for comfort. The elders looked upon them with disgust, even Elder Agenee.

"Behold, this woman's appalling behavior did not stop at that fateful Samnba many moons ago ," Elder Banna boomed. The agitated villagers roared in agreement. "Brothers and sisters, may I have quiet!"

"They should be killed!" One member of the crowd screamed out rashly and earned himself a glare from Elder Banna.

"They should be banished!" This time, it was a woman who spoke up.

"How could she be a white man's lover?"

"How dare she betray us! As if defying a man wasn't enough!" The comments flew through the air so quickly that the Elders had no time to silence everyone. All the while, Hyko clutched at Jaedon, burying her face in his chest. She thought he could hear him whispering "nidtho," but his soothing words didn't calm her down.

"Hyko, I have been told that your...your, um *relations* with this white boy have been going on for months now. Is this true?" Hyko let out a short, sharp breath.

"I never had *relations* with him," Hyko grumbled, feeling her face turn hot. "Not in the way that you are thinking. But yes, we've known each other for months. That much is true." Murmurs coursed through the mob once again. Elder Agenee looked horrorstricken.

"Hyko!" she hissed. "Why would you do such a thing?" Biting her lip, Hyko waited for the talking to die down.

"I saw the first of our people die at the trader's hut because of a small weapon created by the rarroso," she explained, turning her gaze towards Gusto. He furrowed his brow and looked away. "I wasn't able to do anything. From that moment on, I promised myself that I'd do anything to keep something like that from happening again. That's how it all started. Then, I met Jaedon. He's done everything he possibly could to help keep us safe."

"How can we be so sure that this is true?" Elder Banna snapped. Hyko opened her mouth to speak, but no words came out.

"How you fools not see truth she telling?" The villagers redirected their attention to a member of the crowd who'd been broken in spirit long ago. She stood and stepped forward on her boney legs. "She be great aid in escape from rarroso in Kainau. She and boy I seen in caverns. Boy was nice, only follow orders from bigger white man because he puppet for them, just like we been." Jaedon's eyes grew wide when he saw that the woman defending them was the same one who'd dropped the pitcher at dinner months ago, and had wanted his help with the birth of the native woman's son.

"Pata?" Hyko gasped. "But, I thought Jaedon frightened you."

"I judge boy harsh before," she admitted. "Sincere apologies, my son. You can be trusted." Murmurs flew even more furiously. The elders tore their stares away from the odd couple and faced away from the crowd to talk amongst themselves. Pata returned to her place in the crowd, and the villagers went silent. The hostility was replaced with great tension. Only when the elders turned back to her and Jaedon was Hyko able to take a breath.

"If what Pata says is true, neither of you deserve to be killed or banished," Elder Agenee announced. "However, you will be pun-" An obnoxious cry interrupted the elder, sending the multitude into yet another frenzy. A young hunter sprinted over to the village center. He fell to his knees once he reached the platform. Elder Banna's entire body was shaking.

"What made you think that it would be acceptable to barge in on this important meeting like a mindless fool?" he raged. The hunter lifted his head.

"My most sincere apologies!" he cried. "But, it is imperative! More white men. There's more than we've ever seen before, practically a sea of men, headed this way...*with weapons!*"

SENNTO
FIGHT

Jaedon awoke the next morning before sunrise. The men of Tattao were preparing for a serious attack; it looked like most of them hadn't slept at all. He stepped out of he and Hyko's meeting place onto a path covered with puddles. Native men shot him dirty looks as he shuffled past them with his hands in his pockets. The women turned away and busied themselves by spooning out what appeared to be oatmeal into small bowls for the children.

"They say your name is Jaaaedon?" A girl skipped over to his side from behind him. Jaedon had to do a double take; she was no more than nine or ten years old, but she looked exactly like Hyko. Even the way she said his name was the same.

"Umm, yes, that's me," he said slowly. "Who's asking?" She put her hands on her hips and raised her eyebrows.

"Can't you tell, ziolen rarroso?" she cried. "I'm your girlfriend's little sister, Ohn-Tsung. She...she never mentioned me?"

"Uh, yes, she did, but just to clear things up, she and I aren't really officially..." His voice trailed off when he realized that what he was saying wasn't entirely true, and that Ohn-Tsung wasn't buying any of it. Suddenly, two large dark men stormed over to him, grabbing him by the upper arm and dragging him away from Ohn-Tsung.

"Hey!" the girl snapped. "We were having a conversation!" One of the men shot her a glare and snapped at her in their language. The words were unfamiliar to Jaedon, though he did understand "him" and "stop talking." Ohn-Tsung bit her lip and opened her mouth to protest, but the man barked a cruel command before she could speak. Solemnly, Hyko's little sister stomped off, leaving Jaedon alone with the two threatening men.

"You will fight with us," one of them said plainly. "Since you are *so willing* to defend our people." He gave the white boy a vigorous shove forward and laughed. "Better hurry it up. We have women and children to protect." As they headed off, Jaedon heaved a sigh. How was he to fight with them if they all despised him?

"Don't mind Gusto," Ohn-Tsung muttered. She jumped up into view from behind a pile of construction materials. "He's like an overgrown bully. I don't understand him." She held her hand out to him and did her best to get him back on his feet. "Would you like to eat before the fight?" Jaedon stared at the girl and gave no answer.

"Why are you-"

"Talking to a ziolen rarroso?" Ohn-Tsung finished. "My sister is a lot of things, but she isn't *that* stupid. She chooses her friends wisely, and if she trusts you, you're a good kid." She flashed him a genuine smile. That's when they heard the drums. They were low and loud; each time one of them was beat, the ground shook beneath them. The grin on Ohn-Tsung's face was gone in an instant, and she glanced around frantically. Native men were rushing everywhere with battle weapons ready.

"Ziolen rarroso!" Gusto snapped. "What did I say? *Senatowa; fight!"* Jaedon pushed past Hyko's little sister and rushed into the crowd of yelling men. Gusto tossed him a spear, almost impaling him right in the stomach. Jaedon resisted the urge to glower at the man; the ice they were standing on was thin enough as it was.

Tristan was the first to emerge from the trees with Justin and a few of his other right-hand men at his side. Then came London and Cole with several gunmen Jaedon recognized from Kainau. Ever so slowly, the band of white men grew larger and larger, and the army of native men grew quieter and quieter. No longer were there battle cries of any kind, and Tristan smiled the same smug smile Bryce had always worn.

"I don't think I ever expected this," Tristan laughed. "Oh, I always knew you'd be the odd one out, but *this?* Come on Jaedon, a native girl? You can do better than that." Jaedon felt his grip around the spear tighten.

"You never should have come here," Jaedon snapped. "You never should have started abusing these poor peo-"

"Whoa, that's what you consider them? *People?*" Tristan laughed even harder. "They're nothing but filthy animals! You have befriended a bunch of dogs!" He held out his gun and aimed it at the nearest native man. "We'll make this little raid as painless as possible. That's why we're here to kill with guns instead of knives!"

"Take me instead!" Jaedon cursed under his breath when he whipped around to find Hyko pushing her way through the enraged crowd. She wore a determined scowl on her face as she moved, not stopping until she was standing at Jaedon's side. Tristan blinked.

"Well, what's this?" he mused. "A brave soul?"

"I'm the problem," Hyko said. "If it hadn't been for me, Jaedon would've followed orders. Take me. Don't hurt them."

"*Will you cut it out?*" Jaedon snapped. "I can't save you if you keep throwing yourself out there like this and admitting that you're guilty!" Hyko folded her arms across her chest and ignored him. Tristan chuckled and lowered the gun.

"Ah, young love," he sneered. "How *cute*." Hyko took a few daring steps towards the mob of white men, showing absolutely no fear. Jaedon started to follow her, but when he did, a few men pointed their guns at him. "Ah, ah, ah! I would not do that if I were you, Jaedon. The girl is offering herself up as a sacrifice. A peace offering, almost. I view you as a threat."

"Hyko-"

"Let me do this!" Hyko snapped. The pain in her eyes was almost unbearable, but Jaedon sighed and clamped his mouth shut. "If you take me...you can use me for whatever you'd like. I'm the real problem. If I'm gone, you won't have any problems with Jaedon anymore." Tristan narrowed his eyes, still skeptical.

"So you are telling me," he began, "that Jaedon would be back at the beach working, and Bryce would still be alive right now if it weren't for you?" Hyko nodded solemnly and watched as the tyrant readied his gun once again. The man laughed, cocking his head to the side and closing one eye to get a better aim at her. "You foolish little thing." His steady fingers were on the trigger.

Tristan's laughter was cut off abruptly by a loud choking sound. The man grabbed at his neck as he struggled to breath. His face was turning purple within seconds, and before the rest of his men could recover from their state of surprise and rush to him, he was dead. There was absolute silence for the longest of moments before Justin went down as well. Both the natives and the white men stood deathly still as Justin writhed around on the ground, clutching frantically at his throat just as Tristan had. The second he stopped moving, three more men went down. Then four more. Then about half a dozen. The army of native men lowered their weapons and dropped down to their knees to chat prayers.

The remaining white men panicked. Some of them retreated, racing back to Kainau twice as fast as they'd come. Others were infuriated and launched failed attacks at Hyko or any other native they could reach quickly. Each effort ended with the charging white man dropping to the ground and turning purple just like his many fallen comrades had. There was no combat and no bloodshed. Within minutes, over half of the massive army had been killed.

"Were you planning this?" Jaedon asked Hyko, wrapping his arms tightly around her. She looked up at him, completely shocked.

"I...I don't understand any of it," she murmured. "I had only planned to turn myself in. None of this was my doing..."

"It was my doing." Every native man got back on his feet and drew his attention to the village gate. At first, all they could see were limp bodies lying on the ground. However, as Jaedon focused, he noticed slight movements in the trees. Four men climbed out of one of them, holding nothing more than small objects that resembled straws. They were dressed in odd clothing that was not worn by any of the villagers. More men dressed in the same clothes slid down from other trees to escort a familiar woman dressed in royal blue robes out of the woods and towards Hyko. Jaedon let a smirk come across his face as he saw that it was Chief Sauda and her armies.

"But..." Hyko was so stunned that she couldn't get the words out. "I thought-"

"Your people have really made a mess of things," she said, shaking her head. "I walked through every village on my way down here. Absolute destruction." Gusto pushed his way forward, getting so close to Sauda that when he spoke, spit flew onto her nose.

"Woman, how dare you!" he roared. "How could you blame such a thing on us? These white men have been-"

"*Do not speak to me like so!*" Sauda snapped sharply. Gusto scooted back, his eyes wide. "I will *not* be disrespected in such a way, especially after I have risked the lives of myself and my soldiers to save your sorry selves when you should have done so without having to seek help from a city only believed to be a legend!" Gusto and the rest of the army looked as if they wanted to laugh it all off and deny Sauda's words. However, one sharp look from the chief kept them from saying anything.

"But...how?" Hyko asked. "They had guns, and you just had..." Sauda smiled and placed a hand on her shoulder.

"Heshii snake poison, my dear," she explained. "It is far stronger than anything those fools could ever tolerate." She pressed the straw-like weapon into Hyko's hand and headed off into the woods. She flicked her hand once, and the soldiers from the City trailed behind her in even rows of three, leaving Gusto, the army and all onlookers speechless.

AWANN
PEACE

Samnba was in full swing. The early summer air made the night feel young and kept spirits high. The sap punch seemed to taste sweeter, and the fellowship seemed even better than usual. This time, Delfusio did arrive on time, bringing with them their own dramatic yet inspiring survival stories. Hyko watched it all from afar. She longed to go out and be with her friends; she knew that Iatso and Issiio were out in the crowd somewhere. She wanted nothing more than to be back with them, swapping stories like they did at every Samnba.

"Is Enna Leah in her dress yet?" Hyko called to Elder Agenee in the back of her kytah.

"Patience, my dear!" Elder Agenee replied. "She is so small that this dress nearly didn't fit!" Hyko sighed.

"Elder Agenee, I-"

"Hyko, you understand, don't you?" The old woman emerged from the back room with Enna Leah. The few month old baby was dressed in small pink robes that Chief Sauda had given to her as a gift. A white flower was tucked neatly behind her tiny ear. Hyko took the baby and held her close like she always did. A small laugh came from the child and a grin brightened up her face. "Usually it would be the mother and father escorting the infant out for the first time. But, Awa'hi has passed away and the father..." She shook her head and sighed. "So, you will be the escort since you have taken the child in as your own. This means no fellowshipping until after the baby has been presented."

It wasn't much longer before all of the villagers were called together at Tattao's village center. Hyko watched anxiously from the window as Elder Opi stood up to speak. He called Yonej to the platform. Hyko nibbled at her lip until Elder Agenee placed a hand on her shoulder and gave her a reassuring smile.

"Just go out and hear what he has to say," the woman encouraged. Hyko sucked in a breath and nodded. All heads turned to her when she stepped outside. It wasn't the same sort of attention that she'd been receiving for the past year. They didn't turn to scorn her or talk negatively of her. Mothers didn't murmur and gossip as she neared the platform with Enna Leah in her arms. Fathers didn't scowl grimly at her. Many of the people smiled warmly, a sight that Hyko hadn't seen in an entire year.

"We have much to celebrate on this fine summer evening," Elder Opi announced. "We have been given another year. We have been blessed with a new child unlike any we've ever seen before. We celebrate the birthday of a young woman who has been wronged by her own people while she tried to do nothing but help. But, perhaps the biggest reason for celebrating is because the white strangers have put down their arms!" Hyko felt her face burning as a shy grin crept across it. Every man, child and woman cheered except for Yonej. He stood motionlessly with his hands behind his back on the platform.

"Now, it was about this time last year that a young woman and man were betrothed. On that fateful night, this young lady objected. I was stubborn and did not listen. But then, I had another dream." He winked at Hyko and her jaw dropped. "They changed their paths for Hyko and Yonej. As of today, they are freed from their marriage obligations." Yonej gave Hyko one last cold glare before stepping down into the audience. In return, she sneered at him smugly.

"We also celebrate the seventeenth year of our own Hyko, daughter of Peoto," Elder Opi went on. "You have risked your life to help us, and have proved the legends of the City in the Ruins true. You have proven yourself to be wise beyond your seventeen years of age, and brave beyond words." As she stepped down from the platform, the villagers cheered and chanted. She took her seat next to Iatso, Issiio and Ohn-Tsung, glancing around the crowd; there was one person missing from all of the celebrating.

"Hyko," Iatso whispered, nudging her with his elbow. "Take a look." Glancing over her shoulder, Hyko saw the handsome young man hanging back in the shadows of the reconstructed east village gate. She got to her feet slowly and crouched low, making her way out of the gathering and towards him without drawing too much attention to herself. He pressed a gentle kiss to her cheek when she reached him.

"I was hoping that you would come," she said. "You missed it all."

"I'm leaving," he said abruptly. Hyko's smile faded, and she hugged Enna Leah closer to her. He heaved a sigh and shoved his hands in his pockets. "The men are boarding a ship to go home in two days."

"Noka..." Hyko murmured. "But...me and Enna Leah..."

"Is she yours now?" he asked.

"Yes, but...never mind that," Hyko snapped. She looked down at the baby girl who was gazing up at Hyko with a toothless smile. "Jaedon, you...you can't-"

"It's just like you to up and run out without a word," Iatso teased. He, his brother, Ohn-Tsung, her father and Hanjeha were gathered by the village gate. Hyko turned to them, but did not look any of them in the eyes. Iatso lifted her head, forcing her to look at him. "Aren't you going to introduce us to your infamous friend?" Jaedon took her hand and squeezed it.

"Jaedon," she said simply. "This is Jaedon. He and I...well, we're in love." Ohn-Tsung looked away and groaned. Hyko's father laughed and Hanjeha smiled gently. Despite the warm atmosphere, a shiver coursed through Hyko's body and she sighed. Issiio cocked his head to the side.

"You don't look so hot, Hyko-jete," he noted. "What's going on?"

"Jaedon just gave me some bad news," Hyko muttered. "He'll be leaving in a couple of days-"

"And I, um, was wondering if I could have the permission to take her with me!" Jaedon blurted it out so fast that Hyko barely had time to react. She stared blankly at him while he gave her a wink. "I don't think I could bear to leave her now." Hyko drew her attention away from him to look around at her home. The men had been hard at work rebuilding all that had been lost over the course of the year, and the village was looking more and more as she'd always known it to look each day. For once, everyone was joyful and connecting with each other thanks to Chief Sauda and her efforts in the villages.

I can't leave now that everything is so much better, she thought to herself before letting out a sigh.

"But, it will be...I can't..." A strained laugh escaped her lips. "I mean, I know nothing about toilets and cars and su-teak." Jaedon raised his eyebrows and shook his head.

"Nope, you don't," he chuckled. "But, you can learn. I'll teach you just like you taught me." Hyko swiped at the tears in her eyes and turned to her father. He too was wiping away tears.

"My daughter, it is very clear that the two of you share a bond that I could never truly understand," he said. His voice was heavy and laden with sadness. "I couldn't live with myself if I stood in the way of you two being together."

"But...what-"

"Oh hush, child, you're making' my eyes water up!" Hanjeha squawked. "Hyko, you are of age. This decision is up to you." For once, Hyko wished someone would do the deciding for her. Her father shook his head and pulled her into a tight embrace.

"I know it won't be easy no matter what you chose," he said. "You're a mother now, and you have someone that you love."

"But, I also have a family," Hyko muttered. Jaedon sighed and shrugged.

"The choice is all yours, Hyko," he told her. "You've still got a couple of days to figure out what you want to do. If you wanna come home with me, you know where to find me. If not...well, no matter what you chose, I know it'll be what's best for you." He winked and flashed her a grin. *Is it the last of his smiles that I will ever see?* She asked herself as he disappeared into the woods.

EPILOGUE

She always chose red and white flowers. They seemed to last the longest. Her mother had always loved the white flowers; they'd reminded her of purity and new beginnings. Hyko had always felt that it was a bland color. Despite her own personal convictions on the matter, she found herself setting the white flowers on the small memorial for her mother once again.

For Gisipeh, she chose red. For her people, red was the color that represented struggles and achievements. Throughout his life, Gisi had seen both of those things. Her heart still ached for him every time she arranged the delicate petals in the shape of a circle on his memorial. Before he'd died, she'd spoke to him harshly and had never gotten the chance to thank him for being her friend. She prayed to God every night that somehow, her old friend would get the message from wherever he was.

She got to her feet and looked at the two memorials sitting side by side in the grass one last time. Then, she sighed and took Jaedon by the hand. A little ways off, Enna Leah was picking bright yellow weeds and singing to herself, mixing English with the words of Hyko's people. She was still a little cutie, as her name suggested. Her bouncy brown curls fell in ringlets past her shoulders even though she wasn't much more than two years old. Her skin was fair, and her eyes were the most peculiar blend of brown and green with flecks of gold. The older she got, the more Hyko saw the striking resemblance Enna Leah had with her late mother. Still, most said that she looked just like Hyko. Hyko grinned as the girl came dashing over as fast as her little legs would carry her.

"Hyko-jete, look!" She laughed, holding up her bundle of flowers. Though others wondered why Enna Leah never referred to her as "mommy" or "mama," Hyko refused to let the toddler call her anything other than her childhood nickname.

"I see!" Hyko said, lifting the child up into her arms. "You can put them on the table so that it'll look nice for Sunday dinner." The toddler shook her head and held out her bundle of collected treasure for Jaedon.

"Noka," she said. "They for Jae!" Hyko set her adopted daughter down and off she went, dashing away just as quickly as she'd come. Jaedon chuckled and jogged after her, leaving Hyko alone with the memorials. She sucked in a breath and reached into her left pocket, pulling out a journal. She'd turned past the pages of the notebook describing Sauda's great grandmother's adventures and journey to the City and tucked her own diary entry in between the tattered pages.

Amam and Gisi

I know you'd never approve of anything that I've done, but I am glad that you loved me regardless. Gisi, I'll never get over the guilt that I felt when Ohn-Tsung told me that you died. I am so sorry that I wasn't there to help you. Wherever you are-Heaven or Saiytah or somewhere in between-I hope you can find it in your heart to forgive me. Amam, I know I was never the perfect daughter; I never liked the color white, I played in the dirt after my bath, and I spoke out at Samnba. But, I hope you know that because of all of those things, I have become stronger.

As if Enna Leah wasn't enough to keep me busy, soon she'll be a big sister(Odd as it sounds, Jaedon wants to name the baby Somoson if it's a boy, and I was insisting on a name that they use on the mainland where he has grown up). You'd probably hate me if you were still here and I was telling you this. But you've just got to trust me; I know what I'm doing. You'd probably ask me why I decided to take care of Enna

Leah in the first place, or why I ever started talking to Jaedon, or why I decided to marry him.

If only I knew for sure! I suppose these things just sort of happen to me.

Forever the rebellious daughter and best friend,
Hyko,
Daughter of Peoto
Wife of Jaedon, a ziolen rarroso
Mother of Enna Leah

ABOUT THE AUTHOR

Reina McKenzie has been a writer for years, yet this is her first published novel. She has earned several awards for her writing throughout her childhood and high school career. She is currently a student at James B. Conant High School and lives with her family in suburban Chicago. In her free time, she enjoys reading, drawing, singing and studying Japanese as well as Spanish.

17563640R00141

Made in the USA
Lexington, KY
16 September 2012